WELCOME TO CHICAGO

Welcome to Chicago

Erin Finlen

To G:
You can do whatever you set your mind to.
I pity anyone who tries to stop you.

Prologue

Elvie Townshend sat with her legs curled under her, looking, Natalie Humboldt thought, like a cat ready to spring. The position would have been relaxed on anyone else, but the young woman with the reddish blond hair always gave the impression of being a second away from action. For her part, Elvie always thought Natalie looked like an especially fidgety bird, one with long legs like a Stilt or Spoonbill. Right now, she was uncrossing them and recrossing them. Not to mention, she had been running her hands through her long stick straight black hair every time she adjusted her posture. They had every reason to be nervous; they had been going through this interview, or audition, or whatever you wanted to call it, for months. Today, they would find out whether they had passed, whether they were part of the selected team of four agents that would make up the Pathfinders, along with two "captains," who were in charge of everything they did. The purpose of the Pathfinders was to chase down the Interface, a group of, what Bixby Blackwell, another canidate called 'time bandits,' bent on destroying the present by ruining the past. Elvie had pointed out that name was a little too innocent for them, but it had stuck. Besides being selection day, though, Natalie and Elvie were also the last two in the waiting room.

Unfolding herself from the chair, Elvie began to pace, her own thoughts finally forcing her to rise and pace to avoid fidgeting. Fidgeting looked different on Elvie. If she was forced to sit still, it became picking at her cuticles, her lips, her skin, her clothes. But when allowed to move, she paced, and Natalie was now more convinced than ever that she was part cat. Natalie's fidgeting involved playing with her hair and tapping her foot. Which she was trying desperately hard not to do. She was about to break the tense silence when the door to the interview room opened again and the same woman who had been in and out all day called "Natalie Humboldt." She let out a sigh of relief. One way or another, this was about to be over...for her anyway. She cast a nervous smile at Elvie, who gave her an encouraging nod in return before disappearing into the office.

The door clicked shut behind her, and Elvie resumed her pacing, boots echoing on the grey tiled floor, off the undecorated beige walls. The only furniture in the room was the overhead lights plus the two dozen incredibly uncomfortable chairs. The chairs had been arranged in neat rows when the candidates arrived. However, as the day wore on, people moved them. Elvie's original chair was where it had been. She'd moved when the number was down to five, to one that someone, Bixby, she thought, had left leaning against the wall. There were two doors in the interview room, and regardless of whether they got the job or not, people only went through the door to the offices. If this was to save a person from having to walk past other hopefuls who might wonder what happened or to preserve a sense of mystery, no one in the room was sure. At this point, though, she wasn't sure it mattered. She would at least like a hint of whether there was a spot left or if she was finally being sent home. Her eyes flickered over to the door again, waiting, watching, trying not to think the worst or best...either way, they had to let her back. Unless her brain supplied, you were so bad that they were just sending you back the way you came. *Good, great.* Now that thought was there as well. Sighing, she shoved off the wall she had stopped to lean against and jumped when the door to the office opened again. The same woman as before stepped out, her lips betraying a hint of a satisfied smile when she noticed Elvie's startled stare.

"Elvie Townshend. Please follow me." She turned, immediately, and strode from the room, her heels clicking as she walked, and Elvie was grateful that she wasn't a slow walker. Her own boots sounded practically muted as the woman's steps bounced off the plain white walls. There were closed doors on every side, and Elvie tried not to focus on whether or not she could hear conversations coming from the other sides. At last, after the hallway seemed to stretch on and on forever, the woman, stopping so suddenly that if Elvie had been walking behind her, she would have run into her, gestured for Elvie to enter. With a deep breath, Elvie walked into an open office, just as impersonal and plain as the rest of the building had been, but the man behind the desk was anything but plain, filling the room with his personality without saying a word and even though she was taller than him by an inch, the sight of the Governor of Illinois sitting behind the desk made her feel small.

"Miss Townshend, it's a pleasure to meet you at last." He stood, broad shoulders and large hands making up for the lack of height, and Elvie tried to pull herself up taller, pulling her shoulders back and lifting her chin just a little.

"Governor," she took his hand and smiled as best she could. Why was this man, the sole American billionaire to fund the project, the one meeting with her? Why was he the *only* one meeting her? He gestured for her to sit, and after a moment's hesitation, she slowly lowered herself into her seat. The door closed behind her.

"I have to say, I'm not sure how to begin this." He folded his hands in front of him on the desk, without saying a word, as if waiting for her to give him a suggestion. Elvie's nerves finally caught up to her, words spilling out before she could stop them.

"Am I getting sent home?" At his chuckle as blush spread up her cheeks, though she couldn't say whether from embarrassment or annoyance. "I mean, if I am just tell me and I'll go quietly. Is there like a memory wipe or something I have to do?"

"Not for you, no." The answer, in response to a tongue-in-cheek comment about the secrecy of the project until this point, was delivered in a serious tone, and though she hid it well, a chill ran down her spine. Did that mean if she had made the team and if she hadn't, they would have actually mindwiped her? Or were they going to kill her? "The problem I am having right now, Miss Townshend, is how to explain the conditions of your acceptance to the team." Elvie's brow furrowed, and a strange but familiar tension, a feeling of preemptive defense that she had become far too in touch with over the course of this process, settled over her shoulders. The Governor, as if sensing her mood or perhaps it showed clearly on her face, grimaced and nodded, breaking eye contact before taking a deep breath to start again.

"You are Pathfinder Agent number 4, but it comes with some rules that the others don't have. Getting you on the team, while I know that it is for the best and that you are the key to this whole project, somehow, it took more arguing, negotiating, and fighting than it should have. Because, well, because you're—"

"American." She finished for him, her cheeks heating again as he nodded. Elvie pressed the rising anger aside. The reaction she knew would be everything. "I didn't vote for him. Or any of that. I've fought against it all."

"I know. We all know. We've got your records, interviewed everyone, scoured social media…we know it all. I told them that you could be trusted to do the right thing in the event the regime tries to take over this project." He stood and came around the desk to face as equals. She needed to do this for her family and her friends. To save them. They didn't need her now, they needed a better future. "Miss Townshend, you are American. That is true. And it's too our benefit. You're also Polish, Irish, German, Czech, and a smattering of other things. You're one of my constituents, but most importantly, the most crucial part to this entire plan, the reason you need to agree to these rules and make sure the missions are completed is that you are from Illinois."

"So...I have a penchant for carbs, saying 'ope,' and know how to drive on country roads?" Elvie couldn't keep the sarcasm from her voice, and the Governor actually laughed at the comment.

"Well, yes. But you have something else that people from Illinois have in spades." He held her gaze, "courage. You fight for the underdog. The underdog is the one who needs to win this time. Other people from Illinois and even from Chicago tried out, but none of the ones who did had the same sense of justice that your tests say you have. That look on your face is telling me you have what we need." He stopped then, waiting to see if she would storm out, rage about the unfairness, or, after that barrage of compliments, would she preen. She did none of that. Instead, she sat back in her chair, considering...he had mentioned rules.

"What are the stipulations?" Rather than looking pleased at her question as she had expected, he looked more pained.

"You will be monitored with higher standards than the other agents. I am in charge of your behavior, and if you defect or seem to be a traitor of some kind, I will not hesitate to disconnect you from the time machine. And, unless you are in a time period that makes swords and daggers seem out of place, you are not to use a gun."

"Okay." She said with a nod. The Governor raised his eyebrows. "Okay," she said again, nodding. "I'm in. I don't need guns anyway. I've proven that time and again." His smile was just as wide as it was in his 'candid' social media posts, but it was so genuine it made her lips twitch with a small smile of her own.

"Okay, Miss Townshend. Let's get you in with the rest of the crew, shall we?"

The crew did make the initial jump, and they were supposed to make several jumps after that...but...it didn't work. The time machine refused to move from its first landing year. They could change the location but not the time period. They later found out that that happened to the Interface as well. Not long after the jump, they also discovered that the radiation had warped each of them in some way, leaving them with an ability. They all assumed the abilities were static, and so, thanks to the vaccinations and medical treatments, the Pathfinders made their way forward in time, physically unaging, mentally drained, and becoming more of a family than a team. They had to, when sometimes they only had each other.

Chapter 1

Chicago, March 1924

The city of Chicago was a place Elvie had been looking forward to visiting since they had started traveling. Now that she was here, she didn't want to talk to anyone. She didn't want to see anyone. She didn't even want an assignment because she didn't want to get attached and then have to watch someone die…again. She was trying to sneak out of the front door to avoid Shirley or Tony cornering her for an assignment, but Tony was waiting in front of the front door for her. Elvie inwardly cursed the inability to enter the In-Between inside the house as she followed the tall man down the stairs into the command center. Bixby and Natalie were there as well. Bixby was clearly getting ready to leave, and he tipped his hat to her on his way out the door. She smiled at him, in spite of herself. He could make them all angry without even trying, but he was a lovable fellow all the same. Elvie slid into a seat next to Natalie, who she noticed was staring at the floor. That didn't bode well.

"Your assignment," was all Shirley said as she handed Elvie a folder. Elvie opened it and scowled.

"Where's my real assignment?" She asked and tried to hand it back. But Shirley just smiled at her. "Oh, come on." Elvie slumped back in her chair, an uncomfortable metal thing that was usually only used when one of them was getting a lecture. "This is…punishment. Or torture." She flipped the folder back open and looked down at a row of four mugshots. She didn't even have to read the briefs, she thought. The four men staring back at her were people whose stories she had studied obsessively from the time she was a teenager. In some ways, their faces were as familiar to her as her own.

"It's not either." Shirley sighed, already fed up with arguing. Natalie was working on coding something on a tablet and steadfastly refusing to look at anyone. "But it *will be* a challenge. Tony and I think it's what you need to get yourself back on track. Besides, you're the best person for the job."

"But...they're all going to..." her voice cracked a bit, making her stop. She refused to let the emotions show. "I told you I didn't want... Can't I have a recon gig? Just this one time?" She hated how close she sounded to pleading. But the Lincolns, the Johnstown Flood, then having to go to Russia and deal with the Romanovs and their tragedy, not to mention having to keep a crazed monk from killing himself before his assassination, had taken a toll on her. Now, to be in Chicago during prohibition, where they wanted her to 'guide' the North Side Gang? No, she couldn't do it. It would break her. She was sure of it.

"No." Shirley was firm. "There is no one who knows that story the way you do, Elvie. No one else on this team would even be able to tell you their real names, much less pronounce them properly."

"So teach them." But even as she protested, she knew Shirley was right. Wasn't that why Bixby usually worked in Japan? He was an expert in Japanese culture. Wasn't that why, whenever something happened in archeology they put Natalie on it? Natalie was a trained classicist. Elvie was...well, she was the best fit for this job. She just really didn't want to do it.

"Elvie..." At the sound of Natalie's voice, she looked up. Natalie had finally stopped tapping at her screen, and her facewere full of pity. "It's going to be okay. No matter what happens, you will come out the other side." Elvie opened the folder and looked back at the pictures. Her eyes caught as they always did, as they always had, on the so called soulless, spine-chilling stare of Hymie Weiss.

"But they won't," Elvie said, and she tossed the folder down on the desk. She walked over to the coat rack and pulled her coat, the one she'd had for two hundred years that still fit in the baggy way she liked. She put on her hat and stomped out of the house, leaving them sitting in uneasy silence.

Chapter 2

Of course, she had to take the assignment. It was literally the reason she was still alive, or one of them anyway. "Just hold on until you get to see Chicago," she had told herself after the assassinations, after every death she was powerless to prevent. It wasn't like she couldn't take the case, of course. But taking the case meant she had to do it by the book, no improvising as Tony liked to remind her. *Although,* her brain and heart reminded her, *not necessarily perfectly by the book.*

As she walked out of their neighborhood and into the downtown area, making her way east, where she intended to start her preliminary search, she adjusted her posture. She set her shoulders, lifted her chin, and walked like she would fight anyone who interrupted her path. She would, too, given her current mood. She didn't have a set destination in mind, but Elvie knew, in general, that she wanted to make her way towards State Street, she thought that somewhere as busy as that would be sure to give her some idea of where to go. Not as busy as Michigan Avenue and not along the lake, where she would become overwhelmed. The smells of exhaust, smoke, gasoline, people, and the lake pulled at her imagination, and she found herself reveling in the cool grey sky overhead and the early spring air that whipped her face. Going without a plan, she decided to just walk.

Her mind wandered as she walked. She thought of the Lincolns, specifically Robert, and wondered if he was okay. Would he even remember her if he saw her? A real concern, she supposed, as Chicago was one of his many haunts. She didn't look much different, she didn't even look older. But while that might cause him to do a double take, Abe's oldest son had always been no-nonsense, by-the-book, so he would write it off as a coincidence: she was someone who looked like someone that he used to know was all. It would sting, but it was the way it should be, she reminded herself. He was growing old and in a few years would be dead. The date was approaching, as it did all living things. Except her bunch of misfits, of course. And unbidden, she remembered the day that the Romanovs were removed from the palace, and she felt the familiar feeling of nausea that plagued her every step. Nikolas and Alexandra had been objectively horrible, but their kids were just that. Kids. Sheltered children who didn't deserve the fate they had been dealt. She felt a jolt of her power slam through her and forced her mind back to the present.

Which was when she noticed where she had ended up. She was standing on Superior, looking towards State Street. She reached out a hand and touched her fingers to the wall of Holy Name Cathedral, chills ran down her arms. In her time, it was reportedly haunted. That wasn't what had always made her uncomfortable. It was that it was a church. Elvie always felt that if a Catholic Church wasn't making you uncomfortable, it wasn't doing its job. She looked up at the huge stone walls and said a silent Hail Mary. Elvie had been raised Catholic, and while she was no longer practicing, she wasn't even sure what she believed in anymore, just that multiple religions seemed to get all the same things right and wrong. A small part of her retained the need to say her Hail Mary's when she felt that strange religious pull.

Keeping her fingers on the stone wall, she followed it to the edge of the building. Coming to stand on the corner of State and Superior, eyes moving up the building, taking in the massive doors and the stained glass. It was a breathtaking piece of architecture. Elvie compared it to how it looked in her time in her mind, without remembering to pull herself back to 1921, she felt another jolt. But this one wasn't power. It was the disconnect between her thoughts and reality. Because where a parking lot sat in her time, a big brick flower shop stood now. It was strange that the feeling of time traveling was still with her. After all this time, it still startled her to find things different in the places she knew best. Maybe that was why she had been avoiding coming out into the streets of Chicago for so long.

She stood on the sidewalk for a few moments, taking in her surroundings, and then, because she really didn't want to go into the flower shop yet and she was interested in seeing the inside of the church, she walked up to the big door and…hesitated. She wasn't sure why exactly, but suddenly, she felt that she shouldn't go in there. Call it paranoia or an instinct from years of knowing when something important was right around the corner. She turned on her heel, her coat twirling around her as she did, and walked down the street instead, heading north. As she walked, she became aware that she was being followed. She slipped down an alley…at the same moment she turned the corner, she slipped through the In-Between, pictured herself on top of the roof, and stepped out to look over the edge.

A man, who, though he looked like he was young, had seen enough and done enough that most of his youthful innocence was gone, stepped into the alley a moment later. His tan face went pale, even more evident in contrast to his well-maintained black hair. He thought he had been tailing a woman, and now he couldn't shake the feeling it had been a ghost. She cocked her head as she watched him look around. This must be Victor D'ambrosio, she thought. Also known as Vincent Drucci. She knew when he looked up and met her eyes that she had been right. She knew instantly that his reputation as an impulsive prankster was well deserved because his face broke out in a mischievous grin.

"Well," and his voice was pretty much what she had expected, a Chicago Italian accent that was just a bit gravely. But not marred by smoke gravely, gravely in a way that suggested he had taken a punch or two to the throat, and the other guy came out worse. "That is a trick." A few people passing around him looked up and almost collided, but the Sicilian didn't seem to notice. Elvie supposed that when the world was your oyster, you didn't need to care what random people thought when they walked by you.

"I don't know about a trick, I consider it a skill." The smile became dazzling, reaching his eyes, and she felt a tug on her own lips, a desire to smile in turn.

"Are you coming down to me or am I coming up to you?"

Elvie considered him for a moment. She thought about the ways this scenario could play out. Finally, she settled on following her instincts. Now was not the time to introduce herself. Instead, she saluted him, "We'll see each other again one of these days. I'm sure of it." With that, she stepped back through the In-Between over his protests.

Elvie reappeared on North Clark Street, where she decided to go into a nearby diner and just watch people for the rest of the day. She needed to get a feel for how people acted and talked if she was going to blend in. Not that she had ever been very good at that. Or sitting still, so after an hour, she paid and spent the rest of the afternoon wandering the city in a space where no one could see her. In the spot that was all her own. Her nerves were bothering her, and she kept pulling at the straps on the fingerless gloves she wore everywhere to hide the scars on one of her arms. Then, around nine at night, she felt a prickle at the edge of her awareness. Something was very wrong...it seemed she would be meeting Victor again sooner than she had planned.

Chapter 3

April 14, 1865

Elvie sat up and stared around her. Jesus Christ, her head hurt. She should really be dead, she thought as she took in the interior of the building's ancient walls. The walls rose high around her as she fell back on the stone floor, defeated. She had failed, and Abraham Lincoln would die. Had died? Had healing taken long enough that she had missed it all? She pulled her pocket watch out of her coat and opened it. She did a double-take when she took in the dashes where the date should be. Was she dead? She sat up again and looked around, slightly panicked. She remembered the carriage bearing down on her. She remembered the splitting pain in her skull as the horse collided with her. And then…well, she had been pulled away to Alexandria in time. Right?

They all had a spot they had chosen, where the time machine would send them if they needed to be pulled from danger in an emergency. Elvie's was the lost library of Alexandria. Natalie's was in Pompeii. As long as it wasn't a well known place, the time machine would still whisk them away. They had to be careful, of course. People appearing out of nowhere were generally looked upon with suspicion. It was as she was thinking this that she realized how quiet it was. There were no excavators, historians, or archeologists around. She realized that even the sound of birds outside or the wind was strangely muffled. She shouldn't be surprised that there weren't any people here. It wasn't like anyone really knew exactly what this place was yet. But there was still usually someone moving.

"Oh, shit." Panic was tickling at the edges of her brain. She could feel her chest getting tight and a familiar tingling in her feet and hands. Not the time for this, she told herself. She walked around the entire building, and just as she was losing the ability to shut out the panicky thoughts, she realized that the breeze she could feel was fluttering the ground. Yes, actually making the stone beneath her feet look like it was being pulled back. Another, separate stone underneath that looked exactly the same. Like when you got a new phone and peeled the plastic off, Elvie bent down and pulled and found herself surrounded by...the real world. Birds chirped somewhere, the wind blew, and off in the distance, she thought she could hear people moving around. Looking around, collecting herself, Elvie tried to make sense of what had just happened. Returning the curtain slowly to its spot, the noise and wind died away, leaving her in that strange space that felt both there and not there.

She looked at the curtain she had just laid down and was trying to figure out what was going on when a slightly darker sheet caught her eye. It was fluttering too, but less so. Elvie stared at it for a moment. Though she felt as if she knew what was on the other side of this one, she lifted it, just a little, and peeked under.

Elvie never told anyone, not even Shirley, what was behind the other side of the In-Between. She never felt the need to. It looked like a peaceful, dreamlike place that was waiting to be made into whatever she wanted. It pulled at her spirit. The broken, depressed soul that was ready to be done. But the other half of her soul, the vibrant, knowledge-chasing, adventure-seeking part, pulled the other side back, whispered,' We're not done having adventures yet.' Gently, Elvie put the corner back. Taking a deep breath, she pulled the original In-Between again and stepped into what she now realized was the world of the living.

She really should have expected it, she thought, as she threw up behind a bush. It shouldn't have surprised her that the second the adrenaline of realizing she wasn't actually dead wore off, she would feel all of the pain she should have after she woke up. But she didn't. Or maybe she forgot that she had been hit by a carriage, and while outwardly she was fine, her head was still pounding, and the pain turned her stomach inside out. She was getting herself pulled together when she felt her pocket watch vibrating.

"What?" She answered, snapping it open. She usually wasn't so short with anyone, but pain and exhaustion were taking a toll. Add to that the taste of bile in her mouth, and she was ready to scream at anyone who dared cross her. Oh, and apparently, she could now reach different dimensions. It had been a stressful day.

"Oh, thank god," Shirley said. "Your vitals showed straight lines. Not like you were dead, but like you just didn't exist."

"Well, I still exist…my head hurts like I got stepped on by a horse and then trampled by the carriage he was pulling, but otherwise I do unfortunately exist."

"We will discuss your actions when you get back, but for now, I am sending Tony to get you. Stay there."

"No." Elvie whimpered. "Please don't make me travel Tony style. I'm already a sickly mess as it is. Give me like two hours, at least." Shirley hesitated, and Elvie could see her checking the vitals and looking at the screen where Elvie knew she was visible, probably pale, sweaty, and frail-looking.

"Fine…two hours. But then Tony is coming to get you." And the screen returned to a regular watch face. Elvie sighed and leaned against a stone statue. God, how she hated traveling with Tony. It was nice to be able to get places so quickly, but the things it did to your insides were not worth the time saved. So she had two hours to get herself together. She knew if she reached into her coat pocket, it would be full of money to get herself food and a drink or at least an indoor spot to sit, but she didn't want to be around people right now. Instead, she pulled herself together and was about to start walking...somewhere when she realized that she could still see the In-Between, as she had decided to think of it. It was everywhere, she could feel it at the edges of her consciousness, and without thinking, she put out a hand and slipped through to the other side.

She walked, unbothered and uninterrupted, for quite a while. The only problem that she could find, and it wasn't really a problem *to her*, was that her watch didn't work, so no one would know where she was. She wondered if that's what had made her vitals turn to dashes. And if so, she probably needed to get out of here so they didn't freak out and send Tony after her. The thought of Tony and warping back made her stomach turn, though, and she thought longingly of the front step of the house and wished she could just walk up to it from the In-Between without Tony and the queasiness his style of travel provided. Finally, with a deep breath, she pushed aside what she was beginning to think of the Entrance and stopped short.

She was standing in front of the base. Directly in front of the front step, just like she had imagined, actually. She looked around her and watched as the world went on around her. Yes, she was definitely standing in front of their manor. She hopped onto the step, certain she was dreaming, and when it didn't give way, she opened the front door. Tony, who was standing in the living room, apparently getting ready to pick her up, jumped.

"What the fu—" He started as from the basement, she heard Shirley say the same thing, and Elvie knew that she had shown up on the radar as at home. A moment later, Shirley appeared on the stairs.

"How...When...Are you..." She stuttered. Elvie sighed and sank tiredly onto the couch. And then she started telling them about waking up in the In-Between.

Chapter 4

Chicago March 1924

"You would think that the three of you would have learned that this street belongs to us." Angelo Genna said as he kicked Drucci in the stomach. Antonio and Mike, his brothers, held on to Hymie Weiss, who was unconscious and bleeding, but given the man's reputation, he wasn't one to be left alone. John Scalesi and Albert Alnsemi were sitting on Dean O'Bannion, who was barely conscious. The little Irishman was a force to be reckoned with, normally, but the five tough guys had caught them off guard. In the shadows of the nearby street lamps, Elvie could make out swelling on their faces, and Victor's nose looked as though it might be broken. Which, annoyingly, made him better looking, it was the part of his face that had always felt too perfect anyway.

"I guess," Antonio smirked, "It's time to get rid of the pests." He reached towards his gun at his side.

"I really wouldn't do that." She said, keeping her tone calm and measured. To them, it sounded like a female was talking from...somewhere. They couldn't see anyone, and the idea of a woman trying to take on the Genna brothers made all the Italians, except Victor, who was wheezing and trying to figure out why he knew that voice, bark with laughter.

"Darling, you'd better run on home," Scalise said, standing to look around.

"Don't call me darling." It was a pet peeve. It had always rankled, even when Doc called her 'darlin'.'

"Well, *darlin',*" Angelo sneered, looking around him. He was visibly uncomfortable not being able to see her. "Get your ass out of here before we find it. Then we'll add you to the pile of bodies…*darlin.*" Elvie suppressed a groan. Great, she thought to herself. A smartass.

"You have two seconds to tell these dipshits to get the hell off O'Banion's street, or you're going to wish I was a darling."

Angelo, who clearly seemed to be the one in charge, scowled. "Who the fuck do you think you are? And come out and face us like a…" And the cigarette that the man had been holding exploded. Setting his hand on fire. Antonio Genna, who had by now managed to get his gun out and was cocking it, found himself flying backwards and his forearm broken as his gun was taken. The last thing he saw was a halo of blond hair before it pistol-whipped him across the face. Elvie spun and shot Scalise once in the knee. Nowhere near enough to an artery to kill him, but enough to send him reeling backwards and crashing to the ground. She kicked him hard enough to knock him out.

"Finally, I can breathe." She sighed. Vincent Drucci swung Angelo's legs out from under him as Elvie sent Mike Genna's head into a brick wall, and he slid down, unconscious.

Anslemi had stood up by now and was trying to figure out what was going on and what to do, but found himself in a chokehold with Dean O'Banion holding on as he slowly fell into unconsciousness.

"Don't kill him, please." Elvie quickly walked over and, with little effort, separated them. "I would get in a lot of trouble." Everyone must have still been alive because nothing had spontaneously come running down the alley to kill her. She wasn't sure what to do now. Thankfully, she was saved from having to come up with something smart to say by Drucci, who had, by now, placed her.

"It's you!" He yelled and then winced. He must have had a broken rib. "From this afternoon, by the church."

"I told you it wasn't time for us to meet yet." This wasn't ideally how she had planned it either, but what in the hell were they doing in Genna territory? Someone had sent them here, obviously...or so she thought until she glanced out of the alley at a street sign. "North Street...what were they doing here?" She hadn't realized she had said it aloud until a voice she hadn't heard before spoke. The voice was a bit higher than Victor and instead of straight Chicago, there was a small twang farther south in Illinois.

"Why did they think it was their territory?" Dean, his blue eyes blazing with anger and hate, walked over and kicked Mike Genna in the stomach. Elvie would have been irritated by the violence, but considering who the Gennas were, apparently friends with, she felt a pang of envy that *she* couldn't kick anyone in the stomach. But there were consequences to every action, so she settled for watching as the blond-haired man limped over and kicked Angelo and Antonio in turn.

"Who are you?" Victor asked from his spot on the ground near the other dark-haired member of the trio. Elvie could guess, based on the small frame, high cheekbones, and wide-set eyes, plus the way Dean had come over to worry over him, that this was Hymie Weiss, the most terrifying member of the North Side Gang. She was okay with not meeting him tonight, she decided.

"My name is Elvie. And for tonight, that's all you need to worry about."

"Oh no, you're not running out on me again." Victor started to get up and then winced. Elvie winced a little as well. She was pretty sure he had some broken ribs. I should have been faster, she thought to herself.

"I will be happy to tell you everything. Tomorrow...or today in daylight? I'm not sure what time it is..." She trailed off, and she thought about checking her pocket watch, but refrained, it wasn't important right now. "But for now...are you Dean O'Banion?" She turned to the Irishman, who gave her a nod and a hesitant smile.

"Right, so I'm going to guess that at least one of you three has a car nearby. Can you two get him in it and get to a hospital? Or just get medical attention?"

"I mean...yeah..." Dean was watching her, a bit suspicious if she was reading him right. "What about them? You said don't kill them, but they can't just get out of our territory like it's nothing. We gotta reputation." She knew what he wanted her to do, of course, but she couldn't do it, even if she had the stomach for killing, she couldn't have done it.

"Just leave them to me." Elvie said with a salute, "I'll see you three tomorrow, where and when?"

"Four. At the restaurant two buildings down from Schofield's. You know...the place you were standing across from today." Victor was not going to let her forget that she had gotten away from him once. In fact, she was a little surprised he was letting her leave now without more of a fight. No one could stop her if they wanted to, she thought, but it was weird they didn't try.

"Right. Now...go." And she helped them get Weiss's arms around their shoulders and saw them to the end of the alley. She made her way back and pulled out her pocket watch. "Hey, Natalie...when you have time, can you meet me at an Alley near North and State? Please?"

Natalie pulled up to where Elvie was leaning against a tall stone building and got out. She didn't say anything, just raised her eyebrows as she handed her the keys.

"They're here," Elvie said, looking at the keys.

"How do you know?" Natalie didn't have to ask who she meant; there was only one 'they' when it came to the group.

"I was signaled back by a headache and an inability to breathe. It's a long story, but I knew who I was looking for and I got lucky in finding them right away." She hadn't gotten lucky, she had felt a pull as soon as she set foot in Chicago, beckoning her to the alley, to help. She had never felt the pull that strong before. She didn't tell the other women this, but continued, "We are in, what is without question,

O'Banion Territory. But they were attacked by the Gennas and two of their henchmen. They were claiming that this was Genna Territory."

"But...the Gennas align with Capone, right?"

"Torrio first, and then Capone, yeah." Elvie looked at the unconscious Italian's around them. "I took out the one that was about to shoot Drucci, and that's when I could breathe again."

"I have questions about that scenario and your mental health, but I see what you're saying. The plan was to take out a main cornerstone of Chicago Prohibition history, and that would, if I am not mistaken, not only affect one of us, but all of us. It's one of those pivotal things, right?...and you're kind of an important cog in this whole group." The two stood in silence for a few moments. Elvie didn't know what to say to that. She didn't consider herself so important that not being alive would change the course of history, let alone the Pathfinders, but to say so sounded like false modesty. Finally, Natalie, who was never able to stay quiet for long, broke the silence, "So what's the plan?"

"Help me get them in the car. And I'll take it from there...although you're welcome to tag along."

"I don't have much of a choice. You're my ride." And she started helping Elvie drag the five unconscious men to the car.

Thirty minutes and several bruises for the Genna Brothers later, Elvie and Natalie were flying down Halstead. The Gennas were beginning to stir in the back, and though Natalie was not altogether comfortable riding in the car with five angry mobsters, Elvie seemed right at home. Natalie, who was technically a Pathfinder's agent but was more useful around the base, was always jealous of the three field agents, especially Elvie. The fiesty young woman always seemed to get the most exciting jobs. Although Violet had once pointed out that they were, in fact, the most dangerous and usually involved breaking the law in some way.

Elve had never been one to sit in Congress or visit Parliament or royalty (Romanovs not withstanding); she was always out fighting with someone, blowing something up, sailing somewhere new. Natalie was always surprised that she wasn't more jaded, that anything seemed to bring her joy or astound her. So, she wasn't surprised that situations that were legally questionable or just out and outright illegal were the type of scenarios that put Elvie most at ease.

"Do I want to know what your plan is?" Natalie asked, staring straight ahead and wishing that this car had a handle or something. \Elvie was driving like a bat out of hell, and despite her cool demeanor, it was clear she was definitely feeling the time crunch to get the men in the back out of the backseat.

"I mean...it isn't so much a plan as a...thing to do?" She glanced at her out of the corner of her eye. "I can drop you off at a train station? You can wait there for me to get back."

"I'd be more comfortable if you had backup." It was a silly thing to say, she thought. But when she looked over at Elvie, she thought she saw a smile flit across her face.

"I...thank you." And they descended into a silence that was comfortable and companionable. They only got to enjoy it for a few minutes before a groan from the back made Natalie jump, though her body language did not change, the speed of the car had impossibly increased quite a bit...and then they ran a stop sign.

"Good morning, assholes," Elvie said, her voice not that different from when she greeted Natalie in the morning when they were both drinking tea. Seeing Elvie in her element was strange and startling. Natalie was never sure what to expect at anytime on a mission, but in this situation, nonchalance was not even on her radar.

"What the fuck?" The groan was obnoxiously loud, to try to wake his compatriots, Natalie figured. "It's that bitch from the alley!"

"Oh, good, more than one of you is awake." Another stop sign, and Elvie still didn't step on the brake. "That means maybe someone will slip."

"Where do you think you're taking us? Take us back to our territory." It was a command, and Elvie had never taken kindly to commands.

"It's not your territory. It will *never* be your territory."

"That's not what—" Ouch. Someone had just jabbed someone else to be quiet.

"That's not what who said?"

"None of your business. It's our land, and we want to go back."

"I would suggest you tell me. I wouldn't be opposed to dropping you off all bound up like this in front of a police station."

"Try it, you Irish whore. Or is it the Pole you're fucking? I've heard he's quite a terror. Probably beats you up in bed for a good hundred dollars." Elvie swung the car around a corner and slammed on the brakes. Natalie hated that she jumped when Elvie pulled out a pistol. She had watched the other agent swipe it off of one of the Gennas, but had forgotten. She was off her game tonight, Chicago was doing that to her.

"Right, Angelo." And the man visibly paled as he realized she had no way of knowing his name. "I'm not fucking anyone. Just because you wish you could doesn't give you the right to call names."

"Fuck off—" The pistol cocked, and he stopped talking.

"Tell me who told you that was your territory."

"Over my dead body."

The pistol went off, and Natalie was thankful that her hearing couldn't be damaged. The man yelled, and the other men in the backseat erupted into shouts.

"Relax!" Elvie hollered at the top of her voice. "I just shot his leg, and I will do it to the next person who talks that isn't talked to, got it?" The men instantly fell silent, except for Angelo, who was groaning and panting. "Now, let's try it again, and next time I *will* arrange for it be over your dead body."

The man must have seen in her face that she wasn't bluffing, even though she had to be, Natalie realized, because he only hesitated a minute. "A guy showed up a couple days ago. Said he worked for Torrio. Said that he had finally talked the fuckers into letting go of the

North Side. Said his name was Stephen." At the sound of the name, Natalie's blood ran cold. God damn it, why was he here of all places?

"Do you know where to find him now?" Elvie asked. "Because he lied to you. He doesn't work for Torrio. And if you don't believe me, check with the big guy. If I'm wrong, someone will surely track me down." There was a taunt in her tone, as if she wanted them to try and track her down just to show off what would happen.

"He said if we needed him to leave word at The Church of the Holy Family, that's all I know."

"How convenient, because you have a choice to make. We are currently parked at the corner of Roosevelt and Halstead. The Church of the Holy Family is right down the street. You fuck-nuts can get out of here and go get some medical attention from the parish and whatnot, as long as you agree to drop this 'It's our territory because some asshole named Steve told us so' business - pending a check with Johnny, I'm sure. Or you can tell me to go fuck myself again, and I will turn us around and go back up a block or so to the police. Police that aren't in your pocket, I should add." Another bluff, because that would cause some issues in history books, but it didn't show on her face.

"Let us out," Angelo whispered. "I hope I never see your face again."

"That makes two of us." And Elvie and Natalie got out and escorted them to the sidewalk. They didn't bother untying their hands before getting back in the car and speeding off into the night.

Chapter 5

Elvie had driven them back to base at a much steadier pace after they had passed out of the South Side. Though the North Side territory wasn't huge, she definitely preferred it to the other areas of Chicago. She always had, even in her own time. There was no reason for it at first, beyond the fact that it was the glitzy shops and museums and the architecture. Now, though, in 1924, there was a legitimate reason, she just felt safer because she knew the kind of volatility she was facing. The South Side was a backstabbing bunch. The Gennas notwithstanding. In a few years, the South Side would be all hit men.

Natalie was sitting next to her, breathing a little easier now that the angry gangsters were out of the car and she was driving normally. "I suppose we need to head back and tell everyone," he had said, and Elvie had simply replied, "hmm," and kept driving. They passed the street to turn down to get back to the house that was their current headquarters, and she kept going, before turning them down a road that would one day be a lot less easy to maneuver, no matter the time of day, Lake Shore Drive, but right now, at this hour of the night in this year it was deserted. She pulled the car to a stop along the side of the road and got out of the car. Natalie followed her, reluctantly. She'd had enough excitement for one night and wanted to get back to where they were supposed to be. Elvie sat down on a bit of cement and looked out at the lake. After a minute or so, she dropped down next to her.

The thing that Elvie had always liked about Natalie was that she didn't force her to talk. Natalie could fill the silence with a train of thought that could go for hours. Elvie was content to let her chatter while she sat in silence. She would have to do a lot of talking when they got back to Shirley and Tony, but for now, she wanted to sit and look at the lake and collect her thoughts, while Natalie's beautifully accented voice weaved through the night air. If anyone really wanted to know what was going on, Tony would be on the beach with them. About fifteen minutes passed, and Natalie took a deep breath, and Elvie took the opportunity to check on her. What had just happened was a lot for her, and she was used to danger and gunfire.

"Are you okay?"

"This is the most relaxed I have felt in a long time."

"Really? That must be the adrenaline talking." She was surprised when Natalie laughed, a musical sound that sounded like fairy music.

"No, that wore off once you slowed down to a speed under 90. I think," Natalie said slowly, "It's that despite just riding in a car with a handful of incredibly angry, incredibly dangerous men who could definitely kill me with a toothpick, I am still very much alive, sitting on a beach with a woman who could also kill me with a toothpick but is very much on my side. And..." she trailed off a little and then set her shoulders, "I think it's because despite all of that, I can still breathe and I don't feel like the world is out to get me." The last part came out in a rush, like she was afraid of saying it because Elvie would laugh. Indeed, when she glanced at Natalie again, she almost looked like she was waiting for her to say something scornful.

"I know what you mean." She answered with a sigh that made Natalie relax. "We are in one of the biggest, most dangerous cities in the country right now, but compared to you know...our time, it's not that bad. Not to mention, the amount of danger we have handled makes this stuff look like a cake walk...for now."

"True, it's early."

"But, it's *Chicago*, there's a beautiful lake, there's adventure, and things aren't as fast in some ways, yet faster in others. It..." she stopped. She wasn't going to finish that sentence. It felt wrong, and she felt guilty for even thinking it. But Natalie finished it.

"It feels good." Natalie laughed again, this time at the surprise on Elvie's face. "Honestly, Townshend, after all that we have dealt with, this is not something to feel bad about enjoying. It's an adventure, aren't you the one who always reminds us of that?"

"Do as I say, not as I do," Elvie said dryly, making Natalie laugh so hard she fell off the wall she was sitting on.

Chapter 6

"You're going to tell them...? What exactly?" Tony was sitting with his arms crossed next to Shirley. Shirley, who, Elvie noticed, looked very amused despite the united front she was meant to be presenting.

"That I was walking by and saw they needed help." She sounded cool and collected, but inside, she was a bundle of nerves and really hoping that Tony wouldn't ask—

"Didn't a cigarette explode?"

"It's the early twentieth century. It's not like inspections are a thing. Who's to say some gunpowder didn't get into his supply of tobacco?" Across the room, Natalie choked on her coffee.

"Elvie. You really could have handled it better." Shirley chimed in. She was trying to agree with Tony and look like the pair of leaders they were supposed to be, but it was clear her heart wasn't really in this lecture.

"I could have. Probably."

"But…" There was always a but, and Shirley had cut Tony off with the prompt, giving her a chance to explain herself.

"But I needed to make a name for myself. Show everyone I am not to be messed with. And it means that the North Siders will be more likely to see me as an ally, especially since I can handle things without using a gun all the time, than someone who got caught scoping out their base of operations."

"Who did what???" Tony's voice cracked a little, making Shirley wince. Elvie knew she knew about it. Shirley knew almost everything that was said or done on a mission. Apparently, the older woman hadn't felt that this was important information to share. Or she didn't want to deal with the lecture she knew would ensue from Tony.

"It was an accident. I was walking through Chicago and ended up there. I guess, Vincent Drucci noticed me looking at the Flower Shop from across the street."

"And he let you go."

Elvie closed her eyes, took a deep breath, and braced herself before she said, "Well, kind of...I kind of floofed myself up to a rooftop. And he saw me look down."

"Oh my god." Tony was up pacing. "You have to be taken off this assignment. Shirley, I imagine there are other things she could be doing."

"I could trade her with Violet or Bixby. I could send her somewhere else. I am not going to, though." This was unprecedented. Shirley and Tony always agreed on who was put on which assignments. Always. And here was Shirley saying that she wouldn't be removing Elvie, in spite of Tony's insistence. And in front of two agents no less. Granted, Elvie and Natalie weren't going to tell anyone, but it was still noteworthy to *them.*

Tony was staring at Shirley like she had three heads. "Why not? She's already compromised herself. Someone has already seen her..." he waved his hands around the way he did when he was exasperated with Elvie's teleporting. "There is no way this can go on. They'll kill her."

"We will cross that bridge if we come to it. I don't think they will, though. This group of mobsters is slightly more open-minded and progressive than their South Side counterparts. Not to mention, they are religious but are self-aware enough to know they are going to hell. If I remember, right?" Here she glanced at Elvie.

"The quote wasn't explicit that he thought he was going to hell, but yeah, he knew he was a bad person and did bad things."

"Who?" Tony asked.

"Hymie Weiss. His girlfriend or wife or whatever she was says that when they talked about having kids, he wanted them to be good people even though he wasn't. I'm paraphrasing obviously." Elvie said. She wasn't even looking at Tony or Shirley when she spoke. She was adjusting her fingerless glove straps. The recall seemed to take absolutely no effort whatsoever, and she was almost zoned out as she talked, her mind clearly on the task ahead and not the history lesson she had just delivered.

"And that's why she's not being taken off the assignment." Shirley folded her arms and held Tony's gaze. "No one knows this niche of history like Elvie. I doubt that we could teach any of the other agents half the stuff she knows in the same amount of time it will take Elvie to make her way into the inner circle. She's staying on the assignment."

Tony just stared. Anger was flashing across his face. And then he was gone. Teleported somewhere to be alone. Shirley let out a sigh. "That could have gone better."

"Could have gone worse, too," Elvie remarked. "Are you okay?"

Shirley nodded but then looked over at Natalie. "Are *you*?" She was sitting nearby, just staring at Elvie. He looked equal parts amused and impressed. And also, intimidated, Shirley thought.

"I...yeah. I'm fine. I just don't think I have ever heard Elvie so confident in reciting a quote before. And then last night, you knew exactly which Genna you were talking to and where you were going. She's going to be wonderful," she directed this last bit at Shirley. "It's like she was born to be here."

Before Elvie could say anything back, her pocket watch buzzed. She pulled it out as the nervous energy came back to her. "I have to go. I told them I would meet them at a cafe on State Street to tell them everything."

"Are you driving? I think it's hard to find parking during that time period."

"No, I want to walk. It'll give me time to come up with something to say." And she grabbed her suit jacket. Because, of course, Elvie wasn't going to this meeting in a dress. She was rarely seen in a dress if she didn't have to be. In the dawn of the twenties is was becoming more commonplace for women to wear pants in public, and Elvie had embraced it fully. Shirley had scowled when she saw the dark gray trousers, coat, and tie. She said it was too provocative for the twenties. She had been forced to drop it, though, when Elvie had told her she had bought it from a tailor in the city.

"You'll let me know if you need me, right?"

"I will." And then she disappeared up the stairs. Shirley and Natalie saw her dot appear on the map and then disappear. She was in the In-Between.

Chapter 7

Elvie took her time walking up the street. She was more nervous than she cared to admit. She knew she could handle herself alright, but she had spent a long time studying Prohibition Era Chicago. She knew how absolutely horrible these men could be to people who were against them, and as she thought about Hymie, even people who were with them. She really didn't want to be their enemy. But friendship was not an option.

Besides the fact that they were ruthless killers, some of them more than others, she was done being friends with people of the past. It was too emotionally painful when they eventually died. And these men were going out brutally. Their morgue pictures flashed through her mind: Drucci's was sad, though it had a surreal feeling to it, as if it belonged in a movie scene, which suited the man in question just fine; O'Banion's wasn't terrible. It was a picture of a dead man at the morgue. But the picture of Hymie Weiss…that picture had haunted her nightmares for weeks after she saw it the first time. Even now, just thinking about it turned her stomach.

She slipped out of the In-Between a block or two from her destination, and was surprised to see them already there when she arrived. In the light of day, their bruises from the night before were visible, but no one seemed to take notice. Vincent Drucci had a split lip, and he was leaning to one side, as if it hurt to lean the other way, his nose was swollen. Dean O'Banion was keeping one arm close to his chest, he must have dislocated his shoulder in the brawl. And Hymie was the roughest looking of all: a black eye and a knot that was poorly covered by his hair on one side of his head. He also had one leg straight out to the side, his knee probably hurt. She imagined that all of him was hurting. He looked like he had been driven into the ground when she had arrived last night. Drucci, too. At least he hadn't been knocked unconscious, though.

She watched them for a moment before approaching. Vincent and Dean seemed at ease in public, but Earl was tense. He was a stark contrast to the other two, who were, by all accounts, easy-going until they were angered, friendly, and humorous people. Hymie…Earl, she corrected mentally, was a more serious, tightly wound figure. What always stuck out to Elvie when she had been studying the three was the strange look that he had, even in the pictures where he was smiling and at ease, he had a haunted look. Which might have stemmed from being Catholic and also a torturous murder, she always thought. Looking at him now, even from far away, she could see it, hovering around him like a cloud. Violet would have been able to see very clearly what was going on, but Elvie hadn't developed that strange second sight. She could only see what he presented when he thought people weren't watching.

She heard his voice the closer she got, and it was low and even. But sounded like a warning growl. It had a lot of Chicago, not like Vincent's Italian voice or Dean's more southern one; his was all Chicago, just like him, she thought. As she approached, she heard him saying that his brother, Fred, was driving him nuts. Now that they lived together, there was no escaping it.

"I don't know that it's a good idea, you two being in the same house." That was Drucci. She could already recognize his voice; it was a voice that stuck with you. "You two being in a trench together would be fun to watch, though."

"I would rather we weren't in the same city, to be perfectly honest." And then he spotted Elvie. Later, she wasn't sure how he had known it was her, being that he was unconscious when she intervened the night before. She suspected it was just his nature to notice people who seemed to be approaching him. Indeed, he didn't say anything at first. It was Dean who spoke up.

"There you are! Have a seat. We've been waiting!" He was smiling at her amiably, but Elvie wasn't fooled. These were men who had been cracking safes and involved in the murders of other people since they were in their early teens. They wouldn't trust her after just one 'chance' meeting in an alley where she saved their lives. They weren't that naive. They took turns introducing themselves, and then it was down to the business at hand. And it was time for Elvie to make an impression that hopefully didn't get her murdered.

Elvie had a lot of practice slipping into and out of groups of people. It was a skill honed after years of practice. But her senses were a bit jammed with these three. She couldn't tell what they wanted from her. Thankfully, she didn't have to find a way to bring up the night before, Vincent had decided he couldn't wait any longer for answers and started talking before she had even chosen a chair.

"So, I see you outside our store. And then you save our asses that night. I would be suspicious that you were in on the attack, but they seemed pretty surprised to see you, and they aren't good actors." He went to lean forward on his elbows, winced, and returned to sitting slightly sideways in his chair. Mentally assessing where she could sit that would cause him the least amount of pain, Elvie pulled out the seat next to him. She was across from O'Banion this way, which gave her a bit of distance from the man who terrified Al Capone. She didn't feel as unsettled as she expected to, which boded well, she thought. Maybe he wouldn't pull out a gun on her today.

"Stranger things have happened," Elvie said with a smile. Dean looked at her, suspicion evident on his face.

"When strange things happen to guys like us, Miss Elvie, that usually means someone is out to get you."

"To be fair, the Gennas were out to get you." It had just kind of slipped out. It surprised her and them. She was pretty sure they had expected her to at least suck up a little. But that wasn't what Elvie did. Ever. She didn't normally talk back like that, just didn't sugarcoat things to make people happy or kowtow to what they wanted. She cleared her throat and had to look away when she saw Weiss hiding a smirk behind his glass.

"Last night I was in the right place at the right time. Or wrong time if you are a Genna. But yesterday, when Mr. Drucci saw me, I was walking around town just kind of wandering. I actually had been looking at Holy Name before I was looking at the shop. It's a beautiful building." Dean nodded appreciatively, but it was Weiss who spoke up. He wasn't looking at her suspiciously or angrily. Just a kind of curiosity. He had already made up his mind about her.

"Are you Catholic?" Unlike Drucci, he could lean forward and was watching her intently. Unlike all the pictures that showed his eyes as soulless black holes, she noticed they seemed intelligent, but also, she was right, he looked like he knew hell was coming for him. He was 26, and there was no innocence in that face.

"I was raised Catholic." She answered carefully.

"And now?"

"Now, I follow my own path. As long as I am a decent person, I think the higher powers will understand if I don't spend my time in a church three times a week." It had kind of fallen out of her mouth. And this, she realized, is how I die. They'll kill me for being sacrilegious because they're Catholic gangsters, and that's how they operate. Which is fine because apparently I'm broken and can't stop saying stupid shit.

"That's a smart answer," Weiss said after a pause. "I like it..." She felt a rush to not be dead yet. Dean glanced at him. She couldn't tell if he was thinking about what Weiss had said or was confused about his saying it was a smart answer. Victor was watching her with a look of amusement.

"I'm going to use that the next time my ma asks why I haven't been to church."He, too, already knows what he thinks of me, Elvie thought.

"Won't work for you. You'd have to be a decent person first." Earl replied without missing a beat and caught the napkin that came flying at him easily.

"Why would you have helped us?" Dean asked.

"I don't like the Gennas, and I don't like watching people get ambushed and then beaten bloody."

"You don't like the Gennas, but you like us?"

"I find you infinitely more interesting and much more individualized. I also think you are less obnoxiously Catholic, less sanctimonious, and more accepting of people in general. Also, one of you is Vincent Drucci, who jumped a car over a bridge." She glanced at him when she said it. Why couldn't she stop talking? "Another is Hymie Weiss, who's intriguing in a slightly terrifying way, and you're Dean O'Banion, underrated bootlegger and florist, who makes beautiful bouquets."

They all stared at her for a moment, and then Dean smiled. "Well, I'm glad you saved our asses. But I don't know how much I trust you yet."

"Understandable." Elvie took a sip of her water. Her mouth was unbelievably dry.

"Are you tied to any group?" Earl asked, voice low, even, though, surprisingly, she noted not cold and unwelcoming as she would have expected.

"Well, after last night, I'm probably associated with you guys." The answer earned her a smirk from the Polish gangster.

"Imagine us," Hymie said, settling back in his chair, "The first faction to have a woman in the ranks."

"Stranger things have happened." Drucci quipped, winking at her. The rest of the lunch passed in a blur of small talk and anecdotes told mostly by Drucci or Dean, with Earl chiming in with editorial notes once every few minutes. They seemed completely at ease with her, in a weird way. And Elvie didn't mind, she liked listening to the stories and trading barbs with Victor and occasionally Dean as well. Weiss was more reserved and serious, but they seemed to enjoy giving him a hard time just as much.

"So, it is true then? That you jumped a jack-knifed bridge?" Her eyes were on Victor, but she was also acutely aware of the other two men's attention. The man himself was too happy and too proud to share the story. Dean, too, found it amusing. Earl rolled his eyes in the way of an older brother being annoyed but very entertained by his younger brother.

"One of my best moments." He tried to throw himself into the chair and look smug, but it clearly hurt because he immediately adjusted back to the lean he had been perfecting all through lunch.

Victor D'Ambrosio was practically vibrating in his seat as he talked. He leaned forward, even though he was sitting next to her, and his brown eyes flashed with light and excitement. It took all of Elvie's self-control not to smile, afraid that he would think she was laughing at him. Across from him, Earl leaned back in his chair, shaking his head as he took a sip from his glass, giving off the unmistakable air of a man who had heard a story many times before and was about to have to listen to another rendition.

"So," he ran a hand through his mop of black hair, causing the pomade to loosen its hold and hair to start sticking up in places as he spoke. "There I am just minding my own business, driving down Michigan Avenue, not bothering a soul, and on my most perfect behavior."

Elvie bit her lip to keep in the retort, but Earl snorted. "If you don't count the fact that he skipped his bail...you know, after he and Deanie got caught from that teashop. Aside from that, he wasn't bothering a soul." His lips tipped up in a smile as Victor glared at him before turning back to his much less snarky audience.

"Anyway, besides that, I hadn't done anything wrong. But as I'm driving down the street, these two cops are driving past, and they see me...I know they see me, because they immediately pull in behind me. Well, they can't want anything good, right?" His hands, which had been moving the whole time, gesturing as if he was driving a car or snapping his fingers to make a point, stopped face up in front of her, and he spread his fingers wide. "What was I supposed to do, pull over?"

"Yes," came the quiet reply from across the table, causing Elvie to cover her mouth with a hand, hiding her grin, and Victor shot a nasty look at his best friend out of the corner of his eye. That was the only acknowledgment he gave before he continued, almost rising out of his seat in his excitement to tell the story.

"Well, I see them come around behind me, and I'm not letting myself get arrested, so I slam on the gas, and they follow me. We're weaving in and out of traffic, headed for the bridges, when I hear that god awful sound." His hand came down with a smack on the table, and his eyes grew wide. "The steamer was coming through, and in front of me I could see the gates lowering down, and I know these two mugs think they got me." Elvie found that she was leaning forward now as well, his voice and energy pulling her into the excitement, the would he escape, wouldn't he? She desperately wanted to know, and she found herself thinking before remembering that she already knew the answer.

Victor grinned, knowing he had a captive audience, and it was that mischievous, devil-may-care grin that he had, and he shook his head, laughing. "Hell no, they didn't! So, I floored it again, and burst through those gates and just kept going. I cleared that gap," He fell back in his seat, looking pleased and worn out all at once. "Landed on the other side and took off again, it was glorious." Victor stared off into space, satisfaction written across his face, but a huff came from across the table.

Earl finally leaned forward, his eyes, a lighter brown than Victor's but also sparkling with glee, cleared his throat. "He's conveniently forgetting to mention that those two cops made the jump as well, and he got stuck in a traffic jam on the other side. He was arrested. Obviously."

Victor turned to glare at him. "You know you don't have to tell everybody that part. It's not important."

"It's the end of the story. If you're going to tell the story, at least be on the level about it." He ducked as Victor threw a bread roll at him.

"Story doesn't sound as good that way." Vincent shrugged. "You have to know how to enthrall the women, my friend. It's all in the storytelling."

"Is that all it takes?" The other man drawled, an ornery look flashing over his face. "Maybe one of your girlfriends should be informed of your practice runs with the stories."

"Try me, Weiss, and I'll throw every pair of shoes you wear out the window for the rest of your life." Both men broke into laughter, and Dean looked at them with fondness.

"Here's what I think," he said at the end of the meal, after he had paid for them all. "I think the three of us, me too, but especially those two, have taken a shine to you, Miss Elvie. We can't trust you completely yet, you understand…but how would you feel about stopping by the flower shop tomorrow, maybe help us out with some jobs? Eventually, though, unless Earl here is wrong," the Pole choked a little on his cigarette, "I think you'll be a good fit. If you are willing, of course."

Elvie felt her teenage self fist pumping in her head and smiled, "I think that sounds like something I would be very interested in."

"Wonderful."

Chapter 8

Elvie declined a ride from Drucci, opting instead to walk home. Weiss said he was walking as well, which earned him a disgruntled sigh from Victor, who limped alongside Dean on their way to the latter's car.

"They don't really understand the concept of—" Earl started and then remembered who was standing next to him and snapped his mouth shut. They didn't know each other well enough for him to complain about his friends to her, but the gaffe still amused Elvie. Who turned to leave with a wave, but since they were going the same way, he fell in step beside her, a silence that wasn't uncomfortable hanging in the air, and Elvie took a moment to assess the situation. He appeared to be the same height as her, making it less obvious if she stole glances. At lunch, she had found that the easiest way to read him was through his eyes. The rest of his face didn't so much as flinch; it never changed expression. His eyes, though…as he limped along beside her, she glanced over and noticed a small crinkle around his brows, and pain flashed across his eyes.

"You should probably take a taxi," Elvie remarked, making sure to keep her voice neutral and turning her eyes forward.

"I'm fine," He growled as he tried to hide the limp. It was not going well, and he almost fell before righting himself and giving in to the limp again. For Christ's Sake, Elvie thought to herself, she needed to get him in a car before he fell and hurt himself even worse. The question was, could she do it without triggering his temper? Only one way to find out.

"Maybe *I'll* take a taxi." No sooner had she raised a hand than a cab slowed. "Would you like to ride along? I'll pay." She saw him hesitate. It prodded some long-dead urge to push buttons inside her, making her throw in, "I won't tell anyone." It came much more playful than she had intended, her cheeks starting to turn red as he shot her a look that was somewhere between amused and *fuck off*. She had a feeling it was a look he used *a lot*. As if to prove her right, his face instantly schooled itself back to neutral, on instinct more than anything, and she had to bite her cheek to stop the laugh from bubbling out. Unpredictable, her ass, he was easier to read than almost anyone she had ever met.

"Fine." He grumbled, motioning for her to get in first. At first, she thought that he was going to shut the door and send the cab on its way. She would find out later that he had considered it but ultimately realized he couldn't walk that far with his knee hurting as badly as it was. He settled in beside her, his walking stick balanced on his thighs. When he had closed the door, she gave the address of their base on Monroe Street. With a start, Earl blinked at her for a moment before saying his own, just a block down from where she had just said. Elvie was thankful for years of practice not reacting the way she wanted to (cursing Shirley and Tony with everything she had) and reacting the way she was supposed to: she glanced at him and said, "Seriously?"

"Born and raised on the west side of Chicago. Like most of the Polish guys you'll meet around here, I imagine."

"You're Polish? Your last name's Weiss?" That sentence almost killed her from embarrassment. Of course, she knew his real last name. Of course, she knew, even if she hadn't, that a last name didn't mean anything. More than anything, though, she really hated how stupid she sounded, but it was what a normal twenties woman would say. As she watched, he did something strange, he grinned. Not the wide one that she was so unsettled by in the research folder picture, but a small, amused grin. It came complete with an eyebrow raise.

"You playing the fool now?" She felt her cheeks burn again, but he glanced out the window before carrying on. "Real last name is Wojciechowski. My parents are from Poland. I was born here. I'm as Chicago as it gets. And people from Chicago, well, we're a different kind of person."

"Christ, that's accurate." It had slipped out, causing her to wince inwardly, that was very millennial of her.

"Where are you from? You have a Chicago accent...it's just... there's something else in there too." She had noticed him making a face when she spoke at lunch and realized he had been trying to figure this out on his own.

"I'm originally from Illinois, but I have traveled... a lot." She felt herself prickle, wishing to disappear from embarrassment, as he regarded her with interest.

"Are you Irish? Or Polish? I look at you, and it could go either way."

"I've got a little of lots of things." He had an almost supernatural ability to tell if people were lying, so she kept answering honestly. Also, she didn't have the energy to come up with good lies. She was still exhausted from the night before. The questions would have seemed weird, if not for the time period and the fact that Earl had grown up in a world where ethnicity meant whether or not someone was going to beat the shit out of you. Not so much for him, she thought ruefully. From what she knew, he was friends with anyone, no matter where they hailed from. Most people around here were only interested in what they considered good backgrounds and such. Elvie hated it, it made the world too small. The Wojciechowskis, though, didn't seem to put that limit on themselves, and it was a relief.

"How'd you end up over there? I mean, I'm Polish, so it makes sense, but you don't look like you belong in that neighborhood, you look too clean cut."

"Oh, you mean, I look like a goody two-shoes?" She grinned, enjoying the moment as he took his turn to wince, as he had made her do just moments before.

"Looks can be deceiving. We're a hodgepodge group of people that live and travel together." Elvie answered after a moment. "We don't fit in anywhere. This place we're in now worked because we needed a big place for all of us.

"Sounds like my family. They're a good group of people. Couldn't ask for better." He had turned his head to stare out the window now. "My mother, she's great. She's bailed friends and me out of jail more times than I can count. And she's always been there for me. My dad's disappointed in me. He pretty much decided I'm not his kid anymore. I can't say I blame him. I wouldn't want me as a kid."

"I'm sure your dad's no saint." It came out with a bit more venom than she had intended, but the hypocrisy of Earl's father was one of the side stories that had always bothered her. "He's probably got skeletons in his closet."

"He's chosen to forget his past." There was something in his voice that sounded sad. Elvie felt a tug to comfort him, but they had just met, and she still had a healthy respect for her life and safety, so she did the only thing she could think of: she went quiet.

The car slowed to a stop. Elvie looked out and saw her house. She could see where Bixby and Violet were sitting together on the front step. She leaned forward to hand the driver money for her fare, but Weiss reached over and put a hand on her arm.

"I wouldn't be a gentleman if I let you pay. I already let you talk me into taking a taxi. Let me get this," He paused and then added as if he wasn't used to saying it, "Please." She thought about arguing, but there was something in his face that told her to let him have this. Whether it was because he needed it to feel like a gentleman or he needed to feel bigger after last night, whatever it was, he needed to feel like he was helping. Her heart hurt a little for him. If there was one thing that she had learned studying mobsters, it was that they had had it rough before they got to where they were now.

"Thank you," Elvie nodded before she stepped out of the car. She was about to wave goodbye when he called out again.

"I'll pick you up tomorrow, if you want? That way you don't have to worry about what time to be there, and the fastest way to get there?" Or so I don't duck out on the deal, Elvie thought.

"Okay."

See you at 11." Elvie closed the door and walked up to the house. Only when she was inside did she let out a long sigh of relief as if she had been holding her breath for far too long.

Chapter 9

Elvie wandered into the house where she heard Shirley and Tony arguing in the basement. Bixby and Violet had followed her into the house and sat at the kitchen island waiting for her to tell them what had happened at lunch. Natalie had come out of the library and the mechanic shop when she heard the door close.

Her long black hair was in a bun on top of her head, and she still had her blotters on. "Did you have lunch? Was it amazing? Were they nice? Or dickheadss?" Her British accent made the words feel even faster. Elvie had to smile at her friend. The woman was a force of nature. Fast moving and a quick learner. If it weren't for her, they would all be lost. She was a whiz with machines and helped Shirley plan all their cases. But mostly she was so happy to help and hear about what they got up to when they went out that you couldn't help but love her.

Elvie sat on the kitchen counter and told them all about what had happened, leaving out some of the more personal stories and the car ride back with Hymie.

"Are you nervous?" Bixby asked as he grabbed Violet's and his favorite mugs and filled them with their favorite coffee. The two were inseparable when they were in the base together, and they were each other's preferred partner. Shirley had once made a joke that they were twins who had been separated at birth, in spite of the fact that they looked nothing alike. Both had stuck their tongues out at the same time, only adding fuel to Shirley's theory.

"Not as much as I should be," Elvie admitted. "They're not as scary as I had myself psyched up for. But also, they were pretty tired today. We'll see what tomorrow brings."

Natalie leaned on the counter. "Sometimes, like right now, I am really jealous of you." Then they heard Tony's footsteps on the stairs. "And then there are times like now. Later." She grabbed a bottle of water before disappearing back into the workshop.

"She really needs to remember to take those blotters off," Violet said with a smile.

"Elvie! You're back!" Shirley cried, coming around from behind Tony, "How did it go?" Elvie gave Shirley the same rundown she had given the others, even though it probably wasn't necessary: Shirley could have been listening through the pocket watch the whole time. "Any concerns?"

"Not really. They seem like an okay group to deal with. I'll be fine. I always am."

Shirley gave Tony a withering look that spoke of 'I told you so,' that she was thinking quite plainly.

Tony cleared his throat and turned to address Violet. "Violet, you probably have some questions about why you were called back?"

"I assume you want us to work on something here?" Violet rolled her eyes as she spoke. "Or else you missed our company."

"We need someone to keep an eye on things on the south side." Tony held out his hand, and Shirley looked at it, then up at him and walked past him to Bixby and Violet, handing them each a folder. Violet immediately looked down, but her shaking shoulders gave away her laughter. Elvie just rolled eyes; only Bixby acknowledged it.

"Maybe you should just drop the tough guy act, huh, Tony? Shirley'll stuff a folder up your ass if you're not careful."

"And what do you mean you want them on the south side? I can't handle all of Chicago?"

"You can barely handle the North Side, apparently," Tony shot back.

"You're just mad you didn't get to dictate what I did. It worked just fine." Elvie snapped.

Tony cleared his throat again and turned to address Bixby and Violet. "We want you two to work together. The South Side isn't quite as, well, I don't know how to put it. Unless Violet wants to go to work in a brothel, the two of you are going to need to come up with a good cover story to become regulars." Bixby and Violet shared a look, communicating in a way that the others didn't ever understand. Violet shook her head at him.

"I still have some clothes from when Elvie and I had to bust some women out of a whore house in Tombstone. So, send Bixby back. I can do this alone."

"I'll stay," Bixby said, finally. "But yeah, she and I work together on this job. Or at least with someone else at all times."

"Of course," Tony and Shirley said together. They both looked confused at the discomfort on Bixby's face. It had only been there for a moment, but Elvie had seen it too. She wondered what they were most concerned about, Bixby's sexuality or Violet's outspokenness. Neither would go over well on the south side.

"Good, go over your files and find a way to meet them." As Bixby put away the cards and Violet stood, he added, "And please don't, you know, save their lives in an alley and then kidnap an entire car full of people and use that as an excuse to meet them."

"It wasn't an excuse! What did you want me to do? Leave them to die?" Elvie was keenly aware of her voice rising, but seriously. This was ridiculous. "Look, Tony. Sorry you haven't gotten over my one moment of impulsivity, but I have proven myself time and again. You don't like the way I handle things, I'm sure. Guess what? I do not give a shit. You can fuck off, and micro-manage these two." With that, she turned and stormed up to her quarters.

Chapter 10

Bixby and Violet had already left when Elvie woke up the next morning. She hadn't been able to sleep long, she was too excited and restless. The past two hours had been spent pacing, her boots tied, coat hanging off her, undone, and her bag next to the door, ready to leave. She was adjusting her boots and double-checking her glove straps for the third time when there was a knock on the front door. She was standing right on the other side, and she forced herself to count to five. She opened it.

A very tired, clearly annoyed Earl Weiss stood on the other side. He looked like he hadn't slept the night before, and his eyes gave off the same "don't mess with me " look as in one of his mugshots, like he was teetering on the edge of losing his already fragile hold on his temper.

"Are you ready to go?" He sounded like he would drag her out if she said no, so Elvie shouldered her back and followed him down the walk. She noticed he was going to walk again despite still limping considerably.

"Do you want to take my car?" She asked as she trailed a step or two behind him. And a bit to the left. She had watched him yesterday and realized that whenever he made a movement, he seemed to start with his left hand and correct to his right, meaning if he went to fight, he was going to swing with his left first.

"No, I need to walk today." He didn't look back, and Elvie noticed the tension that seemed to be hovering around him. Violet would have a field day with him, Elvie thought, then tried to push the thought out of her mind. The betrayal of Tony bringing back Violet was still too fresh to focus on. She had been working for decades to win back even a little bit of trust after the Lincoln incident, and then he went and pulled this. It was like she hadn't even apologized or proven that she wouldn't do it again ten times over.

"You can walk beside me, you know. I look scary, but I'm not going to start swinging." There was a pause. "Unless you piss me off. Which...granted doesn't take much." It was an hour walk, and Elvie really didn't feel like tailing him by a foot for that long. She lengthened her stride to her normal steps to walk beside him. "You don't seem nearly as scared of Victor as you are of me." He said after they had crossed the street. He actually sounded offended.

"It's not that I'm scared of you." What was the proper way to word this? She wasn't scaredof him, that was true. She was uneasy. "I have just heard that you are easier to upset. And a lot more likely to pull the gun out."

"I don't know that either of those is necessarily true. I'm not the one who...well, you'll see. I do use a gun more, but look at me compared to him. Which one of us is going to be more likely to win a physical fight?"

"I would imagine you can throw a punch or two, though." He was broad-shouldered and, while a future author, not too far in the future (in fact, he was in the city and should know that pretty much everything he wrote about the Northsiders was a lie), said that he was plump, chubby, or fat several times. He wasn't at all. He was tightly wound muscle, but his face did take on a bloated appearance when he had been taking his cancer medication.

"I can." He was quiet for a few blocks, the sounds of traffic and people talking filling in the space. Elvie didn't say anything. Comfortable in her own thoughts, she, like him, didn't need to talk to fill even the most uncomfortable of silences. She took in the buildings, still fresh looking, despite how they looked when she was from...how many of these were still there in her time? She made a mental note to herself to look it up later as they waited for a break in traffic to cross another street. After another block, Earl broke the silence with a pinch of hesitation in his voice.

"Vincent and Dean have both told me, in what I am pretty sure is embellished detail, how you rescued us the other night."

"Mmm. And what is this embellished detail?" *Please don't let it be the cigarette exploding,* she thought to herself.

"Well, you apparently stepped out of a hole in the ground..."

"Nope." Although she wished she could actually do that. It would make a really badass entrance. "I just know how to use the shadows."

"Then you threatened to cut off all their testicles when they called you 'darling.'"

A genuine laugh of surprise escaped at that. "I wish I had thought to say that."

"And you took out two of them on your own."

"That part's true. Actually no. It was three."

"Three?" He didn't even try to keep the surprise out of his voice. Elvie noticed that he had turned to look to make sure she wasn't lying.

"Scalsi, Angelo, and Mike. I'm pretty sure. It was dark, and I don't know that much about the Gennas." Weiss stopped walking, and after a step or two, she turned back, annoyed that he was making this walk longer than necessary.

"You're telling the truth." It wasn't a question. His already big eyes grew even wider as she shrugged and nodded. "Who are you?"

"I'm Elvie Townsend." She saw on his face that that wouldn't be good enough and bit back a sigh. "I told you I've travelled a lot. My job...my old job, I guess, required me to have certain abilities, including the ability to fight people who are pretty dangerous." All of this was true, she realized. He was watching her as she talked with a look that was somewhere between impressed and intimidated. The intimidated part quickly vanished as she assumed he remembered who he was. He might not have been professionally trained, but he had grown up living and breathing street warfare. They would be pretty evenly matched. Not to mention, in terms of impulsivity, Hymie would win every time.

"Were you a spy in the war?"

"Nothing that legitimate."

"That's…impressive. How do I know you aren't an assassin hired to kill all of us?"

"I don't do that anymore. Stuff happened." The amount of work that went into hiding her laugh as he opened and closed his mouth repeatedly was painful as she fought to continue, straight-faced. "Besides, don't you think I would have killed you by now?" That made him laugh. It was the same smile from the day before, startled and caught off guard. Even with how fast her heart was beating, she noticed that the smile had loosened the tension in her shoulders. *Only because it means he's not angry.* She scolded herself.

"I think, as long as you aren't an assassin who was hired to kill us, of course, that you are going to fit in nicely." He fell in step beside her again. "Want to take out my brother for me? He's a pain in my ass, and I can only hold it together for so long before I snap."

"Sorry, assassinations aren't my thing. Now, if you want me to rough him up a bit…I'll see what I can do."

He laughed but didn't say anything else about it. The two passed a few more blocks in silence. Not awkward, Elvie noticed, just two people who didn't need to talk.

"You don't talk much," He said at one point.

"Is it a problem?"

"I actually am enjoying you not talking my head off or peppering me with questions every time I stop talking. Lots of people can't handle silence."

"Lots of people can't handle not hearing the sound of their own voice for too long. Or having to deal with their own thoughts." The last part had slipped out, and for a moment, she worried he would think she was nuts.

Instead, he hummed thoughtfully before speaking again. "I think everyone should have to listen to their own thoughts once in a while. It's a good way to solve problems, too. No one argues except me." Elvie grinned. She knew the feeling well, but she also remembered a rumor about an Earl, his girlfriend, and an omelette. It occurred to her how someone who preferred peace and quiet would get easily annoyed by constant chatter. Keeping the moment light-hearted

"I imagine you give yourself a lot of grief."

"You have no idea." He had stopped walking again, but she noticed this time it was so he could lean against a post. His leg was clearly hurting.

"Taxi?" She asked. But he shook his head adamantly.

"Nah, I need to shake this out of my leg. Walking'll do me good." He shot her a smirk, "unless you need to ride in a taxi. Not used to all the legwork Chicago requires, I'd imagine." The teasing in his voice surprised her, and she breathed out a laugh.

"Earl Weiss, are you trying to antagonize me?"

"Is it working?"

"No, you'll have to try harder." She couldn't hide the smile. So much for not making friends.

"If it means you're sticking around, I'm going to get a lot of practice."

We can only hope, thought Elvie, as the nerves returned.

Chapter 11

Mr. Schofield smiled when Earl walked in with Elvie. "They're in the garage right now, sir. They told me to show Elvie the way, so if you need to..." The older man trailed off, clearly unsure how much to say.

Shaking his head, his genial smile didn't even falter. "I'm okay this morning. But thank you." Elvie knew what they were referring to: his debilitating headaches and fainting spells. She simply pretended to be taking in the flowers (there really were a lot, and she had always wanted to know what the inside looked like) as they continued to talk. After introductions and more small talk, Earl led her to the back, though it was clear that he knew she had heard.

"I have headaches, awful headaches. Sometimes I've got to lie down upstairs when they get unbearable." He spoke over his shoulder as they walked.

"I've had a few of those myself."

"Not from drinking."

"I don't drink..." She didn't really. She would occasionally have something when she was out with Natalie and Violet, but otherwise she stuck to water. "I mean those headaches that come out of nowhere, and they make you want to grab your head, and you wish..." she trailed off. She was doing that thing where her mouth wouldn't stop talking again.

"You wish you were dead." He nodded and turned. His face was serious now. "Once you go through this door, there's no going back. I know you said you've done a lot of illegal things, but I—we are a loyal group. Double-cross us, and you are dead in less than a day. Understand?"

"Yes." Elvie looked in his eyes. He had tried to school them into the look of emptiness that he was known for, but there was the flash of steel back there that reminded her it wasn't just his temper that made him a killer. There was something else, too, a genuine concern that seemed to want to give her an out, so he didn't have to think about having to kill her. "I'm not going to sell you out. I'm in." She felt her heart stutter a little as she said the words. It would have registered on Shirley's computer, and she would be able to try to figure out what it meant later tonight, with the woman who doubled as their pseudopsychologist.

"Right," He regarded her for another moment, and then his face adopted a showman's smile. It unnerved her a little how fast he could switch gears. "Welcome to Sherwood Forest. You are joining the band of Merry Men." He stepped into a huge warehouse-like garage and spread his arms in front of him.

Elvie tried to push aside the surge of affection she felt for him. It was endearing the way he had introduced her, and he seemed to regard her as a member already. It added to her theory that, despite the reputations being reversed, it was Dean who needed the reassurance that she was trustworthy. She straightened her shoulders, schooled her face, and took in the delivery trucks and car parts. It smelled like a car shop, but it was mixed with flowers and cigarette smoke. Elvie noticed the car sitting in one of the corners. The hood was open, and Victor was talking animatedly with a mechanic. Dean was nowhere to be seen yet. It wasn't as loud as she had expected, which was a pleasant surprise. That was until Drucci noticed them and called them over, one hand on the hood of his car, closing it with a slam. She winced at the noise.

A strange thing happened as they walked across the garage floor. Heads turned to see who was coming, regarded her curiously, then they noticed who was in front of her. Anyone who had previously been goofing around stopped immediately and made themselves busy. A din of tools banging and movement rose around the place as everyone tried to make sure they wouldn't trigger the man's whip-like temper. The chill of the March air had crept into the garage, and several of the mechanics wore thick leather gloves to keep their hands from getting too cold. Elvie, even though her hands were in their gloves as always, slipped hers into her coat pockets and fiddled with the coins she kept there to keep her hands busy.

"Did you walk?" Victor asked Earl. "I would have come and gotten you both."

"I offered to drive." Elvie cut in. "He said no." The Pole shot her a look, as if she had tattled.

"I needed to walk this morning. Between my leg and everything else I've got to worry about--" He stopped, glanced around the garage, and ran a hand over his face. "Not the place for this. Sorry"

Victor's Playboy facade cracked for a moment. "You know you're always welcome at my house. Wait, did you say you can drive?" His bright dark eyes fixed on Elvie as if he had just heard her.

"Yes. I'm a fairly good driver, too." She was an excellent driver, but she didn't want to give them the wrong idea about how good. She wasn't sure what they would think was excellent.

"Do you have a car?" She nodded. "Huh. That surprises me. You don't look like the driving type." Afterwards, on her walk back to her house, Elvie would wonder if Earl had been able to tell what she was about to say because he seemed to raise his voice a bit when he spoke.

"You should tell him what you told me, about your old job." Weiss said, leaning on Vincent's car and regarding everything going on around him, while Elvie repeated the story of her 'previous' career. Vincent's face told her he had a lot of questions, namely, how many people had she killed, but Elvie didn't have to answer because Weiss broke in then.

"Where's Dean?"

"Out delivering flowers to a funeral home. Should be back any minute. Then we've got to have a meeting about tonight's jobs, I guess." The Sicilian shrugged. "I wanted to talk to the guys about my car. See if we could make it go faster."

"Faster?" The look he gave Vincent was incredulous. "It goes 120 mph. How much faster do you want it to go?"

Now, Elvie had had a lot of practice in recent years of not laughing when people called sixty mph fast, so she didn't even register that as a strange question to someone from her time. She did, however, register what that meant for the type of car Drucci had.

"Do you have a Stanley Steamer?" She tried not to look too excited. Her own car was a Dodge Roadster. And she loved it. But a Steamer was the fastest car. "Have you gotten it up to 120?"

"No," he shook his head sadly. "Not enough room in the city, and I'm not a fan of driving on sidewalks like Dean. What's yours?"

"Dodge Roadster, sedan."

"Being an assassin pays well." He laughed. "Does it have the electric start? I have a Studebaker with an electric start, but this is my baby."

"It does. Probably my favorite feature. It makes take-offs and getting out of tight spots faster." She saw Weiss glance at her, and she shrugged. Crank starts had been the bane of her existence. Elvie regarded the car next to them. "This is a really nice car, though." It was dark blue and clearly well taken care of.

"She gets it," Victor said, nodding in her direction. Earl rolled his eyes just as Dean pulled into the garage. The car had barely stopped before he turned it off and jumped out.

"You actually came!" He looked at Elvie with surprise. "Figured you'd chicken out."

"Tell him." Drucci and Weiss said together. As all three bosses and a few mechanics listened, Victor whispered comments to Earl about how awesome it was. Elvie told Dean the story of her old employment. When she was finished, he glanced at Earl, who just shrugged and nodded.

"That's impressive. Glad you decided to side with us."

Weiss said quickly, "Stop talking like that." Dean just looked at him for a moment as if trying to decide if the argument was worth having. Elvie could tell by his face and the fact that Drucci sighed behind her that this was an argument they had constantly.

"Let's head upstairs. George'll just have to join in mid-meeting. As usual." Dean led the way, and Elvie was reminded that she still had to meet and get the approval of a fourth member. She really didn't like George Moran. Every time she had studied the history of Chicago gangsters, including the St. Valentine's Day Massacre, there was something about him that just rubbed her the wrong way. Part of it was that he had discarded the Northsiders when they needed him most, pretending not to know them after their lives were taken instead of his. Maybe another part of it was that he had a punchable face. She wasn't sure. Either way, she wasn't looking forward to meeting him. As if he heard her thoughts (or given that she seemed to be having a problem with controlling her mouth lately, she could have said them out loud), Victor smiled at her as he held the door to the garage for her.

"Don't worry. He'll be a pain in your ass at first, but you get used to him."

Chapter 12

Upstairs in Schofield's was exactly what Elvie had pictured. An office with a desk, some chairs, and a couch. There were windows that looked out over State Street, and the room had what she had learned all rooms in 1924 had, a liquor cupboard. Prohibition be damned- most people still drank like mad. They offered her a drink, which Elvie declined. Everyone seemed to start settling into what she assumed were their usual spots. Dean sat at the desk, looking much more businesslike than she had seen him yet. Vincent was watching the street through the window. Earl had settled into a chair, his leg straight out, giving him an air of having sprawled out, which Elvie was fairly certain he wasn't capable of doing. The room was warm, and in spite of Drucci cracking the window still felt overheated compared to the chill of the garage.

Elvie wasn't sure what to do, so she opted for standing on the farthest side from the door, leaning against the wall. The meeting seemed to be more of them all agreeing on who was going to check on what speakeasies tonight and when. Vincent had some business meetings to do during the day and then would be visiting some new cabarets to sell their liquor to that night. Dean apparently had plans to check out a couple with Louie Alterie, and Earl offered to take Elvie to a couple of them, but Dean said he had another job in mind for Elvie's inauguration. He was even going to be nice enough to fill them in when George Moran walked in.

He was taller than the others and stockier and gave off an air closer to that of a football player than of a gentleman. When he was introduced to Elvie, he sneered and said, "We're welcoming women into our ranks now? Why not just hand the north side to Torrio and Capone?"

Oh, Elvie really didn't like him; there was something about him that set her teeth on edge, something that wasn't there with the others. "Is this one of Drucci's conquests? She's blond, and she certainly is a looker. But I don't think giving her a leadership job is a good idea. She'll probably sleep with a Genna—" He had wandered too close as he was joking, and she lost her temper. Before she could stop herself, she punched him straight in the throat. It seemed to catch them all off guard; it had certainly surprised Elvie, who couldn't remember the last time she had let her impulsive temper take over. Moran coughed several times and glared at her.

"You bitch." He hissed and lunged at her. Drucci was on his feet, and so was Weiss. Dean had pulled a gun but didn't seem to know what to do with it. It didn't matter because before Moran could even touch her, she had moved just a hair to the right and caught his right arm, twisting it behind his back and kicking his knee so he had to kneel. She was careful not to break his arm. She bent down to make sure he could hear her.

"I'm tougher than Torrio or any of their little henchmen. Maybe you haven't heard, but I took out three of the Genna gang on my own, so I would think twice before you call me names again."

"You could probably let him go now," Dean's voice broke through, and Elvie was relieved that she was not dead, as she remembered where she was and that she had just attacked one of the main four while in their headquarters by herself. If Tony or Shirley had been watching the footage, she was in for quite a lecture when they got home. If she got home.

She released his arm and let him topple a bit. She looked up at Dean and said, as sincerely as she could manage, "Sorry. I don't know what came over me. I'm usually more controlled." That part was true. She had acted completely on impulse caused by anger at his insinuations that she was going to be some trollop who joined gangs and slept with the members to rise to the top. She was sorry that she had let him get to her…she wasn't sorry she had punched him.

"Why are you apologizing?" Earl asked from his chair, where he was reclining once again. "He's the one who insulted you and us. Then called you a 'bitch…'"

"Not to mention, he was coming at you the second time. Pure self-defense." Victor was now perched on the corner of Dean's desk and smiled at Moran's shocked expression. "Maybe we can fill you in on why Elvie is here after Dean finishes giving her a job for the night."

Moran looked at Dean, as if thinking someone wouldn't have lost their mind and would back him up, but all he said was, "Don't question who the three of us decide works with us. And we don't call women names. Imagine what your mother would say." The subject apparently closed, Dean leaned forward and looked at Elvie, studying her.

"So, is your car up for a bit of a drive?"

Chapter 13

Which was how Elvie found herself driving to the far north end of Chicago that night, the trunk of her car carrying a bag of money, the latest dough from a heist the four Northsiders had pulled off. Do this, Dean had said, drive the cash to their middle man in Waukegan who would get it 'taken care of,' and she was in. One of them. Which, while that excited Elvie, she wasn't thrilled about doing it alone in the middle of the night. Although, as far as initiations went, it could be worse, she supposed. At least they hadn't asked her to kill anyone.

She could take care of herself. But she disliked not knowing what she was heading into. She didn't know who the go-between was or anything about him…or her. She shouldn't jump to conclusions. After Dean had given his orders and filled Moran in on who Elvie was and why she had been welcomed in (which did little to make him like her more; he still glared at her until she left), Elvie had been dismissed until she was to pick up the dough at Schofield's. Not ready to go back to base, she had instead wandered downtown for a long time, until she caught a taxi back to base and absolutely had to get her car.

Now, though, driving her car, the red Dodge Roadster that, after really looking at it, was much nicer than Victor's Steamer, down an unlit country road, she wished she had done at least some digging. As she pulled into the parking lot of a dilapidated church on the outskirts of Waukegan, she really wished she had asked more questions. Because…a church? But going along with fate was what had gotten her this far, so she simply took a deep breath and got out of the car.

Elvie didn't need a gun, but she had one on her tonight, for appearances, and the thing was bulky under her shoulder and made her more than a little uncomfortable. Gunpowder didn't get along well with her temper. Stealing herself, she hopped out of her car and, as quietly as her boots on the dirt road would allow, approached the well-lit church. Maybe she had the place wrong? She hadn't gotten a passcode knock or anything of the kind, so she just…knocked. After a few minutes, she was considering letting herself in when there was shuffling on the other side of the door. It swung open and revealed what had to be the oldest priest she had ever laid eyes on. The man was doubled over and held a cane, his face wrinkled and liver-speckled. But he had two brilliant green eyes that sparkled at her when he grinned, an expression that made him look like Merlin, before saying hello.

"I'm sorry." Elvie started to back away. "I think I have the wrong place."

"Are you Elvie Townshend?" Even the man's voice was old, sounding as if it were coming to her from the back of a cave. Elvie nodded, and with another, brighter smile—a smile that did nothing to ease the confusion, the priest spoke again, "They called and told me you would be coming. Bring in the bag. Oh, wait. I forgot to ask the question, to be sure it was you. What should everyone have to do once in a while and why?"

Despite her confusion, Elvie grinned, her conversation with Earl that morning had been enjoyable to someone besides herself. "Spend time with their own thoughts. No one can argue back." The priest chuckled and motioned for her to get on with it.

"Get the bag, then. I'll make you some tea, too."

Chapter 14

It turned out, strangely, that the whole 'do this really dangerous mission' thing had simply been a ploy to see if she was trustworthy enough not to steal the money. The priest, Father Drennan, was an old friend of Dean's and, as he called them, the boys. They gave him a question and an answer to prove it was really Elvie. He was then supposed to determine whether he thought Elvie was the 'right sort' and phone them when she left. The feeling of relief that she wasn't going to be involved in a shootout was short-lived, her anxiety taking over. It felt like they were underestimating her...because she was a woman? Surely not...still, it was 1924.

"I think I expected something more dangerous than this."

"Ah, but you still have to get back into Chicago after dark. And people will know you came here now. They'll want to know what you know. That's the dangerous part." He handed her a cup of tea. "It's Earl Grey. And boiled with a kettle." He nodded to the old stove behind him. "Just like back home or what it would have been like," he chuckled. "Now, they've told me all about you. What do *you* think about *you?*"

"I...what?" Elvie's brow furrowed, confused. "Say that again?"

"You can tell a lot about a person's character by what they say about themselves. So, I know what they think of you. George isn't a big fan." He looked at her with an eyebrow raised.

"The feeling is mutual," Elvie grumbled into her tea. To her delight, that made the priest laugh loudly.

"I imagine. He's the one who always surprises people when they find out what side of the line he's on. You'd think it'd be Victor, but no. There's something about George that people associate with Capone and Torrio. Anyway," he leaned forward. "What is your opinion of yourself?" He held up a hand before she could say anything, "Remember, I'm a priest, so try not to lie."

That last line made Elvie snort, as if priests were infallible. But she had to do this for the job, and debating theology wouldn't win her points with anyone. She took a moment to compose herself. "I...I don't like myself. I never have. I can honestly say that there is no one who dislikes me more than me. But I am smart. And I can be funny. It doesn't matter, though. I...I don't think anyone should like me, and I can never understand why they do." She had said into her tea, and when she looked up at the man, he was regarding her with a sad smile.

"That probably sounded like a crock of shit. I mean, no one hates themselves that much, but...I do. I have for a long time." Even before the jump that got them stuck. Over two hundred and fifty years of self-loathing...no wonder she was always tired.

The priest looked at her for a long time without speaking. Then he said, "The people who hate themselves are usually the ones who shouldn't. I'm not going to try to offer you counsel, but if you ever want to talk, well, you know where to find me, and Dean has my number." He cleared his throat and leaned forward. "One more question."

"Am I catholic?"

It was the priest's turn to snort. "No, I won't bring religion into it. In my experience, good and bad people are found in all religions."

"That's actually refreshing to hear a priest say," Elvie said. "Not the whole confess it, and you'll be a shoo-in for heaven."

"I've been around too long for that. I doubt if any of the priests in the city would even consider me a priest." He laughed. "And that actually is a perfect lead-in. Hats off to you, Miss Elvie." She saluted.

"What do you think of them?" He paused. "You don't have to answer about George. I think you've made that point clear."

"I don't know how to answer that question," Elvie said slowly. "I mean, I know how to answer the question, but..." She trailed off. "Look, here's the thing. I *know* the things they do. I *know* that they have killed people and all that. I *know*. I swore when I came to Chicago that I wasn't going to make friends with anyone, I've lost too many people. So the answer I would like to give you is that they make me uncomfortable, and they are horrible people, and how did I get myself into this mess?"

"But that's not your answer." The priest was nodding, knowing she felt exactly what she meant. It must have been difficult being a priest and having gangsters as friends.

"No. It's not. Not at all. They're funny. And kind. And smart. They're absolutely crazy, but I want to be around them. In spite of myself, I want to be their friend. Dean's nuts, but he loves those guys. He would do anything for them...they would do anything for him. Hymie is the one who should scare me the most, I think. But he doesn't. He's intelligent and quietly funny. He's got a lot of charm, and he's kind of gotten the shaft in life. It doesn't seem like it at the outset, and he tries to come across as an ass, but he's really just a person with a lot of problems. He's so much more than what he thinks he is and who people want him to be. Then there's Victor. He's...well, he's Victor. He doesn't care what anyone says or does; he's who he is, and he owns it. I would be lying if I didn't add that he is easily the most handsome man I have met in Chicago so far. Plus, he and Earl are ridiculously easy for me to talk to. But they're dangerous.

"I would never want to be on their badside. But I still want to be honest with them. Tell them when they are fucking up." She realized what she had said. "Sorry. I got carried away." The priest waved it off, and she continued. "But, as I said, for someone who didn't want to get attached to anyone in Chicago, I am pretty attached to them, and it's only been two days." Elvie stopped and caught her breath. "Was that an okay answer?"

"Ms. Townshend, I think that was the best answer you could have given." He looked at her with a look of understanding and comfort. Not pity, but as if he wanted her to know she was okay, that she wasn't alone.

Chapter 15

Twenty minutes later, Elvie found herself speeding back towards Chicago. She had been envious of Victor's steamer earlier, but truth be told, she *had* added some kick to her Dodge, and it topped out at 275. She had also fixed the transmission so it got up to speed even faster. She only slowed down when she got to the city. She was driving through the streets, blowing most stop signs. Until she pulled onto Monroe Street and slowed almost to a stop. Up ahead, she could see Earl Weiss walking down the street; he had his pistol hanging from one hand, protection on the dark, dimly lit street, she assumed. She didn't know how she knew it was him; there was no way to tell from the way he stood or his outline, but a pull in her soul told her it was him. That was…concerning. Still, she didn't know why, but an ominous feeling hung over her. Earl looked perfectly confident and content. Which was when Elvie noticed what he didn't see: two men who were following him. They looked like the Gennas. As Elvie drove closer, she could tell it was Angelo and Mike. Angelo was limping from where she had shot him. Then she noticed another shape ahead of Weiss. It was a third Genna brother. She could see the resemblance between him and the other two from back here.

As she watched the third Genna, she found out later that it was Antonio who yelled something at Weiss. Earl yelled something back, a mangled Italian phrase from the sound of it. With him distracted, the other two Gennas made their move. They were sprinting towards

Earl, his back turned. Elvie pushed the accelerator to the floor, and as Weiss turned around to see the other two coming up on them, she swung the car around, cutting off the shot the Angelo had just fired, and a bullet lodged itself in her door.

Angela and Mike swore, and she heard gunfire to her left as Weiss shot at Antonio. Given that Elvie was still breathing, he presumably missed.

"What did I say I would do if I found you on the wrong street again?" Elvie yelled through the window. She saw Angelo realize who she was and felt a rush of pride as the color drained from his face. They yelled at Antonio to run away before turning to run. Elvie took several shots, each deliberately missing by less than an inch. Enough to scare them. Not enough to do any damage. When she turned to see if Weiss was still there, she saw he was looking at her as if he hadn't truly believed what Dean and Vincent had told him, and it was only now that he realized Elvie *had* taken out three men on her own.

"You should probably get in, and I'll drive you home." She heard sirens starting up, and apparently, he heard them, too, because he hopped in her backseat and slammed the door. She flew towards his house. She doubted if the cops had even made it within six blocks of the neighborhood by the time Earl raced to his house and Elvie drove to base at a deliberately lazy pace. She was about to open the door when it opened for her. And there stood Tony, her boss.

"Tony, I don't have time to argue with you about my methods of doing anything." Elvie sighed as she slid around him. "We can argue tomorrow if you want. It's been a busy night, and I am exhausted—" She didn't get to finish because Tony, having shut the door, stepped forward and enveloped her in a huge embrace. It was awkward and surprising, but after a moment, Elvie returned the hug. She enjoyed the comfort. Tony had heard what she had told the priest, she realized, cursing the pocket watch that relayed messages. Still, after having to pour her soul out like that, it felt good to be reminded that she wasn't hated by everyone.

Chapter 16

Elvie had wanted to sleep late the next morning, but that was not going to happen for her. Outside her room, she could hear Natalie and Tony arguing at five in the morning, less than two hours after she had initially fallen asleep. At six, Violet and Natalie apparently ran face-first into each other. Bixby was making fun of them. Which made them both yell at him. The next time she was awakened at eight by Shirley and Natalie having a lively literary debate in the kitchen, she gave up and rolled out of bed. Pulling on her black leggings and a long white button-down shirt, instead of her oversized White Sox t-shirt, in case someone came to the door, she went downstairs to make herself a cup of tea.

"I'm telling you, Shirley," Natalie was saying when she came down. "*Murder on the Orient Express* is the superior book. The twist at the end and the moral factor, it just... It's a masterpiece."

"*And Then There Were None* has all that and more. The character development for such a short book, especially a standalone, is unparalleled, even by Christie herself." Elvie stood in the doorway of the kitchen, watching the two. Shirley noticed her first, but far from caring that they woke her, she dragged Elvie into it.

"Elvie. You be the decider. Which is Agatha Christie's best book? *Murder on the Orient Express* or *And Then There Were None*."

Elvie sighed and ran her fingers through her hair. "You're both wrong. Her best book was *The Murder of Roger Ackroy*d. Or '*N or M.*'

But I think that's just because that's my favorite of hers." She crossed the kitchen as Natalie and Shirley, apparently unsatisfied with her answer, continued their argument, pouring herself a cup of tea. She sat in a big armchair that made her feel like a little kid when she folded herself into it and listened to them argue while she waited for her tea to cool. She piped up at one point that Natalie was right, and if they wanted to narrow the scope down to those two books in particular, *Murder on the Orient Express* was the superior book. Shirley scowled at her and went on a monologue of how the *Orient Express* couldn't hold a candle to *And Then There Were None* because of the sheer originality of the latter.

"Okay, but the moral debate that *Orient Express* gives us is completely different and, honestly, more enduring than *There Were None*." Natalie stood, hands on her hips, her final point clearly winning the debate as Shirley stalked back down to the control room, grumbling. Natalie raised her mug to Elvie in cheers, who grinned back, raising hers. Natalie returned to her lab, and Elvie finished her tea and picked up the book that she had left, unread, on the coffee table the day before while waiting for Earl, too nervous to read. It was a Christie, *The Secret Adversary*, which was probably what had set them off in the first place, she supposed.

She pulled herself out of the story an hour and a half later. She had thirty minutes to get ready, she realized, before Earl had said he would stop by to pick her up. She went upstairs and put on a suit and pulled her combat boots on before brushing her teeth, ran her fingers through her hair, while not a flapper bob was also not long enough to be considered elegant. She considered putting it up to hide under a hat, but...well, what was the point? She made it back down just in time. She was walking up to the door when he knocked. Opening it, Elvie knew that today was a migraine day. He had an odd, glazed look in his eyes that she hadn't seen before.

"Good morning." She said as she stepped out. "Are we walking again, or am I driving?" She knew the answer already; it was extremely chilly this morning, and she was pretty sure he wouldn't want to walk in the drizzle that was starting.

"Good morning, we can drive, if you don't mind?"

"My car?" She'd have to find time to get the bullet hole out. There was probably someone at the garage who could do it faster, she realized. Maybe she could ask…but no. She wasn't a real member of the group. She would do it herself.

"Yes, we can take the car that saved my ass last night." Earl's voice pulled her out of her thoughts as he walked alongside her. "That was some fancy driving."

"I think it's just called driving. But thanks for calling me fancy." She smiled at him, and his lips twitched, trying not to laugh.

He climbed in the passenger seat, and Elvie backed out of the driveway, riding in silence, her thoughts on why the Gennas had attacked Earl…*again.* Interface probably. That was troubling. She made a note to mention it to Shirley tonight.

After a few blocks, Earl looked over at her and studied her profile. She could feel his eyes on her. She didn't know why it made her so self-conscious, except that he seemed to have the ability to strip a person down to the bare bones. It felt like an eternity before he finally spoke.

"Thank you. I'd be dead right now if it weren't for you."

"Don't mention it. Although you did look surprised that I did actually know what I was doing." She shot him an amused glance and couldn't resist a dig. "You agree with George?"

"There's a difference in knowing something and actually witnessing the thing." He paused. "Dean called this morning. Father Drennan said you're one of the sweetest, most charming, straightforward people he's ever met and that we would be idiots to kick you to the curb."

"So…am I fired?" Her heart warmed as he let out that startled laugh that she liked.

"If I can be completely honest, you were never going to be fired. I knew before we even sent you to the Good Father that you were all those things. Drucci did too. It's just...that was what Dean needed to give him the final push towards saying it was okay."

"George isn't going to be happy."

"George can kiss my ass," Earl said without missing a beat. "You handled yourself like a champ, by the way." Elvie just smiled. Inside, her heart was racing, and she felt a bit buoyant. When she told the priest that she hated herself last night, it was, at least in part, because of moments like this.

Good people didn't want to be approved of by mobsters. Yet, Elvie felt like she had won the lottery. She felt a touch of fondness when, out of the corner of her eye, she saw Earl take out his pocket bible and begin flipping the pages. Apparently, he was pretty comfortable with her. She couldn't imagine him doing something so vulnerable if he didn't trust her.

Stop yourself. She chided in her head. You are not making friends, remember? But at the same time, it felt like Chicago, on the North Side, especially was where she was supposed to be. She was home.

Chapter 17

When they arrived at Schofield's, Weiss was looking extremely pale. He waved Elvie in the direction of the garage and said he was going upstairs to lie down. Dean was not surprised when Elvie told him. Drucci grimaced.

"He was tired yesterday, and after last night, I'm not surprised that he's in rough shape today." Victor glanced at the door, as if he wanted to go check on him as soon as possible.

"You did well yesterday, doll. Welcome aboard." Dean smiled. George sighed loudly from the other side of the truck that was nearby. Elvie nodded, fighting the urge to walk around and stick her tongue out at him. "We're going upstairs to have a meeting, but I don't want you around Weiss when he's like this. You never know what's going to happen. So, if he's feeling better tonight, you go out with him for the speak checks? If he's not, maybe I'll give you a job with Victor." Victor gave her a beautiful smile that made her just a little nervous as images of cars flying over bridges flashed through her head. It was annoying that they didn't think she could handle Earl, but she didn't want to push her luck. To be accepted so easily and readily was unheard of, especially with George so adamant about how much he disliked her.

Elvie waved goodbye, fully prepared to go back to the base and use a training room or paperwork, when, as she was walking to her car, she felt a prickle. Her instincts were telling her she needed to know what was said in that meeting. Or that she needed to witness the meeting to understand the dynamics better. Either way, when she slid into the front seat of her car, she slid through the In-Between.

If the In-Between was the curtain between two dimensions, there was also a sheer liner that ran between. It was harder to manipulate, but with practice, she was getting better. She could see the world of the living, but they couldn't see her. It was handy for eavesdropping. Careful not to move too close to where she knew the curtain was, Elvie slipped into the shop and up the stairs to the office. Before she had even walked in, she could hear George complaining.

"She's nuts. You can't trust her. She's probably on the Genna payroll, and she tricked your priest."

"For God's sake, would you shut up?" That was Earl. His voice sounded tired and strained, "I don't want to hear you whine about how you didn't get your way. I want to hear the duties for tonight so I can deal with the fact that my brain is trying to explode out of my skull."

"Oh shut up, ya baby. No one gives a sh—"

"Moran!" That was Dean. Elvie entered the room to see him standing menacingly behind his desk; even at his height, he managed to make George look like a guilty child. "You either let it go or get out." When George didn't move, he sat back down. Vincent was sitting on the back of the chair next to Hymie's couch, and he glanced down at the other man. Even in the dim light, Elvie could tell the two had just shared a small smirk. Honestly, they were like children, she thought with a shake of her head. "Now, before we get to the nightly rounds, we need to talk about the Gennas."

"Oh, not again." Weiss groaned and moved to prop himself up more, and froze. Which was when Elvie felt herself freeze…because he was looking right at her.

"I thought you sent Elvie home?" He said, without taking his eyes off of her. *This isn't good*, Elvie thought.

"I did," Dean said slowly and looked where he was staring, squinting. "Why?"

"She's standing right there." Earl tried to nod his head and winced.

"No, she's not." Victor hopped down and was walking towards where Elvie stood, still confused, waiting for her brain to catch up. "There's nothing here."

"Yes, there is. Elvie is standing there! I can see her plain as day." Then a look flashed across his face, and his eyes rolled back in his head. He'd passed out. All Elvie could think was "Oh fuck."

Chapter 18

Elvie swung her car into the driveway of the base so fast she felt the wheels come back down when she straightened out. She had left when they got Earl to wake up. He had seen her one more time; she knew before she blinked out. How had he been able to see her? Already, a theory was forming. It had to do with the headaches. With his brother, Joseph. It had to do with Earl's rumored cancer and with his heart problems.

Her feet pounded down the stairs before skipping the last two entirely. Shirley must have been anticipating something because she was ready with all the files for the Chicago missions (Elvie hated that it was now plural) in front of her.

"How can Weiss see me?" She asked without preamble. Shirley looked startled.

"You mean, when you are…?"

"Yes. He saw me. He was having a headache. I was eavesdropping on a meeting, and he saw me." Shirley took her glasses off and rubbed her nose. "The In-Between is…what?"

"It's the spot between life and death. Where, if it's not quite time, you have a choice. You can die or go back." Elvie had the answer on the tip of her tongue, though she knew it would lose its credibility if she said it and not Shirley. That's the way it was here. Theories were better if they came from Tony or Shirley.

"So, if he can see you when you are in that space, that would mean he..." She broke up, and her eyes widened, comprehension dawning. "That would mean he was close to death." Shirley looked thoughtful. "Had he been shot?"

"No...he has cancer, or tuberculosis. Whichever it is, he's got about two years before it kills him. He thinks it's cancer, because that's what the doctors told him." She was pacing, and she could feel Shirley watching her, letting her think. "He's dying, and he's always close enough to death that he's able to see when I am over there." Her brain went into overdrive. He could see her because he was already one foot on the other side.

"What? How do you know?" Shirley started flipping through the files. "Holy shit. He does."

"It's suspected that's why he was a little crazy and fought like he did. He knew he wouldn't live long, so he lived like he was going to die at any moment. More than any of the others. It's why he was denied for the army." She was talking without thinking, reciting facts. Shirley was looking at his file, and the mugshot slipped out as she turned the page. Elvie picked it up. "It's also rumored that he had a brain tumor. But not proven. His autopsy results have been missing for years." Elvie looked down at Earl J. Weiss, his big eyes were wider in the mugshot, and there was a bruise forming on one side. But that wasn't what she was looking at. It was the way his left eye was slightly swollen, and the brow seemed more raised than the right.

"Okay," Shirley entered damage control mode. "We can fix this. It was a hallucination. Or something." Elvie let Shirley talk. She wasn't going to lie to him, not about that. For one thing, it was just cruel to say that was a hallucination, but she also had a feeling he knew when people were lying. Then Elvie realized how close he must actually be to death, or at least how it must have felt for his body when he was having those migraines. Her eyes flicked to the hospital ward and back to Shirley. She kept nodding and making affirmative noises, but internally, she was doing calculations. If it were March 1924 and he were to die in October of 1926, that would be a lot of medicine. But they had it. And no one ever checked the stocks, so they would just assume that they hadn't checked it for a long time...if it didn't automatically restock. She wasn't sure how it worked. It didn't matter. As soon as the idea had formed in her mind, she knew she was going to do this.

Shirley was wrapping up when they heard a bang and then arguing from upstairs. It was Violet and Bixby, they called for both Tony and Shirley. It gave her only a small amount of joy to know things weren't going well on the South Side.

"You're okay? We can talk more later if you want to, but you have the plan right?"

Elvie nodded, then watched Shirley run up the stairs. Once she heard Shirley break into yelling, she ran into the hospital room. There was a big container of gauze on the table, and she dumped the gauze into the incinerator and ran to the medicine cabinet. She found the strongest painkillers she could find and began emptying vials into the jar. Then she threw the empty bottles into the incinerator. The yelling upstairs got louder and covered the sounds. By the time Elvie made her way upstairs with the jar, she had almost 1000 pills in there, the drawer was restocking itself, so no one would notice there were some missing. The jar itself would have been suspicious if anyone had bothered to look at the fact that she was also carrying a smaller medicine vial in her pocket. But they were all arguing over something, and no one noticed her slip out the door and into her car, on her way back to the flower shop.

Chapter 19

Elvie pulled back up to Schofield's ten minutes later. She leaned over and filled the small vial to the top, then covered the jar with a blanket that she, thankfully, kept in the car. Taking one last deep breath, she stepped out of her car and walked over to the flower shop. Dean's car was still out front, but Victor's was gone, and so was George's.

Dean walked out of the backroom when Elvie came in, singing an Irish ballad under his breath. She wasn't comfortable enough yet to go upstairs or in the back uninvited, so she had hoped she wouldn't have to wait too long for someone to come up front. Dean's eyebrows rose when he saw her standing there.

"Hello! What are you doing back?" It wasn't suspicious, just surprised. "I figured after the excitement when you got back to town last night, you would want to sleep all day."

"Ha. There is no peace long enough to sleep in my house." She thought of the yelling that was probably still going on. She really needed to get her own place soon. There was a 'For Rent' sign just a few houses down, she remembered. "I was actually wondering if Earl was still here? I have something that might help with his headaches."

"Ah. Yeah," Dean rubbed his neck awkwardly, "He's still upstairs. He had a bit of a problem after you left. He hallucinated and then passed out. It's been pretty bad before, but that was as bad as I have seen in a long time."

"He's never hallucinated before? Or passed out?"

"He's done both, but they have to be pretty bad, and that one wasn't as bad until then. You hang around long enough, and you'll see. He's a good guy, by my standards, but he's got bad moments. Like any of us. You can go see him if you want," he nodded towards the stairs, "Be careful though. I don't know what kind of a mood he's in."

She thanked him and made her way upstairs. She thought about what Dean had said earlier, about Weiss's moods when he had a headache, and his warning just now. She would have to tread carefully if she didn't want to end up as a bloodstain on the floor of the office.

When she opened the door, she expected him to be lying down as he had been during the meeting, but instead, he was sitting up. The room was still dark as he sat with his eyes closed, leaning his head back. She knew he was awake by the way he had stiffened when he heard the door open. He looked better, but he still had big circles under his eyes, and she could tell he was in pain.

"Um..." Oh crap, she hadn't figured out how to address each of them yet. They were such a talkative bunch, she didn't have to. Of course, with Earl, she should have guessed she would be talking first eventually. "Mr. Weiss?" Mr. Weiss? Really, she thought to herself. It must have sounded weird to him, too, because he opened his eyes and stared at the ceiling before answering.

"Did you just call me Mister?" There was humor in his voice, as if it were such a strange concept that it broke through the headache.

"I wasn't sure how to get your attention. I realized I have never actually had to so far." She was still standing awkwardly half in and half out. Dean's warning about his behavior was echoing in her mind. Besides, she had always hated awkward conversations, and she couldn't imagine a situation where telling him about the In-Between didn't end with him finding her to be crazy. For now, the question of his name was enough of a distraction to lighten the mood and the weight in her chest.

"Earl...Hymie...Weiss...asshole...even Henry, all are preferable from my friends to Mister." He closed his eyes again.

"Are we friends?" Her heart stuttered. Did she have friends? That would be a problem, since she wasn't getting attached. But at that thought, the pill bottle in her pocket seemed to grow in size, as if to say, it's a little late for that, you dumb shit.

"I mean...I hope so. But then I guess it's only been two or three days." There was a brief pause. "You can come in by the way. I won't bite, though Dean likes to tell people I'm unpredictable."

She stepped into the room and slowly sank down into the big chair next to him. "I brought you something for those, actually." She held out the pill bottle. And he, slowly, so slowly, it tugged at her heart a bit to see, moved his head to the side and reached out to take it. He looked like he had been sweating, and his normally slicked-back hair fell on his head, making him look younger than he normally appeared.

"I've got painkillers." But he didn't hand it back, as he examined the pills, turning the bottle around in his hand.

Elvie answered, "Not like these." At that, he regarded her for a second. Then he leaned his head forward so he could see her face better. In the small amount of light from the windows, Elvie could see how old he must have felt. His eyes seemed to sit back in his skull now, giving him a skeletal look, and his teeth were just slightly too big, only adding to the unsettling feeling he was giving off. He seemed to be thinking of how to ask the question as he scrutinized her carefully. She held his gaze, not giving an inch. If he wanted to know, he needed to ask.

"That wasn't a hallucination, was it?" The question was out at last, and all Elvie could do was shake her head as the thought that there was someone who could see her now began to overwhelm her. "Then how come they couldn't see you?"

"Well, I think it's because you are dying?" She hedged. She had never been able to figure out how much he knew about his own health. The records were sparse. As it was, he watched her face for a moment, trying to see some lie in her face that she knew wasn't there, before finally he broke eye contact.

"How did you know?" He wasn't looking at her but at a spot on the carpet, his eyes unfocused, and he reached up to rub his temple.

"You can see me. When I'm in the space between life and death. That's the only explanation for why you could see me when I was over there and they couldn't."

"Yeah, I have something wrong. In my heart, I think. Also, maybe my head?" He shrugged, as if he had given up trying to understand. "Most of the time I'm fine, but these headaches…they take me out. So…if that's the space between…are you dead?"

"Not dead. I…have an ability. The *ability* lets me enter that place. I call it The In-Between. I've learned to control it so I can sometimes eavesdrop. I wanted to know why I wasn't allowed at the meeting, so I came upstairs. Then you saw me."

He leaned back again. "Why can you go over there?" He was talking softly, so she lowered her voice too. He wasn't fighting with her, calling her crazy, and there was something about that that made her shoulders loosen a little.

"Hold on, do you trust me?" It was a loaded question, considering the situation, and when he turned his head to look at her, she felt a bit unsettled because his eyes were still unfocused. He looked confused and unsure. Not like the sure and steady person she had become accustomed to.

"Strangely, yes. You seem honest, and you seem to be speaking frankly. But also, you've saved my ass twice, and I'd like to believe that a woman who looks like you would really be on my side."

Elvie was glad it was dark because she had blushed. "Then I'm going to get you a drink. I want you to take one of those, and then I will explain. Okay?" After the briefest of pauses, he nodded.

"That should kick in in about thirty minutes," Elvie said after he had taken two pills. She helped him lie back on the couch. She didn't sit in the chair again; it felt too formal, really. Instead, Elvie leaned against the chair on the ground next to him. She had always preferred sitting on the floor for talking anyway; it kept her grounded.

"Alright, let's hear this story," he said, resting his hands on his stomach, and for a moment, he looked like a corpse. She really hoped these pills worked.

"I died. Well, almost died." She thought for a moment before the reality hit her. For the first time she was ashamed to admit, it dawned on her that yes, she had in fact died that day. "No, I definitely died for a moment. I ran out in front of a horse-drawn carriage. The horse ran me down. Somehow, I woke up from it. In a lot of pain, obviously." That wasn't a joke either. She had hurt for months afterward. "When I woke up, I realized I couldn't see or hear anyone or anything. There was this fluttering, and I saw a curtain. I pulled on the curtain, and it was the land of the living. I let the curtain fall. I saw another one, and I pulled it up and...it was not the land of the living." Even all these years later, the side of the dead knocked her off balance. It had an air of finality that she had never forgotten.

She looked at Earl, who was staring at her with those massive, unblinking eyes. "I had to make a choice. I could go that way, and that would be it...Or I could go back and live my life. Which is what I do. But now, I get access to a place where I can go, but others can't. I have been practicing, and I have it down to where, if I want to, I can see people, but they can't see me. Unless they are, apparently, you." She gestured at him, and he gave a ghoulish grin. "I can also travel very quickly in the In-Between. That's how I got on the roof when Victor saw me outside here."

"Does anyone else know you can..." he wiggled his fingers at her, and Elvie felt a small hiccup of a laugh escape.

"Just the people at my house. I mean, they kind of have to, you know? But otherwise, no. It's just you. I'm sorry you cannot see me. I'm sorry if I freaked you out so much that you fainted. I really did just want to see what the meeting was about." She looked down at her fingers when she finished talking. But something made her add, "As much as I hate to say it, it's nice to have someone else know."

She felt him watching her. If Earl thought she had lied about anything, he would have said so, she knew him well enough to know that at least. Instead, all he said was, "When you talk, it's like listening to someone reading one of those dime novels." Elvie snorted. He looked back up at the ceiling. "Well, after you left, not much happened. If I'm feeling better, you and I get to visit a couple of speakeasies together. But if I don't, we get the night off. Because Drucci has something he wants to do, he said, and no one thought you and George should work together."

"That reminds me. Thanks for telling George to fuck off for me."

"No thanks needed. Any chance to tell that fucker off is fine with me. I don't mind defending your honor." He made a weird noise. "My headache is fading. And my neck doesn't feel like it's breaking."

"The medicine is working, then. I have a whole jar of it for you in my car, but I figured you didn't want me bringing the whole thing in."

"Were you supposed to give me these?" He shook the vial she had given him and looked at her out of the side of his eye.

"No. But no one will miss them. We have a lot." Also, she thought, the only one in danger of needing them is me. She didn't add that part out loud, though she was just a teensy bit bitter about it, if she was honest with herself.

"Well," he said, quietly. "It looks like you and I will be going to check out some speakeasies tonight."

Elvie squealed in her head. Even in her jaded state, she couldn't help but be excited. But all she said out loud was, "As long as you are feeling okay." The reality that he hadn't expected her to care that much was evident when he looked at Elvie with a smile that made her heart hurt.

Interlude

She always got the hard jobs. The jobs that put someone in danger or require more physicality. She didn't mind, though it did mean that she was often the one who needed the hospital wing. She had lost track of the number of times she had had to wear a sling around base because her body hadn't healed itself entirely from taking a beating. No matter how many times she asked for a light assignment, she kept getting the heavy ones. Heavy on her body. Heavy on her mind. Heavy on her heart. Heavy on her soul. And that had been fine. Until now. Elvie was pretty sure this one was going to kill her.

Chapter 20

It turned out that Earl was feeling better that evening and insisted on driving. Which was fine because Elvie was having a silent anxiety attack in the passenger's seat. At some point in the afternoon, after she had left Schofield's for the second time, it had occurred to her that this particular duty that she was being sent on tonight was going to involve a small space with a lot of people and a lot of noise. That was always difficult for her. While also trying to remember what she could and could not say, it was going to be unbearable.

She pulled absently on the strap of one of her gloves. Earl glanced over at her, then back at the road. "You okay?"

"I'm fine." She had said it too fast, and her voice had gone up an octave, on fineAZS%$$$230wq2 making Earl chuckle. She rolled her eyes in spite of her nerves. "Okay, so I'm not fine. But I will be. Don't worry."

"I'm not worried." He pulled into a parking spot along the street and killed the engine. "But you are. And that's odd."

"How would you know?" Elvie grumbled. She was being ridiculous, and she knew it. "Maybe I work best when I'm freaking out."

"You might." Earl conceded. "Although you weren't freaking out last night."

"Listen," Elvie glanced around. "It's stupid. Just trust me when I say you don't need to worry about it." She had finished adjusting her other glove now and started in on the other one again.

"I know it's only been three days. But you know my little secret about the migraines, not to mention you've saved my life a couple of times. How about you let me help?" He paused. "Before you rip the fastener off your gloves." It was a little loose now, Elvie realized as she sighed. She looked over at him. He looked open, honest, and safe. All ways he had no business looking. Besides, he was right; he was open with her. She should be with him.

"I don't like loud, crowded places." Her voice was quiet as she broke the stare down. "They make me...nervous." That was an understatement. She could already feel the tension building in her shoulders. Knowing he was laughing at her, she looked at the floor, waiting for him to tell her how ridiculous that was. Instead, was quiet for a long time. When she looked up, he was still watching her, as if he was trying to figure out how to say something. Or if he even wanted to mention it. This time, he looked away first and then back at her, leaning against the door, one hand draped casually over the steering wheel, as if he didn't hold the fate of her job in his palms.

"I don't like them either." He watched her face. "I can handle loud, but it's when you put it in a small room that I get jumpy." Earl grinned when her eyes widened with surprise, and he leaned forward, pushed her glasses up the bridge of her nose with one finger, and smiled. "But I know this will be a breeze. You've got me with you. And I've got you with me."

"What if I screw something up for you?" She said, voice cracking a little, looking at the button on his vest instead of at his face.

"I don't think you will. You don't strike me as the bringing the police down on a place type of person. You're one of us now, Elvie. Whether you are ready to believe it or not." Elvie looked back at him now. He was watching with genuine affection. It caught her off guard, and maybe it did him, as well, because he cleared his throat before opening his door. "Now, let's get this over with."

When Elvie met him on the other side, he had put his hat on, and in the dark light, his face would have been unrecognizable if she hadn't known it was him. He offered her his elbow, which she tentatively took. "Look at you," he whispered as they crossed the street, "Feels like just yesterday I had to tell you you could walk beside me, and now you are taking my arm without hesitating.

"It was over twenty-four hours ago. That's a lifetime to some babies out there." She murmured back and was rewarded with a smile. One of the unsymmetrical genuine ones that she had decided were her favorites. He raised a hand to knock on a door, but stopped. Turning to look at her, he put his other hand on hers, where it wrapped around his elbow.

"I'm glad you're here. I know we are not what is considered good and right, and you say that doesn't bother you. I just hope you stick around a while. I find things more enjoyable with you nearby." Before Elvie could say anything, her heart hammering in her throat and feeling warm from her toes to the top of her head, he raised his hand again and knocked on the door.

She only had a few moments to recover herself before the bouncer recognized Earl and swung the door open for them. Elvie followed him down the stairs, and the two stood together for a moment before she saw him steady himself and then step into the fray.

Elvie knew he wasn't completely recovered from the headache and fainting spell earlier. But if you didn't know what had happened, you wouldn't have been able to tell, as he seemed to pull a separate personality around him like a cloak. It was fascinating watching the quiet, mild-mannered but witty gentleman become a slightly terrifying menace. He was still quiet, but in a way that said 'Don't mess with me or I will kill you,' instead of just his natural "Don't mess with me."

While she knew better, Elvie found herself unconsciously giving him more space. As if sensing her hesitation, Earl reached back and grabbed her hand, pulling her up to his side, and put a hand on her lower back as he watched the crowd ebb and flow.

"I meant it when I said I'm not going to hurt you. I'm the person you need to fear the least in this room. Because I'm on your side."

He said it softly enough that only Elvie could hear. She was lucky she *could* hear it over the sound of her heartbeat, which had migrated to her ears when he put a hand on her waist. She sometimes forgot how touch-starved this job made her. "Now, Miss Elvie, tell me what you think?"

He was watching the people talk, laugh, and dance. She wondered what he wanted her to answer, because surely there was a correct answer. He didn't seem to be looking at her for once when she talked. Still, she decided to give him an honest response instead of one of her prepackaged ones.

"I think…it's impressive and very against the Volstead, which makes it pretty damn awesome." The 'damn awesome' had slipped out, though if he had a problem with her swearing, he didn't show it. He was watching everything and everyone with such intensity that she was surprised people couldn't feel him staring. After several moments, in which Elvie noticed he still hadn't taken his hand completely off of her waist, he turned his head to look at her. She had been wrong that first day, she realized. He was probably an inch or two taller than her. Not much, but enough that she couldn't look him straight in the eyes without looking up a bit when they stood this close together. He pulled her just a bit closer. His big brown eyes focused entirely on her, and she wondered how she could have ever thought of…how anyone could look at them and think they were soulless. So much of Earl's personality was right there for you to see, if he wanted to let you in. With a perfectly serious expression, he spoke, his low, gravely voice almost lost in the noise around them.

"I feel now is probably the best time to tell you. We aren't really here to see if they are serving our liquor."

"You don't say," she said, tilting her head to one side as innocently as possible. "I'm *shocked*." He laughed a little at that.

"When did you figure it out?"

"Yesterday." When his eyebrows went up, she couldn't hold back the eye roll. "Look, if you're going to check *that,* you do it during the day. Not when there are people everywhere to witness the scene. Also, you would not just check every joint every night; that takes too long, and no matter how many people you trust with it, something would get messed up in all the communication."

"Very good. You're smarter than most women." He must have felt Elvie tense at that because his lips twitched. Her immediate reaction, to lecture him on how absolutely incorrect he was, bowed under the logic of her brain, which had finally caught up to the situation, seeming to have been pushed aside around the time they entered the place. He wasn't serious. It was a test and a distraction. The test: would she let him insult her and her entire gender because they were in public? More aggravatingly, it worked in distracting her from her nerves.

"Most women I know are smarter than men, but we just can't say it without offending someone or making a grown man cry." She had spoken with more bite than she meant, but even after all this time, being considered inferior because of her sex still rankled. She was, as always, surprised when he smiled. This one was more mischievous than usual and wouldn't have looked out of place on Vincent.

"Believe me, I am aware." He had amusement in his voice. "If my ma or my sister heard me talking like that, I'd be in more trouble than Fred in a police station. I wanted to see what you would say. It's nice to see you wound up." She scowled at him for a moment, wrinkling her nose and pursing her lips. Slide down for a split second before flicking back to meet her gaze. Then he looked back out at the dance floor.

"Would you like to know why we are actually here?"

"Yes, please." Elvie followed as Earl led her over to a small booth in the corner. He gestured for her to go first and slid in after her. There was more space between them now, and Elvie was surprised by just how much she missed his warmth. Despite it being spring, evenings in Chicago were still chilly, and Elvie had been feeling colder than usual lately, as if she had a chronic fever or something. Which wasn't possible, of course. She'd been warm for a second, though... *Get it to-*

gether, Townshend, she told herself. He's dangerous and volatile. However nice he might be now didn't change the fact that before the year was out, he would be a force of hatred and vengeance. She wasn't necessarily sure evil was the right word. It wasn't until after Dean that he became 'evil,' per se, and it always made her wonder if it was just the straw on the giant pile of baggage that life had dealt him that broke the camel's back. Besides...who was to say she wouldn't be just as willing to seek out retribution if someone killed one of her loved ones.

A waitress came by, and Earl asked for a gin and tonic, and Elvie ordered just water, which earned a weird look from the girl. When the girl had left, Earl had also looked at her with a question, but she just shrugged, and he let the subject drop, instead looking around until his eyes found whatever it was he was looking for.

"See that guy over there?" Earl asked, pointing one finger ever so slightly towards a tall man sitting with a couple of more guys and a girl on his lap. When Elvie nodded, Earl continued, "That's one of the police inspectors. He's married. But not to the woman on his knee. The man on his left is the city treasurer. He has a drinking problem, and his wife was part of the committee to get the Volstead Act passed. The man on that man's otherside works in the city morgue."

"What've you got on him?" Elvie asked, watching a woman in a green dress slide into the seat next to him.

"It's not him we are watching. It's his wife." Earl glanced away from them then. "She's a problem because even though she frequents here with him, there are rumors that she is a part-timer at a south side brothel." His cheeks were pink when he said brothel, and Elvie noticed he didn't look in her direction either.

"So, are you sending me in to confirm it?" She said it with all the casualness she could muster because while she had experience spying on brothels, she really didn't like the men that frequented them. The violent ones, anyway. The aggressive ones. She was a bit surprised that they were considering her there so early, but strike while the iron is hot, she supposed. Next to her, Earl looked as if she'd smacked him.

"What? No." He sounded genuinely surprised by her question. "We've got a couple of people working on verifying it, but we would never send a woman undercover to find out."

"It would make sense if you were. I wouldn't be offended if you asked me to, you know?" She was watching his face, his jaw clenched and unclenched a couple of times.

"It'd be dangerous and stupid. While I am okay doing those things myself, I don't ask others to do them." Finally, he seemed to relax just a touch. It was odd. Not one person on the Pathfinders team ever seemed to think twice about sending her anywhere, no matter the situation. They didn't even ask if she was okay afterwards, if she wasn't visibly hurt. Elvie became aware that she was the only one looking shocked now. Schooling her face back to neutral, she waved for Earl to continue.

Earl, as she had expected, would be careful about what he said, making sure every word was just what he wanted. Now, he paused before speaking again, putting his thoughts in order after he had been distracted. "We gather information on the people here to use when we are in a pinch. Or under arrest. Or need to bribe people to look the other way." She nodded and watched the dance floor. The inspector was spinning the woman on his knee in clumsy circles and had stepped on her toes at least three times.

"The Volstead Act won't last forever," Weiss said softly, "so people can leave messages here for us for safe cracking jobs and the like. We have to keep our skills sharp. Frankly, I don't think any of us are made for normal jobs." The waitress came back with their drinks and set a piece of paper down with them. "Like this one," he said, reading it and then putting it in his coat pocket. "I'll tell the guys about it tomorrow." Then he was quiet. Letting the quiet sit, Elvie took in the speakeasy. The corner that Earl had chosen was the quietest in the place, next to a door that, from the cool breeze coming from it, led to the alleyway outside. The dark wood bar and the low lights made the women's dresses sparkle even more, and the closeness of the brick and wood walls made the music feel louder than it was. People danced, laughed, kissed, and talked all around them, but it wasn't as overwhelming as she had expected. The band was just starting another song when Earl spoke again, pointing out a woman who had just walked through the door.

"That's the mayor's niece." He glanced at Elvie and shook his head, looking like she imagined the girl's older brother would have looked if he'd found her here, affectionate but disapproving. "She loves these places. And her drink. Surprised she's here tonight, though. Her favorite is the one across town."

He fell quiet again. For the next ten minutes, Elvie was thoroughly absorbed in drama at a nearby table as a woman threw her drink in a man's face and stormed out. In the wake of the exit worthy of a stage queen, Earl laughed.

"We can probably leave now, if you want. I think I've got enough information now."

"If you want to. I'm okay with whatever. Do we have to go to another one?"

"Dear God, I hope not. I'm not as chipper as I seemed in the car." He tossed her a smile, "But I'd be a lot worse if you hadn't helped."

"I'm glad I could."

"Can I ask you a question?" Elvie raised her brows over her glass. "Why did you help? Because I'm guessing you could have gotten in a lot of trouble."

"I could get in trouble, yes." She didn't know how to answer. "Look, you...I like you. And Victor and Dean. Maybe George will grow on me? I doubt it, but maybe." It earned a smile, the smile reached his eyes, which she considered a victory. "I hated seeing you in pain. Knowing or figuring, I guess, that you were close enough to death be able to see me was...hard. I felt like I had a chance to save you. If not, save you, to make your life easier." She took a deep breath and looked back over at Earl, who was watching her with a strange look on his face. "I did it because you're my friend and I hate to see friends hurt." Earl looked down into his drink and didn't say anything for a minute. Elvie worried she had said too much or offended him somehow. But finally, he looked up, and his cheeks were blushing again.

"I'm glad to have a friend like you." He said with a smile. Elvie smiled back and took a drink of her water because he mouth was suddenly very dry. He pulled out a watch and glanced at it, "It's only nine pm. Want to stay a while longer?"

"Sure." She croaked. She set down her water. They sat together, chatting for a while, the surveillance and people around forgotten, scooting closer together on the bench so they didn't have to talk so loud.

Earl told her about growing up on the west side and his stint in Catholic school. She told him about traveling, including what it was like to visit London before the war. She told him about getting stuck aboard a pirate ship by accident and proving herself to be stronger than the captain, which had earned her a free trip to Tortuga, the pirate island, and helped find a way back to the States.

He asked her what she did when she wasn't around them, and she told him the truth, that he might think she was boring, but she spent most of her time exercising and reading, which led to a discussion about books. It turned out that he did like to read a bit, but he hadn't for a while.

"Bootlegging keeps you busy, and so does being sick." He thought for a moment before adding, "It's not considered the tough thing to do, so I learned to hide it. But when I was a kid, my folks didn't have the time, you know. They ran a saloon. But my brothers and sisters read to me until I was old enough to do it myself."

"What did they read to you?" She was genuinely curious. Little Earl Weiss was something people knew nothing about, but it was more than that. She wanted to know because she wanted to know him.

"Fred and Bernard loved to read me things like Robin Hood and Gulliver's Travels. Violet read me the Oz books when we got some used ones." His eyes had a faraway look. "I would ask her to read to me even after I learned to read, because I loved her voice. I still wish I could ask, but you know, it'd be strange." He shrugged. "Now I mostly just read the paper, or occasionally pick up a cheap book at the newsstand or what have you."

"Have you read Robert Louis Stevenson?" She asked, leaning forward. Internally, an alarm rang out, telling her to back off; she was too interested, too curious, but to her relief, Earl didn't seem to care.

"A bit. We had the kids' books of Psalms at home. Frederick likes to say I should read Dr. Jekyll and Mr. Hyde. He's probably not wrong."

"Well, I don't know if it suits you all that well from what I know, but you should definitely read Treasure Island. Or Kidnapped. Or The New Arabian Nights." She paused. "I don't know if that one's available around here. I have a copy if you want to borrow it sometime." Reign it there, Elvie, she thought. It was just that...she couldn't help it. As much as she loved talking to Natalie, Shirley, and Tony about books, she always loved the thrill of introducing someone to something new.

"I would like that. Can you bring it with you when you come to the garage tomorrow?"

"Absolutely."

"Look at you changing me already."

"Am I? Or are you just too nice to tell me to shove off with my 'book learnin?'" She said playfully. She had learned over the night how easy it was to rile him up and how much fun too. He, in turn, had learned the same thing, though he might have already known how to do that before they sat down, she realized, thinking of his barb about women and his quiet prodding to get her out of the car at all.

"Pfft, I was book learnin' with the best of them for a while. You, on the other hand, with that subpar vocabulary over there..." She shoved his arm gently with her elbow, making him laugh.

The bar had started clearing out around them, Elvie noticed as she glanced at her pocket watch. It was one in the morning. "Holy shit." Earl glanced at his own watch, and his eyes went wide.

"We should probably head home." He sounded regretful about it, the same as how she felt.

On the drive home, Elvie realized how tired she actually was; she was spent physically, mentally, and emotionally for a change. So much so that when Earl said he would see her at the flower shop tomorrow, she had gone inside, set five alarms so she wouldn't oversleep, and promptly collapsed, sound asleep on her bed.

Chapter 21

After that first night with Earl, Elvie settled into a routine. She went every other night with either him or Victor. She would go on deliveries once in a while when the driver might need back up, and she had been to see the priest in Waukegan a few times. The guilt that she felt with the mission was always lingering, reminding her that she didn't really belong, that she wasn't being perfectly honest, but after a while, she gave up on trying not to be friends with them.

Earl knew she hated going into the especially loud and active speaks and Vincent knew that she was a good backup getaway driver for him. He also knew that if he got in trouble, it was less of a hassle to call her for help than to get a lecture from the others. Dean, while they didn't work together much at all, enjoyed having her in the shop to talk to when he was arranging flowers. She and George had reached a tenuous truce, but still argued, and the other three knew to keep them apart unless they wanted to break up a fight.

For their part, Bixby and Violet had settled in nicely on the South Side, and Bixby said once that Capone wasn't all that bad, and Elvie had choked on her water and had to be excused from the table. The two had recently moved to live in Cicero but stopped by for visits regularly. She learned from Violet that Angelo and Mike still got ribbed constantly for being shot by a woman.

"It would be funny," Violet had said, "If I didn't know that woman could probably kill them all with a toothpick." Elvie had smiled, unreasonably proud at the comment. She still did odd jobs here and there in other parts of the world, but she was enjoying herself in Chicago and had once or twice caught herself thinking of it as home. It couldn't be home, though, because almost everyone she knew would be dead by the end of the decade. And while she hated to admit it, that thought had kept her up at night. It had gotten to where she barely slept at all, running out at all hours to go find something to do.

Chapter 22

It wasn't long before Elvie had a favorite of the three. She wasn't at all surprised that it was Earl 'Hymie' Weiss. He had always been her favorite to learn about, but getting to know him as a person instead of a historical figure was a whole new experience. She'd met people she'd studied before, of course, but none had she enjoyed getting to know as much as him. He was aloof with most people, but once he had decided he liked you, his personality started to emerge. He was still more serious and quiet than Dean or Victor, but it wasn't in the way Elvie was quiet. Choosing not to talk unless it's important, too shy to be the center of attention. There was a seriousness that came from growing up in a rough neighborhood, with older siblings, and spending time in a saloon during his formative years. It was a seriousness that was born from bitterness at his health, which, while they were more manageable after the medication she snuck him, the headaches still bothered him.

In late March, shortly after she had given up even attempting to sleep, Elvie was standing in the garage next to Earl, listening to George talking about…something. She wasn't really paying attention to him. He gestured wildly, and his large form had the tendency to run into things when he grew too animated, meaning the shop was empty around him as the mechanics and drivers gave him a wide berth. Ernie Barrett, one of Elvie's favorite drivers, was leaning against a table nearby listening, his hat sitting ever so slightly to one side and slipping off his light hair a little more every time he moved. Earl had asked her once how many times he had to pick the thing up in a day, and they had kept a daily wager on it ever since. Her losing streak was up to five days now. Honestly, if being from the future should have been good for anything it was betting but clearly, this was not the case. She was just wondering how much longer George was going to go on for when, next to her, Earl flinched.

It was hardly noticeable to anyone else, and even though she seemed to have a surprising connection with him, Elvie wasn't sure she would have noticed it if she wasn't standing close to him. She glanced at him out of the corner of her eye and noticed his eye twitch, just a little, the color slowly leaving his face. Hadn't he mentioned having a headache earlier? Yes, he was on his way to lie down when George had stopped them. Contrary to what people believed, Earl was polite to a fault, and when George had stopped to talk, he hadn't even batted an eye or complained. Now, though, the headache seemed to be getting much worse and quickly, too.

"Earl?" Elvie whispered. "Let's get you upstairs." But he shook his head and said something about a speakeasy nearby to George. George barked a laugh, and he went rigid again. His hand, shaking just a little, reached up to rub his temple, and he let out a small grunt. Elvie swore internally as she took in every aspect of the situation. They were in a garage. He had just grabbed his head. Ernie was there...shit. She just had time to swivel and catch him, helping lower him slowly to the ground as he fell into a seizure. Everyone in the shop stood around them until Elvie turned and tossed the keys of his car that were sitting next to her to George. "Go. Bring it around now. We've got to get him to the hospital." George looked like he was going to argue, and Elvie regretted immediately throwing him the keys, but to her immense relief and surprsie he listened.

Thirty minutes later, the pair of them were sitting with two chairs between them in the hospital waiting room. Earl, who was no longer seizing by the time they pulled up, was just conscious enough not to need a gurney to take him back with the nurse. George had disappeared to make a phone call, she assumed to Earl's family, before he joined her again. It was warmer out than it had been, and she hadn't taken off her coat yet, so she was still wearing that. Not to mention there was a fire in the fireplace...so why on earth was she freezing again? It had been happening more often now, the cold snaps, and they were always followed by a headache. Not nearly as bad as Weiss's, obviously, but considering she wasn't supposed to get sick...well...there was a reason she hadn't mentioned it to anyone yet. George tapped his foot and shifted awkwardly.

"That was some quick thinking, Townshend." He said at last. George hated silence. It was part of the reason they argued so often. He couldn't just be quiet. Right now, however, Elvie understood. He had just watched his best friend have a seizure on a garage floor. Something that had been deeply unsettling to witness, even as someone who was trained to handle those things, seeing it happen to the man she spent most of her time with lately had been...awful. What had that been like for George?

"Thanks," Elvie said after a beat. "And that was some good driving." George snorted.

"Thank God there were no cops around." He had definitely broken at least three laws on the way here. But they'd made it. "He's gonna be in a real lather about this." Elvie glanced over at him. She knew what he meant...but she didn't know what to say, so she just let him talk. "He hates people seeing him in pain. He thinks they'll think he's weak. Christ and a bunch of the drivers were there too." He sighed and sank back in his chair, falling silent just as the nurse who had gone back with him came out again. She smiled at them when they both stood to greet her.

"He's going to be just fine. The doctor wanted to keep him longer, but he's refusing. Can one of you see him home? And will he have someone with him for a few hours?"

"I'll take him home." Elvie hadn't even hesitated. But then she realized that this was not 2025, and this could have very negative connotations. *Someday, Townsend.* Tony had once *said. Someday you'll stop being so impulsive and* modern. Well, it had been centuries, and it still hadn't happened. She expected George to argue, but he simply handed her Earl's key.

"I'll go get Mary, his ma." He added to the nurse. "She'll be able to stay with him." The nurse nodded and then gestured for Elvie to follow as George hurried out the door.

Hospitals don't change much, Elvie thought as they walked down the sterile hallway, their shoes tapping on the tile floor. The technology does. And the medicine, sure. But the bones stay the same. Maybe that was a good thing? Static and reassurance. Elvie sucked in a breath as they turned a corner, and there, sitting in a chair next to the nurses' station, was Earl. Except...not. There was something different about this version, she thought. He looked pale, tired, vulnerable. When he met her eyes across the room, she recognized the look there as depression, and her heart lurched. His hair was a mess again, and she resisted the urge to smooth it down, knowing he would hate it. The man in front of her wasn't really Earl. This was the gangster that everyone else saw. Beaten down by his own body and life. All his good was behind a wall at the moment, and he wasn't going to let anyone in. This was Hymie Weiss, and he wasn't half as scary as he wanted people to think. She followed him to the car, neither of them saying a word, and when he held out his hand for his key, Elvie looked at it and then back up at him.

"I know you've had a bad day, but even a please won't get me to let you drive. Now, into the car, Mr. Wojciechowski." He glowered at the use of his full last name, a name that she had always known but that Victor had decided to tell her after many, many drinks one night. It had panned out because she now called *him* Mr. D'Ambrosio when he was annoying her. Elvie simply walked around to the driver's side and climbed in...and waited. Finally, muttering under his breath, he opened the passenger door, slamming it behind him. They rode to his house in silence. Mary and George were standing on the front step, waiting.

Everyone looked smaller next to George, but Mary seemed to look even smaller, the worried mother running to her son, who immediately lost all his anger and simply let himself be directed inside.

"Thank you," she said, turning back to Elvie, and this was the moment that the time traveler finally felt intimidated. Mary was the female version of her youngest son. Dark hair, dark eyes, and a serious countenance. "I'm Mary Weiss, his mother." In her head, Elvie had a million questions for her, but bit them back. Knowing now was not the time.

"It's nice to meet you, Mrs. Weiss. I'm Elvie Townshend." She held out her hand, and the older woman smiled, pleased by the lack of pretense and shook it, a strong grip that didn't surprise Elvie at all.

"I've heard a lot about you from the boys. They like you very much." Elvie glanced at George, who was shifting awkwardly on the corner, and Mary, despite the situation, laughed a little. "Well, maybe not all of them. But George is a prickly thing."

"Hey!"

"Well, you are," Mary called back and then turned to Elvie. "I have been dying to talk to you but..." she gestured at the house.

"Now is not the time." Elvie finished. "Is there anything else I can do for him?" Mary shook her head, smiling sadly. "He'll be back to himself shortly. You'll see him tomorrow." Elvie nodded and handed her his car keys.

"I just live right over there." She nodded towards the big house, with brick walls and a busted front step that they had chosen to be their base of operations in Chicago. "If you guys need anything, don't hesitate to ask."

"I really appreciate that." Mary smiled and then headed up the stairs and inside, leaving George and Elvie standing on the sidewalk. George opened his mouth, and Elvie held up a hand.

"I swear to God, George, if you offer to walk me home, I will punch your lights out. Again." She stepped around him and called back. "See you tomorrow." Elvie knew, though, that even if she did see Earl tomorrow, he wasn't going to be himself, not right away anyway. She did not expect him to shut her out entirely.

Chapter 23

Every time Elvie would walk into a room after that, he would walk out. She did deliveries and other jobs with Victor because he would always find something else to do. Elvie was stung, but she didn't push him. Then, one day, after a delivery, she was walking to her car. She saw him watching her leave through the office window, a sad, tired look on his long face. She smiled and waved. He lifted a hand but then stepped away. The next day, she had asked Victor about it.

"He's embarrassed." Vincent sighed as he drove them along Lake Shore Drive. They were headed to his place to have dinner with his wife, as she was tired of hearing about Elvie but never meeting her. "Idiot thinks that you won't see him the same way now that you saw him having a fit on the garage floor. We keep telling him you won't care, but he doesn't listen. You know how he can be." He sounded exasperated, and Elvie wondered how many times was spent over the course of Earl and Victor's friendships arguing over things like this. "I'd say he'll come around, but he's being more stubborn than usual about this."

Elvie had simply nodded, pushed the thought to the corner of her mind to examine later. She enjoyed her time with the Druccis, except Cecilia scared her a little…okay, a lot. She was loud and expressive. Her bleached blonde hair flew when she moved, and Elvie had a hard time determining whether or not she was angry. An issue that Victor shared as he tended to say things to Cici as if they were questions instead of statements. Throughout dinner and coffee after, Elvie was freezing, pulling her jacket tighter around her when no one was looking and shifting closer to the fire. As they walked to the car, the headache arrived again, just a dull ache tonight between her eyes. When she got a moment alone in the control room, she needed to check her stats. For now, she enjoyed watching Victor and Cici banter, a sweet back and forth that she had never expected from him.

When he took her home, Elvie had gone back to thinking about Earl and his new coldness. Victor talked, in the seat next to her, mostly yelling at other drivers and commenting on people's driving. She thought he hadn't even noticed she didn't say anything, but he surprised her when she got out in front of the house. Leaning over so he could see her on the sidewalk, his voice took on a serious tone, "Elvie. It might help if you talked to him. I know you want to give him space, but he misses you, and I can tell you miss him. You guys need each other. And one of you has to break the ice, and we both know it won't be him." He drove away, leaving Elvie standing, exasperated and tired on the sidewalk. With a long-suffering sigh, she looked at the stars, wondering to herself if it was too late to run away to Antarctica for a couple of decades.

"He is a pain in the ass, isn't he?" Came a voice out of the darkness, making her jump. No one ever snuck up on her. The other agents tried, and if anyone even came close, they got a prize of some kind. Elvie was well aware of it all and would act surprised if she was feeling kind, but none of them ever genuinely snuck up on her. Looking around, turning in a circle, Elvie couldn't see anyone, further disorienting her.

"You probably can't see me on that side, right now. I haven't mastered this like you." The voice had a slight rasp to it, a scratchy throat, but there was something else…something familiar about the cadence, Elvie thought as she considered what the voice had said. With a slight hesitation, Elvie stepped through her side of the curtain, her eyes widening when she saw a man of about twenty-three standing on the other side.

He was a little taller than her, with a ruddy complexion, brown eyes, and brown hair. But that wasn't what grabbed her attention. No, that was his slightly hooked nose, his cupid bow lips, and his ears, sticking out just a little from his head. She knew that nose and that mouth. The one she was used to was hesitant to smile and usually set in a firm, serious line, at least when first meeting people. This man, though, looked as if he were holding in a smile, and his eyes danced with mischief that gave him the air of a fae king. She knew at once who he was and also hoped that she was wrong. That it was impossible.

"Joseph Weiss?" Her voice came out a little hoarse. Was she seeing ghosts now? Joseph had died in 1913 at a sanatorium in New Mexico, after a battle with tuberculosis, exacerbated by the stress of a murder trial. He was the oldest Weiss child, and Elvie had always suspected his death left his brothers, at least the younger two, feeling that they had big shoes to fill, while missing their sibling. He shouldn't be here, and she shouldn't be talking to him. And yet...

"A pleasure to finally speak with you, Miss Townshend." He gave a bow that reminded her of Earl during his tour of the garage, with his flamboyant gestures and over-the-top showmanship.

"How are you here? And how do you know who I am?" Elvie crossed her arms, trying to appear more intimidating than she felt. In truth, she was completely thrown by this whole situation. If Joseph wanted to, he could attack her and win. Anyone could, because she was clearly in a lucid dream.

"I've been watching...from that side." He stuck his thumb over his shoulder, indicating the side of the dead. "The barrier's been a little less firm lately, and I was able to push through it just now. I was hoping you would be able to hear me."

"Well…shit." Elvie sighed loudly. She'd often wondered what would happen if a dead soul decided to come back through. Now, it appeared—wait—"What do you mean watching?"

"I was there that night you met Dean and Victor. I've been keeping tabs on my family." As he talked, his voice seemed to lose a little something, and his posture changed. "I can't stay for long, on either side, apparently. I always end up being pulled back to Albecerque. That night, I was trying to figure out how to help when you showed up. I got pulled away, but I've been quite enjoying watching you with the lot of them. You pull them out of their shells."

"I don't think Victor needs me for that," Elvie said, drily, making Joseph bark a laugh, so different from his brother's yet also the crooked smile. "Why have you been—"

Joseph held up a hand and cut her off. "I can't stay long, I'm going to go back to the desert soon. If you want more answers, you need to come find me. Which shouldn't be a problem."

"But—"

"What I wanted to say was that Victor is right. My brother is a pain in the ass that way, and he won't be the one to open that door back up. I also wanted to tell you to talk to him, like Victor did. You two need each other. And I don't just mean that in a metaphorical way. Something's coming…" he twitched, and he seemed to be dissolving.

"Oh no, I need answers." Elvie lurched toward him, but he was already gone. His voice left her one last message.

"Talk to my brother. Then come find me in New Mexico. I'll answer your questions there."

Chapter 24

The next day, Elvie wasn't supposed to be at the shop, but she went anyway. She had not slept at all, instead she had walked to Earl's house, turned on her heel and went home where she paced a hole in the floor of her own workshop, a large room beneath the control room, waiting for dawn. In truth, she wanted to talk to Earl not because of Joseph's promise to answer her questions but because she missed him terribly. She missed talking to him or just walking in silence. She missed his subtle eye rolls whenever someone annoyed him. Elvie missed her friend and it had been so long since she had had a genuine friend that the abscense of him was startling. Yes, Elvie told herself, it was only friendship and nothing more.

At last, she made herself do some research and repairs on her car, when it was late enough in the day that she knew Earl would be there, Elvie showered, dressed, and raced out of the house before anyone could speak to her.

It was a warmer day, and the door to Schofield's was open to the street, trying to entice visitors with the scent of flowers, though it was hard identify the flowers over the regular city odors. Dean was at the counter when she walked in, arranging some flowers. He started to greet her, but she held her finger to her lips.

"Is Earl here?" She whispered.

Dean nodded, "Upstairs running some numbers. Tell me you are here to get him to cheer up." She winked and slipped up the stairs silently. Once she was sure that Dean couldn't see her anymore, she slipped into the In Between and stepped through the office door. Earl had his head bent over a ledger and was tapping a pen on the paper absently. He didn't hear her walk in and didn't notice her until she stepped right in front of the desk. He looked up, startled. Then she stepped out of the In Between, and the sounds of the traffic flooded in.

"Hello." She said, surprised by how unsure and shy she sounded. He'd never brought out this side of her, and it was a strange feeling, leaving her exposed and a little sad. She averted her gaze, looking away as he stared at her. "I'm sorry for sneaking up on you, but I knew if you heard me coming, you would find an excuse to leave." He still didn't say anything, just kept staring at her, in that disarming way of his, the one that made her talk without thinking and spill everything before she could think better of it.

"I want you to know that I don't see you any differently after what happened in the garage or at the hospital. I still find you a bit intimidating and all that stuff. I still have a healthy regard for my personal safety, or however I phrased it that day... but mostly I miss you. You're the best friend I've got around here. I'm sorry you're embarrassed, but you don't need to be. Like, why should you be embarrassed anyway? You can't help how much it hurts. It's not like I'm going to judge you for that anymore than shooting someone and I'm still here. Clearly. Besides that, I really prefer you for speakeasy checks. I don't have to take care of you because you don't get drunk. You're a much better dancer, by the way, and you don't trail off in the middle of a sentence because of a lady's rear in a nice dress. You are infuriating, sure. It's the kind of infuriating that I like the best and..." Had she just said that out loud. Her cheeks began to heat as she felt a blush creep up them. "And...And...could you say something?" She was aware she had stamped her foot just a little at the end, but seriously. Wasn't he going to do anything except stare at her? After a moment, a small smile spread across his face.

"Elvie, why are you apologizing to me?" He stood, coming around the desk to stand in front of her before, well before she threw her arms around him in a hug. She had never thought of him as a hugger, but she felt him smile into her hair, and he squeezed her back. He was the most tightly coiled human she had ever known, and she could feel how tense he was, but after a moment, he relaxed, and the hug became warm and comfortable.

He pulled away, put his hands on her shoulders, "I'm sorry, Elvie. You have to understand. I'm used to being the toughest guy around, and when stuff like that happens, it shatters that illusion. I don't know what expectations you have of me, and I felt like I had disappointed you. I was so embarrassed and then...well..."

"You didn't want to have to apologize first?" She guessed, and he gave her a playful scowl. "Listen, Earl, you never have to remind me what you are capable of. I know all about you. I know your reputation and that you shot your brother. I know about most of the other stuff you have done, or at least the idea. Don't worry, I have a respectful fear of you." She had meant it to be funny, but instead he looked down at the floor between them. His voice when he spoke was sad.

"I don't mean that I would want you to be scared of me. I just mean I want you to think...I want you to *know* I'm tough." He didn't meet her eyes, still. Elvie was always amazed at how sentimental things were before her time. This felt like a more intimate moment than she had intended. Except that could have just been the person involved. That's how it had been with Earl from the start. Everything felt more intense. *You two need each other,* Joseph had said. Was this part of that? Or just who he was?

"Trust me," she said, lifting his chin with one finger so he would look at her. "I am well aware of how tough you are." The moment still felt charged and after a second, Elvie bounced on her toes, a nervous habit she seemed to be picking up from Vincent and asked what he had been looking at, turning to the ledger he had been going over.

"Just trying to figure out how much money I need to set aside for something." He sounded like he had had enough with the task.

"Who are we bribing?" Elvie flipped the ledger towards her.

"What makes you think we are bribing anyone?"

"Are you insulting my intelligence?" She shot him a look. And he grinned.

"No more so than usual...ow!" She had poked him with his pencil. The two spent the afternoon in the office goading each other, Elvie perched on the desk or pacing the room as he made tallies and did calculations in his book, telling her what she had missed when he was working on his own and she told him about Victor throwing up in the river one evening and having to take him home to Cecilia, nervous the whole way. Dean and Victor opened the door when the shop was closing to find them laughing hysterically at Elvie's impression of George.

Chapter 25

The problem with going somewhere new in the In-Between was that she didn't quite know where to visualize to get herself there. Having never been in Albequerque, New Mexico, Elvie just decided to think of the place and Joseph, if he was actually there and hope for the best. It was a method that had gotten her this far, no point in giving it up now, she thought dryly, looking around at the walls of the sanitorium as it materialized in front of her. Elvie looked to her left where she saw him. Leaning against a wall nearby was Joseph. He tipped his hat, which he had gotten from a hat she didn't know. Her face must have shown it because he chuckled and took it off spinning it in his hand. As he spun it, it changed from a flat cap to a straw hat to a more modern fedora.

"It turns out I have some control over my wardrobe here." He tossed it in the air and caught it as it turned back to a flat cap. "I'm still learning the ropes, but I can't get through to your side."

"I don't think I can help you with that," Elvie said, blinking and appearing perched on a low wall just next to him. He grinned, so unlike his brother, Elvie thought, and yet he seemed to trust her implicitly, and she didn't have any reservations about him.

"Well, not yet." He hopped up next to her. "You and Henry make up?"

"He goes by Earl now," Elvie avoided looking at him, instead turning her face up to the stars, which could be seen for miles, unlike in Chicago. It was the thing she always missed in big cities, the night sky.

"He'll always be Henry to me. You didn't answer my question."

"Yes. We are back to friends." No more beating around the bush, she decided. She needed to know how he had come over to the middle. "So, how did it just happen that you were able to pass over here. I thought souls moved on after they went through that side."

"Have you ever seen it happen?" He looked at her curiously, head tilted to one side.

"I...no." Elvie had avoided that side of the curtain as much as possible, the emptiness that she had felt when she looked through had been terrifying enough. "I just assumed since I never saw anyone over there..."

Taking pity on her, Joseph answered the unspoken implication. "Most people do go on. But I can't. I've seen a few others over there who couldn't either. They seemed to think there was something they were waiting for. They weren't completely wrong, I don't think. I always felt like I was waiting for someone to tell me what to do. I knew I was going to be needed somewhere. So, you wait." He shrugged, though his face looked pained. He had turned his own face up to the stars when he finished, trying to hide it, but she had already seen.

"When you arrived in Chicago, I was able to get through to the middle. I had just been watching from there, but now the divider moved a little more each day. And one day, the day you met George, actually, I pushed through." Elvie had no idea what to say. She had no doubt he was telling the truth, but a million questions flooded her mind.

"So...why do you think you are through now?" She asked slowly, trying to keep her voice even. The implication was that he had a job to do with the Pathfinders. Or at least her. But what could he possibly do from in here, and what if he didn't stay in here? It would be lonely for him, she thought, her heart lurching. But he was *dead*. He couldn't come back.

Joseph had been quiet, thinking about what to say, and at last he sighed and looked down at the ground with a shrug. "I can't say for sure." He met her eyes. "It's something to do with you. And my brother. And his friends. I'm supposed to be on that side. I can feel it."

"That's not possible." Elvie's voice was quiet as all the implications sank in. The damage it could do to history, for one thing. But then a little voice snuck in, *what if it meant you didn't have to say goodbye this time?*

"Elvie. Look at me." She did, and his earnest brown eyes, so different from the ones she saw every day, and yet still so full of desperation to do something more, to be something more, were pleading. "Haven't you ever felt that you have this ability because *time* or *God* or something wanted you to?" Elvie felt herself nod, despite not wanting to and he nodded back, fast and eager. "That's what this feels like. I don't know how I'm going to get over there. But I know I have to. I know I have to help you on your mission, and I know you, my brother and his friends are the key to beating whatever it is you are trying to fight." Try as she might Elvie couldn't force herself to think that he was wrong. In her heart she knew it, too. But to pull someone out of here…she wasn't strong enough and she wasn't sure she should.

"I don't expect you to do it tonight. I don't even know what I expect. You just need to know that when the time comes, you have to pull me through." They sat in silence for Elvie wasn't sure how long, before she hopped down from the wall. She knew he was right, in that bone-deep instinctive way. She also knew she couldn't deal with that right now.

"I have to go." She said, and without another word, she left New Mexico and landed on the front step of the base on Monroe Street.

Chapter 26

One day, when things had gotten back to normal, Elvie was leaving base, still having not gotten around to moving out. She opened the door where Earl was waiting, the two of them always going together by unspoken agreement. As she was walking out Natalie yelled for her to have a wonderful birthday. The note in her voice meant that she had known Elvie wasn't going to tell anyone. Raising an eyebrow Earl said only "Happy birthday" but she saw a look that on anyone else would have been considered surprised, not concerning. On his usually serious face, it was full of mischief, and she couldn't help but feel a bit worried.

Victor found them a couple of blocks later. The conversation had been normal the whole walk so far, but as Earl held the door for Elvie he grinned at her, that strangely impish smile back and she resisted the urge to put a hand over his mouth to keep him quiet. The door had no more than latched behind him when he leaned forward, putting an arm around Elvie to tap the Sicilian on the shoulder to make sure he was paying attention.

"Did you know today is Miss Elvie's birthday?"

"It's your *birthday*?" Victor sounded so pleased that, if Elvie hadn't known who he was and how he had celebrated his own birthdays, she would have been surprised. Instead, she wanted to run and hide before he could get any ideas.

"We don't need to acknowledge it." She said, holding up her hands, pushing Earl back just a bit. She was the only one who wasn't Victor or Dean who could get away with it. A fact she took an obscene amount of pride in.

"How old are you, anyway?" Earl asked. She had hoped her wouldn't ask, and she tried to deflect.

"Mary wouldn't like you asking me that."

"She's not wrong," Victor's smooth voice cut in with a laugh. "But my mom wouldn't care. How old are you today, Elvie?"

"Twenty-five." It was where her body was frozen, so it wasn't a lie and it wasn't like she could say 277 years old or whatever it was now. She had stopped keeping track. Shirley remembered all their birthdays and made sure they each got a cake but otherwise, they didn't count the years anymore.

"You're older than both of us?"

"Apparently," she grumbled.

"I knew I liked older women....I didn't know Earl did, though."The Pole, who had been leaning against the door frame, fiddling with his prayer book, didn't say a word, but Elvie noticed his ears turning red. She looked down at her lap momentarily, trying to suppress a grin before she recovered herself.

"Watch it, D. I'll rat you out to Cecilia for flirting."

"You wouldn't dare."

"In a heartbeat." She poked him in the side.

"From behind a bulletproof door? You're terrified of Cici, and we both know she'd come for you first." He grinned at her. Elvie was going to relax just a little when he said the words that made her stomach drop. "We're taking you out tonight, right, Weiss?"

"Oh, definitely. Dinner and drinks on us." Earl had put the prayer book away and was leaning back with his eyes closed.

"Please, no. You don't have to." She didn't know how to say she hated celebrating her birthday and being the center of attention. As Drucci pulled into the parking lot behind the flower shop, she could think of few things worse than Drucci trying to get her to drink and singing her happy birthday.

"What kind of friends would we be if we didn't celebrate your birthday?" The youngest of the Northside bosses smiled at her and squeezed her knee. "You're stuck with us tonight, kid."

"You can't call me kid anymore." She pointed out, grumpily.

"You'll always be a kid to us."

The car had barely been put in park before Drucci was out and headed toward the shop.

"He's going to tell everyone, isn't he?" She watched him bounce his way inside while she waited for Earl, who set his own hat on her head.

"Come on, birthday girl. Let's get you inside before he calls them all out to sing for you." Elvie groaned loudly and tried to turn around. Earl grabbed her hand and pulled her into him. There was a rumor, wildly untrue, she was certain that he was a ladies' man, a player. Moments like this, when he used the charm he hated people knowing he had, she wasn't so sure. "Let me celebrate your birthday. It's one of the only things I've got going for me right now." And then, with a grin, he added, "Please." And she hated that her knees gave a little when he said it.

"Fine," she shook him off and, still wearing his hat, moved towards the building. "But if I'm grumpy with you, it's your own fault."

Elvie spent the day hiding in Dean's office, where the man himself was conducting meetings. She made herself almost invisible in one of the big chairs, and they pretended she was a bodyguard when anyone who didn't know her walked in. Victor wouldn't let anyone walk past her without telling them to sing her Happy Birthday. Earl wasn't much better, but he had gone out for a meeting around noon and hadn't come back yet. Dean brought her a tiny cake from a bakery down the street and a bouquet of Gerberas, her favorite flower, which, after he left the room, made her tear up.

At five o'clock, she was lying on the old couch with the book she had bought herself the day before. When the door opened, she slowly moved the book just enough to be able to see and smiled when Earl walked in. He looked nervous, but as soon as he noticed her watching, he put on his serious face.

"These are for you." And from behind his back he held out two books, *Men Like Gods* and *The Outline of History,* both by H.G. Wells. She had mentioned wanting to read more of his books in passing when she and Mr. Schofield had been in the greenhouse together, talking about books one day. Earl had come in at the tail end of the conversation, and yet he remembered that.

"Thank you!" She threw her arms around his neck and kissed his cheek." His ears turned red again. Elvie stepped away to look at the books. "Can I just go hide somewhere so I can read them and not go to dinner?"

"Oh no," Earl laughed, taking her elbow gently and guiding her to the door with one hand, grabbing her jacket with the other. "You're not getting out of this one." At the bottom of the stairs, Vincent, Cici, Viola, Dean, and even George with his wife, Lucille, were waiting.

"Come on. This party's not going to start itself!" Vincent was at the door before Elvie had gotten down the stairs.

"Don't worry," Earl whispered in her ear, "I have a plan to get you out before he gets really drunk."

Chapter 27

True to his word, as soon as Vincent lost control of his volume and had pulled Cici onto the dance floor, Earl held out a hand, as if indicating that he wanted to dance with her. She let him guide her onto the floor. He pulled her close so she could hear him.

"Now, we just have to work our way across the floor and out the door."

"Won't they notice?"

"Well, Dean and Viola are making goo-goo eyes at each other, so they won't be here much longer. Victor...you saw him. And I told

George. So, I think we're in the clear." He was guiding them through couples without making it look obvious.

"You seem to have a lot of practice at this, Mr. Weiss."

"Not with Mr. Weiss, again!" He feigned exasperation, as he always did when she said it, her favorite way of needling him into smiling and laughing. They passed under the lights of the dance floor before, with one last twirl, he gripped her hand, pulling her up the stairs and out into the night.

"Where are we going?" She could tell he had a destination in mind, he was walking with purpose, and he hadn't dropped her hand. They had gone back to her car when they left the flower shop, so she could drop her things off there. At first, she thought that was where they were going. Except they weren't headed in that direction at all.

"It's a surprise." He called back and then pulled her arm so she was beside him. "Don't worry, it's the kind of surprise you will love."

"I don't know that I expected this out of you."

"Hush." For once, she did, letting him lead her into the ritzy shopping district. Her eyes went wide when she realized where they were headed. The giant, gothic pillar that was the Old Water Tower. It had survived the Great Chicago Fire and had been renovated only a decade ago. Elvie was not entirely sure what they were doing here, she was certain Weiss didn't have a key to the building.

Well, maybe he did without a second thought, he pulled open one of the big wooden doors and motioned her in ahead of him. "I'm glad you wore your boots." He grinned, a Cheshire-sized smile. "And I hope you aren't afraid of heights."

"Are we going up?" The question came out at an octave Elvie was unaware her voice could reach. He just nodded impatiently to the stairwell. The two climbed and climbed, Elvie glancing down occasionally to see the spiral stairs straight below them. When they reached the top, there was a sloping desk off to one side. When Elvie walked closer, she sucked in a breath when she realized what was on it: the original plans from 1913 of the design for the Water Tower District.

The window to her left gave her a view of Michigan Avenue stretching south, and the streetlights gave the world a beautiful, magical glow. Elvie turned and stared at Earl, who was sitting on the window ledge opposite adjusting the cuffs of his suit jacket and fiddling with his wrist watch, avoiding looking directly at her, almost nervous looking, she thought.

"How...?" She turned and looked at the plans again, her fingers tracing lines, finding the streets she memorized growing up, watching the city from afar as if it were some beautiful wonderland. She could see buildings that she would one day adore that would be built on the site of buildings in the plans. Her gaze caught on the Adler Planetarium in the very bottom corner.

"I called in a favor." He had come to stand next to her now. "I've heard you wax poetic about Chicago often enough that I knew you would want to see this view. That you would have wanted to see the top of the Water Tower."

"You have no idea..." she breathed. Tiliting her head back to look at the domed ceiling overhead, she felt as if she was in a dream. A very happy, surreal dream. These moments didn't happen to her anymore...and yet she could feel her lips turning up into a smile that she knew would hurt her cheeks. "I used to wish that I could live here. That I would make it an apartment, in the heart of Chicago, just for me."

"It'd be a bit small."

"Just a bit," she chuckled. "Look at that view." She sighed happily as she looked out at the city, leaning on this windowsill. Earl stood next to her, their shoulders and elbows brushing.

"If there is any city in the world that could be equal parts beautiful and terrifying...peaceful at the same time as being bloody, it's Chicago." Earl was looking at the street now, too. His eyes were unfocused as he kept talking, "I always thought, growing up, that New

Yorkers must have this beautiful city the way they talk about it. No rats. No street gangs. No fighting. Then I visited and nah. They're just better at hiding it. Chicago…it's a city that knows what it is and isn't ashamed. I love it for that." Elvie was watching him now, instead of the view. She wondered if he knew he could be describing himself, too. He knew who he was, and he didn't hide it or seem embarrassed by it. Her heart thudded in her chest as she swallowed another wave of emotions.

"Earl…thank you. Thank you for this. It's the perfect way to end my birthday."

"Even though I wasn't supposed to know about it?" He said, tapping her foot with his and giving her a wry smile.

"Yes, even though." She laughed. "I guess I should thank Natalie tomorrow."

"Oh, no you don't. Save all the thanks for me. I'm the one who rescued you from Victor's evening which will end with a car full of his dinner I'm sure."

"Ew. Yes, thank you for saving me from that."

"I'd do it for you everyday if I could, Elf." He had started calling her that one day and it had become his pet name for her. If it could be a pet name between friends. The two stared at each other for several moments before Earl finally broke the tension, clearing his throat and looking back out at the busy street below.

"Maybe I'll fake a headache tomorrow so I don't have to deal with Victor's hungover ass."

Chapter 28

Elvie finished her work with the Northsiders early the next day. She and Earl had stayed in the tower of the water tower until the sun peeked over the horizon, talking about everything and nothing at all, just passing the time as friends did. If she had been a regular person, she would have been exhausted. Thankfully, Pathfinders were wired to not need as much sleep, and they all went through years where they needed next to none. Elvie rarely managed to sleep more than four hours on a good day. Now, with fatigue that couldn't be fixed with sleep, constant chills, and strange headaches, she was thankful, even more for a night like the previous one. She'd felt warm and safe and happy. Earl had been grumpy and sour from lack of sleep, but he'd offered her a smile before disappearing for the day again. Elvie had fixed a few trucks in the garage and decided to call it a day. Pulling her fingerless gloves on a little tighter and wrapping her coat around herself, she pushed out of the garage door and ran smack into George Moran.

"Sorry," she mumbled as she went to step around him. The idea had popped into her head to go talk to Joseph and she wasn't interested in stopping to talk with anyone let alone George. He was normally content to let her go without talking to her as well but today he was feeling like an argument.

"That's all I get, huh?" His laugh was mirthless and cruel and she turned, confused.

"What?"

"A half ass sorry. You must not think you can get anything out of me, since you don't care to be nice to me." He turned to walk away but Elvie had never been one to let an insult slide.

"I don't care to be nice to you because I think you're a spineless piece of shit who wouldn't think twice before turning his back on his friends." Well, she hadn't meant to be that harsh. Maybe she was more tired than she had thought. Slowly, his eyes wide, his cheeks flushed, madder than a hornet, George stalked towards her. Elvie, not in the least afraid, put her hands in her pockets and stood her ground.

"Excuse you? You have a lot of nerve to say that, considering you're trying to sleep, you're hiding something from everyone." He was right in front of her, barely a hair's breadth between them, and he was taller by a could two or three inches. But she just raised her eyebrows.

"And what am I hiding, George?"

"I don't know but you are using us…them. You want something or maybe it's information. You'll sell them out or move on. I know your type, Townshend. You've got Earl wrapped around your finger and you'll leave him a broken mess after you get what you want." Depsite being determined to not let him get to her that insult, no matter how untrue hit a little too hard and she glared at him, her hands out of her pockets now, curling into fists at her sides. The spring winds whipped around them and she wished with all her might that she could disappear before she did something stupid.

"I would never hurt him. Or backstab or use the Northsiders. I thought I had made that clear. I am not you, George. When I am in a gang, I am in, no matter how hard things get. Unlike some people who run when things get hard." That barb landed better than any punch she could have thrown.

"Bullshit!" His voice raised several octaves and Elvie felt a rush as she clenched her fist tighter ready to swing. "You're nothing but a dirty, lying manipulative bi—"

"What the hell is going on back here?" Standing in front of his car was Victor, and Earl was leaning against the hood, arms crossed, eyes burning. Victor, who had spoken, looked between them, and Elvie unclenched her fist. She couldn't cause a rift between the Northsiders. She swallowed and sighed.

"Just...another argument." Her voice was a growl. She was lying...George was right. But how the hell do you tell people that you're from the future? And she would never ever use Earl or Victor or anyone. But what if they thought that too? Maybe not right now, but someday. Suddenly, she wanted to be very far away from everyone. "I'll be going."

"Elvie, wait!" Earl started around the car before she could turn, and Elvie quickly shook her head, taking a step backwards.

"No, really. I need to get going. I can't...I can't be late." And she was off at a brisk walk as fast as she could go without outright running away. Earl, recognizing someone who needed a moment with their emotions, let her go. When Elvie peeled out of the parking lot, she was wiping tears from her eyes that he, thankfully, didn't see.

Elvie had never attempted to take her car through the In-Between before. It normally just traveled with the base. But she knew that if she went and dropped it off at base she would have to answer questions. Questions she didn't want to answer, namely, "Why are you crying?" And "Where are you going?" The answer to both was: *I'm not talking about it.*

She wasn't interested in dissecting what it meant to be crying because she felt like a liar and double-crosser when she desperately, so badly it hurt, wanted to tell Earl the truth. It wasn't like this was a new life for her; she'd slipped into and out of people's lives so often for years that it shouldn't have even been a thought in her head. And yet...and yet after all this time, this was the first time she could remember wanting to stay and put down roots. No. That wasn't right. What she wanted was to change their future. To keep all of them from being killed. That's why she had been on her way to New Mexico in the first place, especially after last night. If she could bring Joseph to the living side with her, couldn't she, in theory, bring back Dean, Victor, Earl? Especially Earl...oh, she'd let his future play out just like it was supposed to...but on October 11, 1926, she didn't have to say goodbye. Shaking her head, realizing how crazy she sounded, Elvie pulled to a halt outside the seemingly empty sanatorium and put her head against the steering wheel. Elvie tried desperately to pull herself together.

The door to the passenger's side opened, and Joseph slid into the seat next to her. "Jesus, automobiles really have gotten nicer in the last decade." Elvie let out a huff that was supposed to be a laugh, but she was shaking too hard to tell. Joseph sighed. "George sucks."

Her head shot up. "You were there?" Joseph nodded, eyes wide, bewildered at her apparent surprise. "How did I...how did your brother not see you?"

"I told you, I haven't figured this whole thing out yet." Joseph shrugged in a gesture so innocent and boyish that Elvie felt a pang through her heart so sharp that she rubbed her chest. Earl would never have gotten to be so innocent and boyish. Joseph had died at twenty-three, and while he was still more mature than any twenty-three-year-old should have to be, he was still younger than Earl was now, and mentally and emotionally, he was younger than his brothers had ever gotten to be. Earl, at twenty-three, had perfected his cold stare that he was famous for; he had been in the news for shooting his brother and blowing up safes. He was supporting his family, his parents, and siblings, and carrying the weight of the world on his shoulders, and he would never make it to thirty. Fresh tears welled up, and she shook them away as Joseph, oblivious to the crisis she was having, continued.

"I can see over there, but no one can see me. Not even you. I've tried to get your attention. You just so happened to already be stepping through the wall that first night, and that's why you could hear me. I think."

"Okay. So, we need to figure out how to get you through. And we need to do it soon." Elvie said, pulling herself up straight and shaking her hair out before opening her door. "Let's see if I can pull you." Joseph slid across the bench following her out into the dry desert heat. Elvie, after adjusting her fingerless gloves to make sure they wouldn't slip off held out a hand. Joseph shook his head.

"I don't think it will work." At her raised eyebrows, he looked…lost. "I don't think you're strong enough yet to pull me out on your own. I don't know how I know these things, but I can see what's about to happen. How something won't work and maybe why? I don't know, but if you try to pull me through, it'll be like you—"

"Let's just try it." Elvie cut him off, insulted at the implication that she couldn't do something after her fight with George. After crying for the first time, it felt like years. She wanted a win, and so she grabbed his hand and pulled. It was like walking through sludge as she started backwards, as if she was slowly sinking underwater. She could feel the correct side behind her; she was almost there…but then, when Joseph's hand hit the wall, it was like the sludge became cement. She had the sensation of drowning, and after trying and failing to pull Joseph through. She released his hand, and the world let her breathe. As she gasped for air, Joseph had his arms crossed and was looking down his nose, in that way twenty-three-year-olds did that, which was so aggravating.

"I told you. You need to be stronger." Without so much as a word, Elvie shot out her leg and used her foot to pull Joseph's out from under him. He hit the ground with a thud, and when he glared up at her, Elvie smiled the evil smile she saved for George and the Interface agents.

"Don't be an asshole, and it won't happen again." To her surprise, Joseph laughed, his was lighter and easier than Earl's

"I knew my brother liked you for a reason." He held out his hand and Elvie helped him up.

Chapter 29

Back in Chicago, later that evening, Elvie walked up to Natalie's workshop door and knocked, tentatively. One never knew what they were going to get when they walked into the mad scientist's workshop. If you weren't careful, the door could be rigged to shock you. Or explode. There was no telling. Sure enough, the sound of something being taken apart came from the other side of the door. After a good thirty seconds, the door opened, revealing Natalie with her straight black hair tied up in a messy bun, her blotters resting on top of her head, and a handful of wires.

"Elvie! It's you! I didn't think you'd be back tonight." The taller woman stepped aside to let her in, gesturing to some stools by the workbench that took up the entire center of the room. Elvie had always loved the way her name sounded in Natalie's London accent. The 'v' became an 'f,' turning her from a normal person into a fairy creature. Which was how it felt sometimes when you walked into her workshop with its dancing lights and inventions strewn about the place. It was a shop right out of an old Dickens story.

"Hey, Nattie. How's it going? And why wouldn't I be back tonight?" Propping one foot on the stool and leaning her arms on the workbench, she followed Natalie's progress around the shop, putting things back and picking up new things before finally landing back at the giant table top. Her green eyes were dancing with excitement, so she must have been working on a new invention.

"You've been gone a lot. I know you're not sleeping again. And you were in New Mexico so I thought maybe you'd just stay the night there or something." Natalie held up a hand and the old car engine that sat in the corner threw a piston at her. Such was the power of Natalie, to manipulate machinery.

"How did you know I was in New Mexico?" Elvie leaned forward and tried to catch the other woman's eye, even though she had a pretty good idea what the answer was. "I was in the In-Between the whole time, and that's not supposed to show up on the tracking system." In addition to not being able to use the In-Between in the house, they still hadn't figured out how to get the system to recognize its location. While not being able to get out of the house was annoying, Elvie didn't mind that she couldn't be tracked when she was in the In-Between. Natalie looked up at her with wide, innocent eyes.

"You were? Are you sure it was the whole time?" Unamused, Elvie just waited. "Oh, fine. I updated the pocketwatch systems the other day. I didn't think it would work, so I didn't tell anyone that I added my proto-software for the In-Between into it." Her face transformed instantly from embarrassed to overjoyed. "But it worked? You were really in there the whole time?" In spite of herself, Elvie nodded and watched Natalie dig on a shelf for a notebook, chattering the whole time about how amazing it was that it had worked so well. She scribbled notes down, and when she finally looked up, Elvie watched as it took several seconds for Natalie to regain her footing in the world of what was happening right now and not the one with her millions of ideas.

"Anyway, sorry about that." Moving back to what she had been working on, Natalie picked up a wrench. "How is the job treating you?"

"It's fine." Natalie glanced up with a face that told her not to lie and Elvie sighed. "It's wonderful. It's the best job I've had yet." Natalie set the wrench down.

"But..."

"But, I want to tell them so badly. Earl already knows about the In-Between—"

"He what!?" Natalie yelped but Elvie waved her off.

"Shirley wanted me to lie to him. Play along that it was a hallucination but…I just couldn't do that to him." She looked down at the desk and rolled around a wayward screw as she talked. "This hasn't been like my other jobs. No matter what I do, I get more attached. And then today…" she trailed off, unsure how to say it. Because saying it made what had happened real.

"I saw your fight with George." Of course she had, Elvie thought. The stress meter on her profile had probably been off the charts, which made her current predicament all that much more worrisome. "I thought the way you controlled your emotions and your power was admirable." She had been examining a small motor while she talked and didn't notice that the younger woman had winced and grown pale when while she talked. The headache was back, but that wasn't an issue for right now.

"That's another big problem, Nat." Elvie said quietly. Natalie froze and put down the wrench, staring at her with what looked like horror.

"You did control your power, right?"

"There wasn't a power to control." Elvie's voice cracked. "I think my power changed."

Natalie put her tools down and leaned forward. "Why do you say that?" Elvie pulled the glove on her right hand off. She always gloves but her right hand was more or less clear of any scarring. "I broke the skin with a screwdriver this morning working on a car. Since it was self inflicted, even by accident, it shouldn't have healed, right?"

"Right…are you sure it was that hand?" Natalie walked around and looked it over. Elvie knew what she was seeing: not one scratch or bruise.

"Positive. You know I'm left-handed." She watched realization dawn on Natalie's face, so she asked the question that had been bothering her all day. "Do you think it's because…you know…I died and came back? Or because I go over there?" Natalie just shook her head.

"Maybe? I don't know. Let me look into it; maybe there is something way deep in the system. Don't tell the others about this. If our powers can change, we don't need to freak anyone out. And if they can, we need to figure out what caused it first."

"I have an idea about that. What was it you said, all those years ago?" Elvie slid her glove back on, strapping it tightly around her wrist. "That the power was linked to what we wanted most or what was the strongest impulse. Yours was to understand how things work and fix them. Bixby's was to fit in. Violet's was to understand how people felt. Mine was tied to my desire to express myself and be accepted. What if my desire changed? What if now I just want to save people?"

"You can't, Elvie. You know that. Remember what happened the last time you tried?" The carriage was bearing down on her at Natalie's words, but this time, Elvie changed the memory. It didn't hit her. She stepped through a curtain into a world and was safe and unharmed.

"Maybe there is a way around the rules." Elvie looked up at Natalie, who looked like she wanted to tell Elvie to hush, someone could hear her, and also wanted to know more. Natalie pulled out the stool in front of her.

"What are you thinking?"

Chapter 30

For the next week, Elvie spent her days avoiding everyone as much as possible, just as Earl had done to her. She couldn't stand to look at them, knowing what she knew and hearing George's insults ringing in her ears. She knew she wasn't using them, that she wasn't manipulating them, and that she would never hurt them, but that didn't change the fact that he had struck a nerve when he said she was hiding something. It had already been difficult not to tell them everything; now she was afraid it would come spilling out any time she opened her mouth. And so, she did her job with someone else or on her own when Dean would let her, worked in the shop, and then pulled left onto Superior Street and up to the Sanitorium in New Mexico, where every day she tried again to pull Joseph through. It wasn't getting eaiser but Joseph was looking less pale and gaunt every time she saw him, which she took as a good sign.

Then, on one of the first days in May, Earl, Dean, Vincent, and Louie Alterie were delivering a shipment of booze to a client that they had learned about through one of the vault jobs. Elvie hadn't been invited; in fact, she had told them she couldn't come because she was looking into an apartment. She was walking down Monroe, close to where the "for rent" sign and the landlord who had promised to let her in were waiting, when she felt a strange lightheadedness. It was an anomaly. The Interface was pulling something…but whatever it was hadn't set off her watch or the base's alarms yet. There was still time to stop it from becoming a problem. Her being able to sense it first meant that it must be something she was uniquely equipped to deal with. Then, it hit her like a freight train. The new liquor clients had suggested a strange warehouse. Elvie hadn't thought much of it when she heard Dean mention it; abandoned warehouses were a common spot for first meetings. There were also common spots for dumping bodies and committing murder, she thought now, mentally kicking herself as she tried to remember the address they had said. She was beginning to panic, though, and when nothing came to mind, she reached out, just a little, through the In-Between.

She didn't know when she had developed this sixth sense, but if she needed to find him fast, she could think of Earl, and she would feel the pull of him and send herself in that direction. Given that this was an emergency, her power must have been even stronger than usual, because she found him immediately. He was much farther south than she had expected. She let herself be pulled quickly, and for a second, she thought she had been wrong, because she found herself in the middle of one of the buildings on the Pullman Factory grounds. She pulled just a little on the In-Between, and she could see what was going on. She was standing behind Earl, just a bit to the left, and he hadn't noticed her yet. You didn't need to be a mind reader, she thought, to know he was wondering which of the lunatics had decided to make a drop here on Pullman land, during the middle of the day. All good questions that she would have asked and been able to fix if she hadn't been avoiding them for a week. Now, it seemed that the Interface was trying to get them arrested...or killed?

There were three cops pointing guns at the men, and Dean was doing his best to charm them. It seemed to be working, too, so why was Elvie feeling the effects of time change? And then it happened.

Alterie had either been stepping back to grab a gun or just adjusting his stance, but whatever he was doing knocked over a board next to him. The sound frightened an already tense policeman who, for whatever reason, shot his gun at Earl. The bullet hit him in the leg, and he went down. Elvie didn't have eyes for anything else. She might not have been a doctor, but she knew enough to know that the amount of blood and the way it was coming out meant that the bullet hit the artery. She bent down on the floor next to him, and of course, he could see her now.

"Elvie, what are you—"

"Shut up. Don't say anything and don't move your leg." She did not have time to register that she hadn't disappeared and that the time change light-headedness was gone. She just knew she had to help, not because then the timeline would be thrown out of balance, but only because she didn't *want* him to die. She ripped open his trouser leg where the bullet had entered. Elvie hadn't tried her new power on anyone except herself yet, and now seemed as good a time as any. She ripped off her left glove and pressed a hand to his leg, making him jump. The bleeding slowed and then stopped, and when she removed her hand, the hole was gone. She looked up and stared at Earl, who was staring back at her. She imagined she looked just as confused as he did. But she didn't have time to say anything, she felt so tired she thought she might faint.

"Get the hell out of here." She hissed, pictured her front step, and disappeared.

Louie had taken off when the shooting started, and Dean could be heard trying to start the truck as Victor ran over to him. Dean clearly hadn't seen what had happened, but Victor's face showed that he definitely had. He stared at Earl and said, "You want to explain how your pants ripped themselves open and your leg no longer has a hole in?"

Earl stared at him, not sure he would have had the words to describe any of it. The sirens in the distance and Dean yelling at them to hurry the hell up broke him out of his thought. "Later. Elvie and I will explain later." Without hesitation, Victor nodded and led the way towards the truck, where they barely got the door closed before Dean was tearing out of the factory building.

Chapter 31

When Elvie had shown up on the doorstep, the door had been locked, and she knocked weakly on it. She was exhausted. All of her body hurt, her bones, her muscles, even her blood seemed to be moving slowly. The only thing moving at normal speed was her brain, which was sounding alarm bells of all kinds because she definitely did too much too fast. A little voice in the back of her head pointed out that Joseph would have a hard time saying she needed to get stronger now. Natalie had heard the alarms for the vital monitors ring in her workshop and was closest to the door. She flung it open, and Elvie stumbled in.

"I…I…I'm going to pass out." Natalie just caught her before she slumped to the ground.

When she woke up, she was on the couch in the control room, a blanket pulled over the top of her, and her boots on the floor. She also felt an ice pack on top of her head.

"Elvie!" Shirley yelped and hurried over. "Thank god." She put a hand to Elvie's forehead and sighed. "The fever's gone."

"The fever?" Elvie sat up. "What fever? And don't you have questions about…" she trailed off, a strange thought occurring before she could say more.

"Yes, you were in the In-Between for a long time, and then you showed up on the doorstep, set the vital monitors into a frenzy, and collapsed. Natalie brought you down here, and your fever was one hundred and three. We pumped you full of fluids and all the usual stuff, but it wouldn't break. It finally broke about an hour ago. Do I have questions about why you were off the map for so long and show up with a fever? Absolutely, but making sure you are well is the first step." Shirley walked back over to the vitals screen and started clicking through so that all of Elvie's internal biology was on display on the screen. "I also want to know why you have blood on your hand."

"I...don't know," Elvie said slowly. "I had the feeling of time changing and that I had to stop it. I did...stop it." not a lie, a complete one at least, "and I don't remember what happened with the blood, and I don't know how I got the fever either." She had some ideas, though. But she wasn't sharing them with Tony or Shirley, not yet anyway.

The steps on the stairs were the only warning she had before Natalie was there. "You're awake!" She ran over and threw her arms around her. Elvie felt a bit bad; she could feel the dried sweat in her hair and on her skin. "Are you okay? What happened in there?"

"I don't know..." still not a total lie. She had no idea what had allowed her to move a fatal bullet wound but she wasn't going to complain.

"I imagine you overexerted yourself by staying in that long, and then the stress caused your body to have a sort of meltdown," Shirley said. "Everything looks good now, though."

Natalie and Elvie exchanged glances behind Shirley's back. If Tony saw it he didn't seem to think it meant anything. And then she told them what happened when she felt the change.

"Any idea what caused it?" Tony asked.

"None," Elvie shook her head. "Someone must have tipped off those cops. I'm not one hundred percent sure who, but I can guess."

"We'll ask Violet and Bixby to snoop around and see what we can find. Do you think the North Siders might know?" Shirley asked. Elvie shrugged. She had no idea what the North Siders were thinking right now, least of all Earl and she had noticed Victor was still watching him before she disappeared. That would be an interesting conversation, but not one she was prepared for right now.

"You'll have to find out, when are you—" But Natalie was cut off by Shirley.

"She'll find out tomorrow. Right now, she needs to get upstairs, shower and sleep."

"What time is it?" Elvie asked.

"Six in the evening." Bixby answered. "Apparently, you showed up at two and have been out since."

"I'm going...to do what Shirley said." Everyone looked surprised, even Shirley. It wasn't like her to give in so easily. They all stared at her. "But don't get used to it." She gave what she hoped was a grin, not a grimace, and walked upstairs, where she indeed showered and immediately went to sleep, promising herself she would talk to Earl tomorrow, even if it changed things.

Chapter 32

She woke up at seven the next morning, having slept for twelve hours. Her brain was ready to go. Spinning with ideas about what she could do with her new ability and what this meant for Joseph's situation, stuck as he was in that space between life and death. On the other hand, her body was not. Every joint ached, and her muscles were tight, as if she hadn't trained properly in months and then had a fight with the entire Interface cold. She was sore everywhere. She considered just staying in the base today, which was quickly ruled out when she just thought sent her anxiety into overdrive. Getting up and ready for the day, she looked in the mirror and sighed. She had dark circles under her still, her reddish blonde hair was trying to escape from its clip, and her glasses kept sliding down her nose as if even her face was too tired to keep itself arranged.

No one else was moving yet, at least not anywhere Elvie went, and she enjoyed having some privacy. In her privacy, she could worry about how her role with Northsiders would change. And, she thought, of course it would change. Just like it would here when Shirley and Tony found out she was a walking healing machine. She was no longer a person to her new friends, she was sure. Elvie would have lost her humanity in their eyes and become simply a tool to keep them alive. The thought burned, and she tried to comfort herself with the thought that at least now, when she left, it would be easier.

Just as she was pouring herself some tea, there was a knock at the door. She glared at it, willing it to go away while also trying to determine whether or not to ignore the caller. The upstairs of the house was decorated for the time, but anyone entering a private quarter or the control room would be completely confused. She had just decided to ignore it when the knock sounded again. A little more urgent this time. With an inward growl, she decided to go see who it was before they woke the whole house...then she would have to talk to someone about her mission, and she avoided that as much as possible.

Elvie creeped towards the door not making a sound and looked through peep hole. Stepping away, frowning, Elvie shot a glance at the clock on the wall. It was eight thirty. Early for them. Which meant they had questions. She would like to think they were up early because it was had just happened that way. But she knew better. Even without opening the door, she could see Earl had big circles under his eyes, and Vincent looked grumpy.

Well, now you're in trouble said a voice in her head. She really thought she would have had more time to come terms with everything before being confronted by the pair of them. Another four hours, at least. She took a deep breath and opened the door. She looked from one to the other and then finally found her voice.

"Morning. Aren't you two up early?" Elvie had put on the attitude that she rarely used with any of them except for George. Cold, businesslike and closed off. If they are going to try to exploit her let them try. But she wouldn't be friendly about it.

"I was okay with leaving it until this afternoon, but this asshole was insistent." Vincent sounded like he had been dragged here under duress. He wasn't a morning person normally. And that was when his mornings started at noon. "Can we at least get breakfast while you two tell me what happened yesterday?" Elvie wanted to say no, they could tell him right here, but they hadn't demanded her to come with them but Victor turned his eyes into big brown puppy eyes, pleading silently for food and coffee. She looked at Earl. Part of her hoped she would see the ruthless mobster, Hymie, looking back. Instead, she just saw how tired he looked. And was that concern written there, too?

He met her gaze and just said, "Please?" Elvie almost growled at how quickly her convictions rolled over for that one word from him.

She sighed, "Fine let me change."

"Why?" Victor looked her up and down. "You look terrific, a little strange, but terrific." Elvie looked down. She was in her customary black leggings and had a dark red plaid tunic with a black belt on top. She hadn't planned on going anywhere until this afternoon, and Tony would be beside himself if he found out. She would deal with that problem if it came up, she decided. Besides, compliments from Victor were also genuine. She shrugged and went to grab her boots, jacket, and bag.

Victor was driving, which was not normally a problem. Today, though, he was clearly in need of food, coffee, and to go back to bed. Elvie thought the car would flip a few times, the way he was taking corners, and she remembered how much she loved seatbelts. As he screamed to a stop in a parking lot in front of a diner, she missed airbags, too.

"This is probably the most thankful I have ever been for a diner." Earl grumbled, getting out first. "I thought I wouldn't live to see it."

"What happened to 'I want to do this *now*, Victor?'" The other man did a passable imitation of Earl, and it made Elvie smile to herself as she shut the car door behind her. "Isn't that what you said when you woke me up at the ass crack of dawn?"

"I wanted to pick up Elvie. Not die on the way to breakfast."

The pair continued their bickering with Elvie trailing behind all the way to the table, and kept at it until the waitress dropped off a whole pot of coffee and two cups.

"You two come here often?" Elvie asked dryly.

"Watch it there, miss. I'm tired, and I might think you're trying to take me home." Victor winked as he poured himself a cup. He grabbed the sugar container and added more than Elvie had ever seen anyone use. It was almost comical when she noticed Earl took his black. There was a slight, uncomfortable silence as they decided how to proceed.

Victor took a sip of his coffee, and Elvie looked at Earl. "How's the leg?" Choking and hacking as Victor choked on his coffee-flavored sugar filled the diner.

With a grin, Earl answered, "Like I was never shot. Also, I'm not dead, so there's that." The waitress dropped off Elvie's water and handed Victor a towel before walking away.

"Always a good thing," said Elvie into her water.

"That was a new trick, I'm guessing?" He was looking at her out of the corner of his eye as if to look at her full on was painful. She was about to answer when Vincent seemed to have recovered himself.

"Wait, wait. You two: back up." He waved his hands. "How does she—how do you know he was shot in the leg?"

"To be fair, I didn't say shot..." Elvie said softly as she pulled at her glove straps. Earl pushed his knee into her thigh, comforting her with his touchand reminding her that she wasn't alone. She could do this. He might not see her the same, but he was still there, she realized. For now, that was enough. If things hadn't changed, he would have died yesterday. She pushed back gently with her own knee, saw his lips turn up at the corners before she spoke again."There's something I need to tell you or show you. Although I don't know how to do it here." She thought for a moment, then she motioned for Earl to let her out of the booth. "I'm going to walk outside. While I'm outside, I want you to tell Earl something. Something that I couldn't possibly guess you would say, and when I come back in, I will be able to repeat it. Word for word."

"What?" Vincent looked confused.

"You won't believe me if I just tell you," Elvie wasn't sure he'd believe her when she showed him, but Earl had believed her right away, and Victor was definitely more prone to believing things like this than Earl was.

"Trust us," Earl said, settling himself back in the booth, motioning for Elvie to go.

With that, Elvie walked to the front door and then stepped back into the diner in the In-Between. Approaching the booth, she heard Victor's voice, skeptical and grouchy.

"So, what? I can say anything and supposedly she will be able to hear it from all the way out there?"

"Not quite," Earl was watching her and she leaned on the booth next to where Vincent was sitting. "She can hear it because she's right next to you."

"Oh come on." The Sicilian was clearly exasperated. "I'm supposed to believe she's invisible now?

"D, this is me. Does this seem like a joke I would even attempt to make?" The look on Earl's face didn't come close to pleading. It was instead, 'I risked dragging you out of bed before eleven for this. You know I'm not shitting you.' Vincent sighed, exasperated, but he seemed to be at least playing along.

"Fine, let's see. What can I say…what can I say…OH!" Elvie saw his characteristic smile slide onto his face. She walked around to the other side, so she was leaning over Earl's seat, resting her arms on the back. To his credit, he didn't so much as glance at her.

"If Elvie's really here than you definitely wouldn't want me to make a comment about how—"

"Do not. Do. It." Earl was stiff and staring at his coffee cup, color creeping up his cheeks.

"Elvie, if you are here and you are listening, *Mr. Weiss* here is absolutely dizzy for you. But he thinks that you would never go for a guy like him because he looks like him, and let's be honest, I look like me. Oh AND he's too chicken to do anything because he's a good Catholic boy. I think it's a bit late for that, don't you think, Hymie?" By the time he had finished speaking, Earl had sunk lower into his seat. He was red from the tips of his ears all the way down his neck to his collar.

She didn't say a word, but she did look around the diner. No one was paying the two men in the corner the slightest bit of attention, and so, because she really wanted to get him back for purposely embarrassing Earl and because she knew he would argue the point with her, she hopped over the back of the booth. It startled Earl, who jumped, and as she slipped out of the In Between, she crossed her arms and looked right at Victor.

"HOLY HELL!" He would have fallen over if he had been in a chair. And he looked like he might actually jump up to the top of the booth seat. "Where did you come from? You walked outside. I saw you."

"I could repeat back you said," Elvie said, ignoring him, leaning forward with a devilish grin of her own "Or I could tell you and *Hymie* here, who by the way can see me when you can't, that looking like you doesn't mean much if I prefer someone with brains, some semblance of self awareness., and who isn't at risk of giving me three different kinds of sexually transmitted diseases should he decided to try it with me someday."

Drucci stared at her open-mouthed, and Earl turned his head slowly and raised his eyebrows at her. Looking at him, from his wide brown eyes to his dark hair and his cupid bow lips, she heard herself talking again, "Also, you aren't bad looking at all, you're actually better looking than that dipshit when you don't look like murdering someone. Especially when you don't plaster your hair to your head." She stopped herself thankfully, feeling she had said too much. But it didn't seem to have upset things, because he gave her a small smile, still embarrassed but a bit less like he wanted to sink into a hole in the ground.

"Okay, so are you like a ghost? Or what?" Vincent asked. "A *rude* ghost by the way," Elvie explained to him what the In Between was and why she could go there. Then Earl took up the thread and told him about finding out that he could see her all the time. Then they had to tell him why. And he didn't handle it well at all.

"You're dying?" The food they had ordered when Elvie had been telling her tale was now cold and forgotten. Victor looked like he might cry.

"I mean, yeah. It's kind of obvious. And it's not like in this line of work we live long anyway."

"That's not the point! The point is maybe you'd be lucky and get out of this and live to a ripe old age if it weren't for...that."

"It's the only point I can do anything about." Earl held his gaze, and a silence descended over the table. Then the Pole turned back to Elvie, "So, now that he knows everything and you know more than I would like you to, let's get back to my original question. Was that a new trick you learned yesterday?"

She nodded, drawing shapes in the condensation from her water on the table. She hadn't let herself think about what had happened yesterday much at all. She had obviously thought about how it had affected her and what she had done in a practical sense, but every time she started to remember the actual event, she remembered the pure panic that had washed over her. Panic came back when she thought of how her fear wasn't from a professional standpoint. It was a much more selfish reason, and she wasn't ready to admit it to herself yet.

"So, not only do you have access to this space that is somewhere between the living and the dead," Victor was talking slowly, walking himself through the ideas. She had known he wouldn't be hard to convince. This was the guy who had cooked up plans to get himself into the White House. "You can do all that, and now you can heal fatal people?"

"It would appear that way." Elvie didn't look at either of them. This was it, where they started coming up with ways to keep themselves—well, ways to keep Drucci alive forever. She braced herself as Earl opened his mouth.

"You disappeared as soon as it happened. You looked like a ghost. You never look like a ghost when I see you like that." Before she answered, Elvie considered asking him what she normally looked like in the In-Between, but stopped herself. Now was not the time.

"It takes a lot out of me, apparently. As soon as I did it, I felt like I was going to faint. I just made it back to my house and inside the door before I did. They tell me I had a fever that wouldn't break for four hours, and they were all worried I was dying."

"Did you tell them? What you did, I mean?" Earl knew that when Elvie had told everyone about the In Between, it had changed her relationship with the people in the house. Putting her as a weird outcast who got very dangerous and far away jobs (although he didn't know that last part).

"No. I didn't want them to find out and use me for...well, using me as a tool. I also don't want to do it very much, so if you two could try not to get shot much?"

"You almost died because you saved him?" Victor looked incredulous. "Would you do it again?"

"Seems so," Elvie looked up, confused at the last question. Was he serious? "And of course. It wasn't his time. I'd do it for you, too." She knew it was true, although chances were she would more than likely need to use it on him than use it on Earl anytime soon. "As I said, just try not to get shot too much. I can't be getting fevers randomly all the time."

Victor smiled, "Oh no, you look like death today, Elvie. I don't want that on my conscience."

"Wait, you mean you guys don't want to like...use me for emergency situations?" They both looked offended, which she supposed she would have, too, if the situation were reversed. Look how she had reacted to George saying something similar.

"No way." Vincent gasped. His face was comical as he spread his hands wide. "What do you take us for, Torrio's men?" Elvie snorted.

"Elvie, we don't want to use you for anything. You're just a member of the gang, like the rest of us. I've told you that before." Earl looked a little angry, but she couldn't tell if it was at her or if he was having one of those days. "Besides, I'm pretty sure the amount of bullets it would take to take us down is beyond your power."

"Well…right now…" She heard Joseph telling her she would get stronger last week. "But maybe someday."

"You aren't practicing that one. We might be criminals, but we don't want anything to happen to you."

"I…okay…" She hated that she felt like crying again. She'd gone almost five years without doing it once, and now it seemed to be happening regularly.

"What's wrong?" Earl leaned forward and pulled on her arm gently to turn her towards him.

"I'm very emotional about that for some reason."

"You moved a fatal bullet wound and almost died because of it less than twenty-four hours ago." Earl put his hand over hers on the table. "It makes sense."

Victor left to pay the bill, and Elvie leaned back in the booth and closed her eyes. This had gone much better than she had anticipated. Drucci had even said he wouldn't tell the other two until Elvie was ready. But it was still going to be a very long day. Her head hurt, and her body ached all over. She had to help unload a couple of shipments and then reschedule her meeting from yesterday.

It would have been enough on its own, but at that moment, a crash on the street outside broke the regular hum of the diner as a post box went flying past the window. Oh, she really didn't have the patience for this.

Chapter 33

"Dean?" She asked Earl as they both rose to go investigate.

"Probably," sighed the man next to her. "We're going to have to pay to replace that." The two followed Victor out the door and looked in the direction the box had come from. Sure enough, there was Dean's car, and standing on either side of it were Dean and George.

"Did you see that thing fly?" Dean grinned George had wandered past them down the street to make sure no one was hurt.

"Everyone okay?" She asked when he got back.

"Yes, thankfully." He was scowling at Dean. "You got lucky that time. And next time, don't do it with me in the car."

"Did you guys have breakfast without us?" Dean didn't even acknowledge George. The Irishman's cheeks were pink, and he had on his jolly smile. "Don't suppose you would want seconds?"

The three looked at each other. Drucci and Earl shrugged, and Vincent added that he wasn't paying this time. Then they all looked at Elvie. It would be fun to sit in there with them all and listen to them badger each other and talk about their lives, but she felt so tired, and she wanted to go home and rest before the shipment. She only had two hours before she had to be at the shop.

"Not today. I'm going to go rest and change into something more practical before I go to the shop. I'll see you all later."

"Suit yourself." George shrugged and went into the diner. Dean, annoyingly, patted her head, the aggravation added to by the fact that she was two or three inches taller than he in her boots. Victor smiled and gave her a hug. She loved his hugs; they were always warm and genuine. She let herself be enveloped by it.

"Take care of yourself, kid. I'll see you later, for that delivery." Then he turned and followed the others, leaving her and Earl on the sidewalk next to the car that now had a dent in the front fender. Elvie was fairly certain she would be the one replacing the fender.

"Don't disappear for a week again." His voice was more serious than she had heard it directed at her, and she knew her face showed surprise because he winced apologetically. "Listen, I pushed you away. You and George got in that fight, and you pushed me away. Let's call it even. I don't know what George said to you; he won't tell me, and I doubt you will either. But I have missed the hell out of you for the last week. You have worked with everybody except Victor and me. I hate it." His face was earnest, and he looked so upset that Elvie just blinked at him for a moment before she found her voice again and was able to speak without emotions poking through.

"Okay." She nodded, faster than she meant to, and she knew she looked ridiculous. She found it hard to be embarrassed by Earl, though. "I'm sorry. I was in my own head about something, and I felt like you guys would be better without me."

"That's not—"

Elvie cut him off. "It might be. It probably is. But I won't disappear again. I promise." He looked like he was going to argue with her, but Dean knocked on the window inside the diner and startled them both.

"We're going to deal with what you just said another time." Elvie almost made a comment about him being bossy, but he kept talking. "Victor's right, though. You don't look well. You can take the day off if you want. I'll drop the booze off at Frank's."

"No, no. I got it. Just need to go rest." She was going to wander the city, she knew, but he didn't need to know that. "Now, go. Have fun." She nodded toward the diner, and he sighed, resolving that she wouldn't listen.

"Thank you for saving my life...again."

"Earl, at some point, you'll have to stop thanking me. I'll save you every time I can." He grabbed her and pulled her into a hug that felt like saying a million things and not saying them at the same time. When they let go of each other, he gave her one last worried wave before turning back for the diner. Once the door was safely closed behind them, Elvie started walking. She didn't cross to the In-Between. She wanted to think, and for this kind of thinking, she needed background noise.

The hum of Chicago on a weekday was perfect for it. People shouting and coming and going. As she made her way back to base, she basked a little in the late spring sun, and even the smells of exhaust and sewage seemed reassuring. *I guess that's what happens when you almost die*, she thought to herself. She turned onto her street and saw Bixby and Violet's car in the drive. She really didn't want to hear about the South Side or answer any questions about where she had been or information she might have had...information she had forgotten to ask about.

Quiet as a ghost, Elvie slipped inside, waited for the inevitable moment when Tony raised his voice at something Bixby had said, and snuck past the control room stairs and up to Natalie's door. Her first instinct was to go in immediately, but then she remembered that it had taken Violet two years to grow back her eyebrows after she did that and pulled out her pocket watch, typing quickly: "Let me in the workshop, please. Before they notice I am here."

The door opened a second later, and Natalie motioned her in. Once the door was shut behind her, Natalie looked her up and down.

"You look like hell."

"Thanks. That's the third time I've heard that today, it's doing great things for me." Elvie followed Natalie as she made her way into the very back of the workshop, behind a massive wall of old gears and metal springs. That was Natalie's 'office area.' Although there was no desk, just two very big armchairs and a clipboard with an end table on one side that was flooded with blueprints and designs. Natalie perched on the seat next to the end table, her feet folded under her, leaning forward. Elvie sank into the opposite chair. She was freezing again, but the chair and the whole room were warm and snug. Maybe she should stand up; she would fall asleep if she wasn't careful.

"What happened yesterday?" Natalie had waited longer than Elvie had anticipated. She'd expecting a message on her pocket watch as soon as Natalie realized she wasn't home.

"I healed what should have been a fatal bullet wound." Elvie rubbed the side of her head where a headache had started. She should really get this looked at...but that meant tests and answering questions about herself...she'd handle the headache herself. "It would have changed the timeline drastically. Maybe that's why I could do it."

"It wasn't on yourself then?" Natalie was scribbling in a notebook she had pulled out of the stack. They were supposed to keep records in the system, but they had all learned long ago that anything you didn't want explicitly shared with Shirley, Tony, or the future was to be written in a paper notebook. Elvie had shelves and shelves full in her room, and she knew where Natalie hid hers. Bixby was buried in a chest off the coast of Japan as if he were a pirate. Violet...Elvie didn't know about Violet. She had always been Elvie's antithesis. She could feel others' emotions, and as such, they didn't interact much, since Elvie was always keeping a tight lid on hers. Violet said they were louder. Elvie had said that was bullshit, and it hadn't ended well.

"No." She left it at that, and Natalie looked up. Her eyes slits as she tried to figure out the answer on her own. She opened her mouth to say something when there was a knock and the sound of the door to the workshop opening.

"Nat! You in here?" It was Bixby. Natalie shut the notebook and glared at Elvie.

"You're going to tell me exactly what happened eventually. I can't help if I don't know." She whispered. And then louder. "Back here, Bix."

Bixby appeared, his curly blonde and brown hair bouncing as he walked around the wall that separated the nook from the rest of the workshop. He ruffled Elvie's hair before sitting on the floor against a wall.

"Not interrupting anything, am I?"

"Just girl talk." Elvie said as she smoothed her hair, which was pointless. It was already messy, but she hated people messing it up. "No, Violet." To her surprise, Bixby closed his eyes and let out a sigh that sounded like it came from the very depths of his soul. "Is everything okay?" Involuntarily, she shivered, and Natalie reached over the wall and pressed a hidden button. The bricks came apart to reveal a fireplace that lit itself. Elvie gave her a thankful nod.

"We are here today because word somehow has gotten around that Violet is having a thing with someone high up in the ranks of the Torrio-Capone gang." Bixby winced as Elvie and Natalie both yelled.

"I know. I know. But it might not be true."

"Might not be? Or isn't?" Natalie was tapping her fingers on the arm of the chair, a sure sign she was unhappy. Bixby scrunched his nose and looked away.

Elvie got up and started pacing. "How high up, Bixby?"

"I really have no idea. I just know she's been sneaking around a lot. I wouldn't have thought much of it but..." He trailed off, catching himself.

"But?" Elvie and Natalie said together. Bixby shifted uncomfortably.

"She's been getting flower deliveries. Really nice flowers, big bouquets. She always burns the card, but I mean, they're red roses. Obviously, it's not just a fling." He pointed at Elvie, suddenly.

"But you can't really talk. Everyone knows you and Earl are together!"

Elvie laughed, incredulous. "We are not."

"You're not?"

"No. Is that what they say down there?" Man, they really would believe anything, wouldn't they?

"Well, they say you two are together a lot. That you guys have been seen dancing together at speakeasies." He got very quiet as Elvie folded her arms and stared at him. "What?"

"I've also danced with Dean, Victor, Ernie, Frank, James, Albert, and one very drunk Louie. Do they think I'm with them, too?" He hesitated. And Elvie stamped her foot. "Oh my god. What the hell!"

"You know what it's like nowadays, Elvie. Women who hang out with men are considered...floozies."

"I'm going to floozy you." Elvie snarled. Bixby scooted closer to Natalie's chair.

"Capone says—"

"I don't give a shit what that two-faced, backstabbing, sloppy son of a bitch has to say." Elvie snapped, and the amount of venom in her voice surprised even her. She paused and rubbed the bridge of her nose, under her glasses. "I'm sorry...I just...it's..." She couldn't finish because there weren't enough words to describe how much she absolutely loathed Capone and Torrio.

"He's really not that bad, Elvie." Bixby tried, and Natalie groaned, putting her head in her hands.

"How can you say that?" Elvie's voice rose several octaves. "He's awful. You know what he does! You have a file, at the very least, you know how this ends!"

"He's nice enough to me. And Violet. He welcomed us in as managers of one of his joints. We had to prove ourselves, of course, but that's not difficult." Elvie's fists clenched and unclenched.

"Does he know where you guys are, Bixby?" Natalie asked suddenly.

"No," Bixby shook his head. "I disguised us before we got in the car to come here. If he was watching our building her just saw a little old man and woman get in the car." Bixby's ability was to change his own and others' appearance, almost without effort. It was definitely handy, especially on dangerous jobs.

"Why did you disguise yourself, if he's so great?" Elvie asked. "Surely he'd understand you're visiting family."

"You know it's not that simple." Bixby scowled at her, but Elvie was already heading for the door.

"It really is that simple, Blackwell." She called back. "He's just really good at hiding his true self. I hope you don't experience the real thing firsthand." She slammed the workshop door behind her.

Chapter 34

Schofield's was quiet when Elvie arrived. She'd walked from the base to cool her temper. Honestly, Bixby was completely oblivious, and the more Elvie thought about Violet and the rumors and the roses. She and Violet were opposites in every way, but surely it wouldn't extend that far, right? Well, obviously, it wouldn't extend that far. She wasn't romantically involved with anybody. She took the stairs two at a time and grabbed the delivery things off of Earl's desk. There was no sign of Victor, and for all his faults, it wasn't like him to be late.

"Just you today, Miss Elvie?" Ernie was waiting for her when she entered the garage, his hat not even close to the center of his head. She glanced at the clock on the wall. It was time to go, and if you were late dropping off liquor, things could go sideways in a hurry. Victor knew where they were going. If he wanted to, he could catch up.

"Looks like it." It occurred to her that this was her first time doing a delivery by herself. She didn't let Ernie see any of her hesitation; she began flipping through the papers until she found that day's delivery schedule. "Just two deliveries today, it looks like. One on Clark and one on Pierce." They climbed up into the truck, and Ernie started the engine.

"I know both of those places." He said, glancing at the addresses.
"This will be a quick day then," Elvie said, a silent prayer of thanks

for that. She still felt exhausted physically. After Bixby's news, she was now mentally exhausted as well.

"I'm surprised it's just you today," Ernie pulled the car smoothly out into traffic. "No offense meant, of course."

"None taken. I am surprised too." She was surprised that Earl hadn't mentioned there was a change of plans this morning. Or that he hadn't called to tell her that she was doing it with just her and Ernie.

"Ah, well, I'm sure you can handle any trouble." He sounded sincere, which didn't surprise Elvie in the slightest. The story, the very embellished story that Victor and Dean had told everyone about her first encounter with the Gennas, had spread through the Northside and then through the city's underworld. It had made her something of a legend on one side and completely loathed on the other. At least according to Bixby and Violet.

The drive to the Clark Street location was a short one, and the drop off went smoothly. Elvie put the envelope containing the payment into her pocket, next to the papers with the list of dates and deliveries, and they headed to the Pierce Street location. The feeling that something wasn't right hit her as soon as they pulled in. There was no reason for it, just a tickle between her shoulder blades that said that something was amiss. She was about to tell Ernie to drive away when he jumped out of the cab to open the back gate. Elvie sighed. It wasn't like she could just leave him there.

The man who came out to greet them was a small, mousy-looking man whom Elvie had met three times. She had been here twice with Earl, and once with Victor, and the man, Frank, she remembered, had never been nervous. Not even when he made an off-color remark, and Earl told him if he did it again, he'd be at the bottom of the river. Frank hadn't so much as blinked then, but now he was visibly shaken, and his greeting was a stuttering, jumbled mess. When he didn't move to help unload the truck as usual, Elvie caught Ernie's eye and just barely inclined her head, the signal for him to get back in the truck.

"Is something wrong, Frankie?" She asked as casually as she could. She decided not to move for her gun, not yet.

"I...well...I...um..."There was the sound of a door closing behind him. As Elvie sucked in a breath, Frank whispered, "I'm sorry." Footsteps sounded behind him in the shadows. Seconds later, Mike and Antonio Genna stepped out, flanking a man who Elvie knew worked for the Interface.

"He sells their booze now, Townshend." She backed into the truck and knocked twice. The engine started, and the tires squealed. Ernie was gone before the bullets could hit his tires. Frank had ducked behind some nearby barrels. Elvie stood on her own in front of two Gennas and an Interface agent. She knew all three of them wanted her dead.

Chapter 35

Natalie was doing research in the control room when Elvie's blood pressure spiked. It was such an odd occurrence that she and Shirley did a double-take.

"Where is she?" Shirley asked as she pulled up the map on the biggest monitor.

Natalie read, "Pierce Street? She said she was helping with a delivery, I think. Maybe things went south." Except, Natalie thought to herself, things had gone south on missions before, and it had never caused a noticeable spike in blood pressure on Elvie. Granted, she had never had a day like yesterday. She pulled up the pocket watch feed and swore.

"Is that one of the Interface agents?" Shirley gasped. "And the Genna's?" She reached for the SOS button, which would send a distress signal to Bixby and Violet's watches, letting them know Elvie needed help. Natalie's hand shot out and grabbed Shirley's arm before she could press it.

"We can't! It would blow their cover." Natalie frowned, trying to think quickly of a way to get help to Elvie. Then it hit her. She stood up so fast her chair tipped, and she bolted up the stairs.

She grabbed the phone and, in a more demanding tone than she ever used, ordered the operator to put her through to Schofield's on State Street.

At Schofield's Flower Shop, two things happened at the same time: the phone rang, and their delivery truck screeched to a stop in front of the shop. Dean let Mr. Schofield grab the phone as he ran out front to check on Ernie. He was supposed to have gone with Elvie and Victor on a delivery. But neither of them was anywhere to be seen; instead, Ernie, panicked, nearly ran into him on the sidewalk.

"Sir, Mr. O'Banion, you gotta go help."

"What happened?" Ernie started talking so fast that not one thing he said made sense. "Slow down. Help who?" Dean grabbed the man's shoulders and hung on. He could hear Mr. Schofield yell for Earl. That was strange, very few people ever called the shop looking for the surly Polish man. Something told him that whatever the phone call was about, it was the same thing he was about to hear from Ernie.

"On Pierce Street. The drop off...the Gennas were waiting with some guy I've never seen before. Elvie sent me back. I came here as fast as I could."

"Shit." Dean turned to go back inside to get his keys and his gun, but the door flew open. It was Earl, who had been upstairs resting. He looked like hell, and he had brought all of hell downstairs with him.

"We have to get to the Pierce speakeasy." Was all he said. In his hand were Elvie's keys. She had dropped them when she arrived, they imagined. Her car was in front of the big delivery truck.

"I can drive. Let me get my gun." But when he came back out, Earl was in the driver's seat. Dean hadn't even shut the door before the car was in motion. "Who was on the phone?"

"I don't know. They didn't give me a name. Just said they saw the Genna's and Elvie at the speakeasy drop-off point, and we'd better get over there."

"Somehow I don't think you're that worked up about our territory."

"On a normal day, Elvie would be fine. But she's not herself today." He barely stepped on the brake as they flew around a corner so fast that Dean slammed into a door.

"Where is Victor? He was supposed to be going too." Dean asked, setting himself right again. He was quite enjoying himself. He had no doubt that Elvie could handle herself, though he did want to be there if she needed them. Still. Seeing his friend worked up and driving like a bat out of hell was entertaining.

"I don't know that either. Haven't seen him since he dropped me off after lunch." He slammed on the brakes as two Italians ran in front of the car. It was Mike and TonyGenna and they were running like they were being chased by tigers, a bloody trail following them. Earl and Dean looked at each other.

"I think we underestimated her." Dean said with quiet awe. Pierce Street was only three more blocks away and he car swung onto Pierce St just in time to see a garbage can fly through the air and a very angry, very pale Elvie stepped into the alley.

Chapter 36

Elvie hadn't wasted time with words. She wasn't great at talking under pressure anyway. Instinctively reaching for her old powers, forgetting she didn't have them anything longer, she cursed. Elvie hated using guns, she always had. She was more of a swords and daggers fighter, to be honest, and because of that, Natalie had equipped the sleeves of Elvie's jackets with hidden daggers. She let one drop into each hand and caught both the Interface agent's hand and Mike's hand, forcing them to drop their guns. The only one left armed was was Mike Genna and he seemed to be rethinking things.

"What's wrong, Mike?" Elvie purred, pulling out her own gun. "Remembering what I did the last time we met?" Frank, in a rare moment of thoughtfulness, knocked over some boxes and caught Mike in the knees, causing him to fall forward. "Well, thank you, Frank. Although, you should probably go inside." Frank didn't need to be told twice and ran back for his saloon. The man from the Interface was scowling at her. "I'll be right with you." She said, leaning down to pick up his gun where it landed, keeping one trained on him.

Elvie kept her own gun pointed at Mike, put the other in her hoslter and knelt down, grabbing the Anthony Genna by the collar. "I would suggest, that unless you two want me to tell Torrio that you were causing trouble on my streets, that you home run as fast you can. She grabbed Mike's shotgun and wrenched it away. Anthony's gun had fallen far enough away from him that he would have been an idiot to make a grab for it. He stumbled up and Mike grabbed him as they started to walk away.

"I said run." Elvie hissed and shot two shots. One hit Mike's right hand, and then the other skimmed past Anthony's side. They didn't waste any more time and were gone before Elvie could blink. She turned her attention back to the final man. She was pretty sure his name was Derrick. "Now, Derrick...it's Derrick right?" The man frowned, he had been sure she wouldn't remember his name. It had caught him off guard. "What do you think you are doing?"

"The Interface has taken a special interest in Chicago. You got the better of us yesterday...somehow. I thought my aim was very good." His voice had an edge, like he was trying to goad her into overreacting. She really wanted to, especially since he had just admitted that the Interface was behind yesterdays warehouse ambush. But she couldn't, not here anyway. Elvie cocked her gun. She was normally opposed to violence but she had a feeling that she knew where this was going and she was already running on empty. Her patience was at an end.

"Why are you so taken with Chicago?" The man opened his mouth, but Elvie cut him off. "I have been dealing with Interface bullshit trying to destroy the North Side for three months. I am tired of it. Hurry up, before I blow out both your knees and you have to crawl back to whichever hell who you crawled out of." She wasn't kidding and he knew it. Elvie had a reputation built on rumors and half truths and some less than savory truths long before Chicago. The Interface, and especially, this man knew she would get what she wanted.

"If we take Chicago, we take out the Pathfinders...maybe." A sly smile crept over his face. "But if we take out the North Side, we're pretty sure it takes out you. Which will definitely end the Pathfinders. And if we end Hymie Weiss it definitely ends you." He winked. "You're already soft for that evil shit. He's just like you, black soul and the world will be better without you both." Elvie didn't have total control over what happened next but looking back she would wish she had slightly better controlled of her temper. She took out his knees, and kicked him so hard, Derrick flew across the the alley into the brick wall and collapsed to the ground.

"Look at you," he coughed. Letting your temper fly." He got to his feet and pull a box out of his pocket. She knew from experience it was their teleportation box. Before he could press the button. She had stepped through the In-Between and was directly in front of him. She grabbed him by the throat and squeezed.

"Before you press that button, here's a message to take back to Steve. Chicago is mine. He would do well to stay the hell out of it." She dropped the man, who with fear in his eyes pressed the button and vanished.

She was angry. She was could feel energy buzzing through her and was thankful there were no streetlamp around. Instead she physically picked up a trash can and heaved it as hard as she could across the street. The physical release of throwing the can helped the buzzing, but the noise set her teeth even more edge as the can bounced across the street, knocked over the neighboring buildings' cans as well. She was rolling the cans back when she heard a motor approaching. Wondering if Ernie had made it to the store already and sent help, she looked up and was surprised as her car came speeding around the corner. She was relieved for a moment, now that she knew Ernie had made it back to the shop unharmed, until two men, one blonde and smiling, the other other dark haired, looking like he was about to commit murder. Dean was looking around like he wanted to applaud, as Elvie and Earl stared at each other without speaking. All she could think was that she hoped that Frank had the good sense to stay inside.

Which, of course, he didn't. Taking tentative steps out of his speakeasy, Frank came into the alley way. That was when Earl saw him and drew a gun.

Chapter 37

"No. No, no, no, no." Elvie was in front of Frank so fast even she wasn't sure if she used the In-Between or not. "I don't think he wanted anything to do with this." She was aware that she had no idea if that was true and said a silent prayer (she was doing that a lot lately) that it was. Then, she found herself adding that if it wasn't true, Frank would at least have the brains to lie.

"It doesn't matter," Earl growled. He wasn't Earl anymore, instead the rage filled, impulsive mobster, Hymie Weiss was holding the gun. His hair was a mess and the brown was gone from his eyes, his pupils huge as he seemed to have lost himself to his emotions. "He betrayed us."

Elvie rolled her eyes at the melodramtic comment. "Okay, again. He might not have had a choice. Can we hear him out, at least?" Her eyes slipped past him momentarily to Dean, as if hoping he would step in but he seemed to be taking everything in with an amused stare. Elvie felt herself scowl involuntary and his smile got bigger.

She took a tentative step forward. She was pretty sure that Earl wouldn't do anything to her but she really didn't feel like getting shot on top of everything else today.

"Elvie, you're new still. But this is how these situations are handled. Get out of my way." His voice was rough, ragged, and quiet. He wasn't looking at her, but he hadn't shot her for moving, which was a step in the right direction. She took another step closer and then another until she put her hand on the gun and lowered it. Keeping both hands visible, she slid the hand on the weapon up to his hand and squeezed his wrist, as gently as she could. The physical contact and small pressure startled him. His eyes shot to her, and she saw the amber brown of irises begin to come back.

"Please?" She said softly, holding his gaze, willing him, the *real him* to hear her. "Please, don't kill anyone today."

Earl was quiet as he looked her over from head to toe, and Elvie watched as his pupils shrank and his shoulders relaxed. At last, after what felt like an eternity, his face softened and Elvie breathed out a breath she didn't realize she was holding. "Are you hurt?" He asked, as Dean stepped around them and pushed Frank into the speakeasy, muttering something about talking and letting them have a moment.

Offended, Elvie scoffed. "Of course not." I can handle the Gennas and some piece of shit suit." The disdain in her voice made Earl arch his brows in amusement.

"I don not doubt you could, normally. But after last night, I wasn't so sure. I'm sorry we weren't here with you. When I find out where Vick was—"

"I'm right here," came the familiar drawl. Victor was walking down the alley towards them. "I was picked up after I dropped you off for 'suspicious behavior.' Ernie told me what happened when I got to the garage." He looked at Elvie, who realized belatedly that she was still holding Earl's wrist. He had the grace to suppress his smile when she dropped her arm to her side, before he continued. "I'm sorry I wasn't here to help. Judging by the trail of blood that leads down the street and the lack of blood on you though, I'm guessing you handled it....well, like yourself?"

Elvie decided not to answer that, instead she address her most pressing question. "*Was* the behavior suspicious?"

"No, there should have been *no* suspicions about what I was doing." Coming closer, his eyes widened. "Holy hell you look worse than this morning." She glowered at him and was about to snap back when Dean yelled for them from the doorway.

"You guys are going to want to see this!" His voice different than usual, Elvie thought. He didn't sound shaken but she definitely sounded less confident than normal. Vincent motioned for her to go first, and she hurried to Dean. "It's not the normal Genna garbage," he said when she walked in. She had no doubt that the Interface was responsible for the whole thing and was just using the Gennas to get what they wanted.

The inside of the speakeasy was not as destroyed as Elvie had seen after other shakedowns, in fact, it looked like the shakedown had been half-hearted at best. Dean showed them to Frank's office. Inside was a woman in her mid thirties as well as two children, a boy, of around ten years old and his little sister, five or six who he held protectively close. Elvie felt her stomach drop as she realized why the family was here.

"This is my wife, Miriam." Frank said, hurrying over. "And these are my kids, Mickey and Delilah. Everyone, this is Elvie. She works with Deanie and the boys. She just sent Genna's running. Not sure where the other guy is. I don't think we need to be scared of her." Elvie waved. Miriam whispered hello, but was staring at her lap. The boy just nodded, his face as still as stone as he took in the situation. Delilah, on the other hand, squinted one eye and turned her head a bit.

"Are you a gangster, too?" She had a sweet, childlike voice. Elvie wasn't sure how to answer, but the girl was sounded so confused that she forced herself to say something that wasn't too incriminating.

"I suppose I'm a bit of one." Delilah's face scrunched even more in confusion and she tilted her head even farther.

"How? Aren't only boys gangsters?"

"Nope, not true." Victor had walked in behind her. He was looking at the kids with his completely normal, casual face. If Elvie hadn't come to know him so well then she would have thought he was oblivious. As it was, she could tell by the spark in his eyes and the way he kept clenching his teeth that he knew damn well why Frank's wife and kids were here. "It depends on how tough you are. Not what's between your legs."

"We kind of adopted her, anyway." Dean added as he and Earl entered last. Elvie watched the color drain from the latter's face as he took in everything. His eyes landed on Miriam. His lips thinned as he put it all together, taking in Frank's family.

"Frank, tell them what you told me." Dean said before he disappeared again, closing the door behind him. Frank started talking at a brisk clip, as if he were desperate to tell them. Which, after staring down the barrel of a gun, he probably was.

"Well, you see I was here waiting for your delivery. Next thing I know in walks that weird guy and Tony Genna. Tony goes 'You gonna be selling our beer now.' And I say, no. Cuz you know, I only sell Deanie's." Elvie shot a quick look at Earl and noticed his lips twitch, he hated to be wrong. "When I said that, he starts trashing the joint. Nuttin' I hadn't seen before, you know. I tink you've done it yo'self there, Mr. Dru—"

"What happened next, Frank?" Drucci spoke over him with a pointed tone and look, bouncing up on the toes of his scuffed black shoes. Even though the situation was quite serious, Elvie bit her lip to hide a smile as Frank rallied from the interruption.

"Right, well then that other guy tells him to stop and dat one in da suit says, 'He'll do whatever we say.' And then in walked Mike. And...and...and..." he took a steadying breath, "And they were with him." His voice cracked. "He had a gun on my kids."

"He came to our house, Frank," Miriam said, quietly, glaring at her husband. "You always said they'd never bother us at our own house." Frank started to protest.

"Ma'am," Earl cut it, politely, of course. In the quiet of the office it sounded louder than his voice actually was. Elvie was pretty sure Miriam hadn't realize he was there, since she startled when he spoke.

"With all due respect, Frank was half right. *We* wouldn't have bothered you at home. You're not a part of this this life."

"We'll take care of it though." He smiled at the kids and said "How does a fancy hotel stay for a few days sound?" The kids' faces lit up. Again, Frank and Miriam started to protest.

"Paid for by us, of course," Earl added before they could say too much. "Elvie, how about if you and Vincent give them a ride to their house. You guys pack bags for three or four days." The kids cheered and Elvie had to smile, as did Victor and Earl. The change in the boy was immediate. Mickey's serious face transformed into a sunny, happy one that made him look more childlike than even his sister.

"You too, Frank." Elvie said. "We will deliver the liquor after we get this straightened out. The four of you just hole up in the hotel." When they opened the office door, the sound of Dean's raised voice, calling someone, probably Johnny Torrio, every expletive in the book, spilled in.

"Look at you," Earl softly said to her as he passed her, "making decisions as you do it all the time. I think it's safe to say you're one of us now." His smile was a secret one just for her, dropping as soon as Victor and the others got close enough. His hand brushed around her waist before moving in the direction of Dean's voice and tossing her keys over his shoulder, in a very odd gesture for him. Elvie barely caught them, her heart rate stuttering, wishing he were still there. That he had lingered a second or two longer.

"Can I driver your car?" Vincent asked from behind her bringing her back to the present with a crash. "Pretty please?" He had been begging her to let him drive it for weeks, and since Earl had driven it she didn't have much choice now. She gave an exaggerated sigh and tossed him the keys. He let out a whoop and led the kids to the car, Miriam and Frank trailing behind and Elvie bringing up the rear, fiddling with her pocket watch.

Chapter 38

Getting everyone packed and back in the car didn't take long, the kids would have taken nothing if it meant getting them to the hotel faster. The hard part was getting them settled in the hotel. Victor had decided on the Drake, stating that it was close enough to the North Side base for them to keep an eye on it, and the kids would never forget it. Elvie hadn't realized how fond he was kids. It made her smile, just a little, every time the rough and tough gangster with a reputation for danger would say something or tickle one of the two kids.

While Victor was helping Frank and Miriam get checked in and obtain a bellhop, Elvie was in charge of taking care of Mickey and Delilah. It was no easy task, since the children were normally a rambunctious pair, according to Miriam. It appeared the excitement of the hotel stay was the equivalent of giving them cups of sugar. Mickey was also infatuated with Victor, his driving, and all things automotive. He was asking Elvie all sorts of questions about cars and where Victor had learned to drive like that (once he had gotten used to the car, he had begun zipping in and out of traffic and around corners. Elvie wished she could have leaned over and pressed the seatbelt button she had installed). She did her best to answer in between helping Delilah, who, having taken to her quite keenly, was very interested in becoming 'tuff' like her. The girl had insisted that Elvie teach her how to punch and kick.

Which is why when Dean and Earl walked into the Drake's lobby, Elvie didn't notice because Delilah had chosen right then to attempt a "spinning' flyin' punch kick mavooer" and almost knocked over a lamp and came close to taking out several passing elderly guests. Elvie stuck her tongue out at their retreating backs as she helped the girl back to her feet. She was just answering a question about the top speed of the car (she lied and said 150, knowing he would never believe the actual top speed) when she saw their parents approaching with a bellman and the three North Siders in tow. Earl wasn't even trying to hide his smile, making her wonder how much he had seen, and Dean appeared to look more like his jolly self. Only Victor looked worse for wear, which, considering they had arguably had the more difficult job that included child wrangling *and* he had spent the better part of his afternoon at the police department, was not a surprise.

"Thank you all." Miriam reached over and pulled Elvie in for a hug. The twenties were certainly an affectionate time, Elvie thought as she hesitantly patted the woman on the back. "You have no idea how much this helps."

Dean smiled, "Don't mention it."

"Seriously, we've got a reputation to uphold," Vincent added ruffling Mickey's hair as the boy stared at him in awe. Elvie pulled both kids in for hugs before helping them load things on the bell cart.

"You should be able to go home by tomorrow. But to play it safe, your stay is paid up for three nights anyway." Earl said as Delilah pulled on his arm. "Yes?" He looked down at her, confused, Elvie had noticed kids weren't immune from the energy that Earl gave off in public and avoided him. Delilah's interest came as a shock to the four friends, none more so than the Pole himself it appeared, the look was one of confusion and a little fear.

"You should have Miss Elvie teach you how to throw a punch." Delilah said and then pulled him down a little bit by the sleeve. "She's got...*spunk*." Elvie hid a grin behind her hand. Victor turned a snort into a cough. Earl, though, smiled at the girl, nodding. He got down so they were on the same level, talking as equals.

"She's pretty impressive, isn't she?" At the question, Delilah nodded. "Did you know she's also really smart? And a darn good driver?"

"No, but it doesn' supise me." The girl said, seriously. Earl reached into his pocket and pulled out a small card. Elvie knew it was one of the cards he carried that had the Schofield office number on it.

"It shouldn't. I've become quite fond of our Miss Elvie. But do you want to know a secret?" Everyone was riveted, especially Elvie, who had never seen Earl interact with a child before. Delilah nodded and waited for the secret. "She really loves kids and teaching them. She doesn't talk about it, but I've seen it a few times now, like how she was with you?"

"Yeah! Did you see my spin?"

"I did. It was so good! You are going to be quite a fighter." He looked at Elvie out of the corner of his eye. "I bet that if it's okay with your mother and father, if you call the number on that card I gave you sometime, Elvie would love to teach you to read and write and take you to the library."

"Isn't that what schools for?" Delilah asked suspiciously.

"Technically, but I've learned things are much more fun when Elvie is involved. No one knows books and stories like her." As Earl had spoke Elvie had felt herself blush, a warm tingly feeling had spread throughout her whole body. To be known was a special kind of feeling on it's own, but he had gotten her so right in that small description that she thought she might cry. No one had known her so well in a long time or cared to know her. Her heart had been trying to process the sweetness of his interaction with a child only to have it swelling to three times it's normal size. Good God, she was losing it.

Delilah looked over at her then, and Elvie hoped her face looked more together than she felt. "Is that true, Miss Evie? Will you teach me?"

"Absolutely. If it's okay with your mother and father, of course." The two parents exchanged a look and shrugged. If this was the worst that came out of this day they seemed okay. Delilah cheered and ran over to hug Elvie. The tears were definitely going to spill then, and she blinked them away hurriedly.

"Alright," Frank said, clapping his hands. "Let's head up." The rowdy family of four made their way to the elevator, Mickey trying to ride on the bell cart and Delilah skipping ahead. The four North Siders watched them before turning to leave. Dean and Earl in front and then Victor, trying to supress a yawn, and finally Elvie, staying a bit behind to collect herself. Earl was holding the door when she got there.

"How did you know all that?" She asked when he fell in step beside her. "You sounded like you've known me forever?"

"You aren't the only one who watches people, Elvie Townshend." He said and gave her his elbow, and the two followed the Dean and Vincent down the street to the cars. Vincent and Dean, had their heads together and Elvie wondered what they were discussing. She knew she would have to be getting home soon. She had sent a recording of what Frank had said to the base, and she would need to get back to debrief, but for now, she tightened her fingers on Earl's jacket sleeve and took in the feel of the early summer Chicago air, mixing with the feeling that she was where she was supposed to be.

Chapter 39

Base was chaotic when Elvie got back. She shouldn't have been surprised. The confirmed presence of the Interface, combined with what had happened to Frank and Miriam, was alarming. Shirley and Tony were very much up in arms. However, Bixby and Violet were at the Four Deuces tonight, as per usual. Bixby had tried to get out of it, but he was supposed to be bartending and had to go. Elvie wasn't even sure Violet had any idea what was happening. Which meant that the chaos was coming from just Natalie, Tony, and Shirley. And mostly just Shirley. Natalie had been to the convenience shop down on the corner and gotten Shirley cigarettes, which she was flying through at an alarming rate.

"What could they be thinking? Bringing in civilians like that?" Natalie asked, for what must have been the fourth time. They had been going around and around the same questions for the last hour, ever since Elvie had gotten back. Her headache and the chills were getting worse. She had had a very busy last few days. More so than usual, and while she had known about the Interface's presence in Chicago for months this was the first time she had been able to offer proof that it was effecting other people.

"What does it matter what they are thinking? Does it really matter when there are children involved?" She asked, her voice weary. "I don't know what you want to do about it. We just have to keep them from screwing things up. That's all we can do without altering timelines. Until we have an idea of what they are planning on a larger scale, we have to proceed as usual."

"We can't just let them get away with this!" Shirley snapped at her, her voice shrill. Elvie looked at Tony across the table, pleading.

"She's not wrong," Tony started slowly. He held up a hand when Shirley started to protest. "Listen, she's not wrong. We can't necessarily do anything to counteract what they do. It could set off alarms for the South Side and compromise Violet and Bixby."

"Elvie, can't you like…sneak up on them and take them out?" Natalie looked over at Elvie, who felt her anger prickle. If it was that easy, she would have taken care of the Interface ages ago. Did they really think she wouldn't have done something by now if she could?

"Not without knowing where they are specifically and how enmeshed in the timeline they are. Don't you think—"

"It seems to me that you have gotten a bit too caught up in the *romance* of Chicago right now, Elvira." Shirley interrupted. Tony's eyes went wide and Natalie stared at her like she had three heads.

"Excuse me? Also, that's not my name." Elvie tried to keep her voice calm. She tried to remain patient. But she should feel her blood pressure rising. She was unsure why Bixby and Violet who weren't even here were off scot free, they never reported anomalies or anything and here she had provided proof. She had also been in New York last week to deal with an anomaly and France last month. But *she* was too caught up in the atmosphere of Prohibition Chicago to notice…what exactly?

"You're off your game. You're too emotionally attached to the people here. If you weren't you'd have no problems running in and catching the Interface." Shirley was trying to find someone to blame, Elvie knew but that didn't make her better. Not today, at least.

"If I remember correctly, you are the one always telling me to think twice before I rush in. And didn't you send me to Hollywood last month because you had a headache?"

"That was a mistake, just like keeping you on this assignment." She was practically yelling now and was standing up, leaning over the table, like an angry parent or teacher. "You think you belong here, and you don't. You don't want to mess anything up on the South Side because you don't want to mess anything up for you and your gang." She was gaining speed now and when Elvie opened her mouth to protest, Shirley talked over her. "You're being selfish and you've lost sight of the future. What would your family say back home if they saw you today?" The alarm downstairs had reached a fully siren's wail but it didn't matter because the only sound Elvie could hear was the blood in her ears by the time Shirley had finished.

"I don't know...who you think you are. I don't know if you think you have access to all the thoughts in my head." Her voice was shaking when it finally came out, and Tony and Natalie had both moved away from the table. Elvie stood up slowly. "But every single day I go out, and I risk my life. I watch people make decisions that I know will get them killed because if I stop them, everyone I loved back home will die. Or cease to exist. Meanwhile, you sit here in the base watching things through a computer screen and acting like you know half of what goes on out there. But, sure, I've lost perspective. It's easy for you to sit there in your chair on your ass and judge me, but let me tell you, Shirley. I would never risk the lives of children because of my own personal feelings. And before you tell me I am too involved around here, remember you told me to stay here." She paused and took a breath. "Then go soak your damn head." She grabbed her keys off the table and left without another word.

Chapter 40

When Elvie had stepped out of her house, she had almost reflexively stepped into the In-Between. It was where she normally went when she didn't want to be found, and for now, she would stay here until she figured out where she wanted to go. As usual, she had no idea where that was, just that she couldn't be there. She wandered across the small yard trying to calm herself down and, as she always did on days like this, just kept walking.

It hurt more than she would ever admit out loud, Shirley thinking she didn't care about the timeline. Because of her love for the future, her family was the only thing that had stopped her from blatantly interfering several times before, and recently, it was a thought she had to push forward much more often. This was a different feeling than in 1865. Then she *had* been thinking about the future and how Reconstruction and civil rights might have gone better if Lincoln hadn't been assassinated.

Now, it was personal. More personal, anyway. That's why being called selfish by Shirley had hit so hard. It was what she called herself every day when she wondered if there was a way to save the people she had begun to think of as home. Because she wasn't ever going back to her own time, her original home, and her heart was longing for a place where she was loved and accepted, outside of who she was to the mission.

It occurred to her that the sounds of the city, the traffic, and people talking and yelling had disappeared. She looked around her at her surroundings. The building in front of her was an old, derelict house next to an even older church. She had thought herself to the priest she had met that night in Waukegan. "Yeah, alright, subconscious," she grumbled aloud. No one could hear her in the In Between. Well, no one but Earl, and he wasn't here.

Stepping out into the living world, she wondered what the worst thing the priest could say was, couldn't be worse than all the things she herself had thought. With that less than reassuring thought, she climbed the steps of the church. Being a Tuesday afternoon, there was no mass, so, even though she was pretty sure the door was unlocked, she knocked tentatively. From far back in the church, a voice called for her to come in. She pushed the heavy door open and slipped inside, shutting it quietly behind her. The ancient priest was sitting at a small desk on one side of the stairs that led to the altar. Any doubt that he would remember her disappeared when he looked up and smiled at her.

"Well, Miss Elvie! How nice to see you. What brings you here today? I didn't get a call from Dean, so I assume it's not business." His eyes were just as bright as that first night and Elvie realized at last what it was she liked about him as she shook his hand before sitting in the pew across from the desk. He was simply a good soul.

"I was wondering…if I could ask you something?" Elvie asked slowly, unsure of how she was going to phrase this.

He leaned forward and folded his hands together. "I am all ears."

"Well…" What was the best way to phrase this? She wondered. She took a deep breath as her heart hammered in her ears as she got ready to ask the question in the only way she could think: bluntly. "Is it wrong that I have become so attached to people who do such awful things? Does it make me a bad person? Is it wrong that, while I can see the bad things I also see the good in them and want to stop them from leading themselves to an early death? Should I want to stop it?

And why should I be more worried about the deaths of them, people who have...you know..." she didn't want to say it in a church, "than all the good people that die everyday?"

"There it is." He chuckled. "Earl mentioned you are a recovering Catholic."

"Oh, do we have a club?"

"You should, I'd host your meetings." He smiled at her, and even though her insides were still coiled up inside her, she felt herself smiling in response. "Let me ask you a question to answer yours: Do you like them because of the bad or the good? Do you like them because they break laws and rob safes? Or do you like them because they help people who need them? Do you have a soft spot for them because they don't get the same recognition as...certain other mobsters who do the same things but call attention to the good while hiding the bad?"

"What difference does it make?" She looked at him curiously. "What difference does it make why I like them if they are still on the wrong side of the moral spectrum?"

"Elvie, there is a difference between the man who thinks he is doing something good and ignores all the bad he does and the man who knows he is doing something bad and knows it's wrong but does his best to be a good person in every other regard."

Elvie looked down at her hands. "I don't know who I am anymore. I thought I did before Chicago. But they've changed everything."

"Are you saying you want to give them up?" He tilted his head. There was no accusation in his voice, just calm patience, as if he already knew the answer.

"No. That's what scares me the most." She felt tears prick her eyes. "I'm not a killer, but I work with them."

"You and most of Chicago." He laughed humorlessly. "You already think you are bad, Elvie. I can't change that. But you're not. You've found a place you like, you've found people who seem to understand you, and you understand them. They let you in, as if you were a missing piece of their puzzle. So, no Elvie. I don't think it makes you a bad person to want to help the people who have come to think of as family."

Chapter 41

Elvie was sitting on top of her car on a dirt road in the middle of nowhere. The grass around her was about three feet tall, and wildflowers were scattered everywhere. The sun was setting and Elvie was staring up at the sky, watching the first stars appear overhead. She had been sitting here for an hour since leaving the church. The first thirty minutes of which she had spent out in the field just wandering, using the pocket to play music, a modification that Natalie had made to it, and that Elvie had loved her for.

Now, as she lay on the hood of her car and watched the stars appear, she was beginning to wonder where she went from here. She was too far in, too invested in the guys and their mission. Dean, she wasn't as close to. In truth, his brand of psycho made her more than a little uncomfortable. Earl could switch to murderous in a heartbeat, that was true, but there was usually a clear trigger. Dean didn't always have one. Sometimes it seemed like he shot just to shoot.

Earl and Victor, she was more attached to than she would have originally thought possible with a person of history. They had become her closest friends and people who could make her smile in spite of everything. They were also strangely protective of her. They never wanted her around when they thought someone would get shot. And even though she had proven herself time and again by now, when they were out together, the two were usually nearby. The one time a man had grabbed her and pulled her onto his lap Hymie had been across the room faster than Elvie had known he could move and personally threw the man onto the street, a broken nose and split lip later. After he came back, he hadn't left her side for the rest of the night. Elvie smiled at the memory.

"You look relaxed." Tony's voice came from her left.

"Is that a problem?" She didn't look at him. Maybe if she ignored him, he would leave her in peace.

"Are you planning on coming home tonight?"

"No." She really had no idea what she was going to do after she left this field. She'd already been to see Joe today and he was more solid than ever, he didn't seem to have a hint of illness left in him. "I might go get a hotel room. I don't fit in very well at base anymore. Well, I never did, but it's worse now." Tony shifted beside her, but she didn't look over at him.

"What Shirley said...was wrong. She didn't mean it, and she shouldn't have said it. She was freaked out and angry."

"I know, she's gotten that way before."

"I've never seen you react that way." She could feel his eyes boring into her.

"Because I was having the same thoughts about myself. I feel selfish for enjoying myself and becoming friends with them. For the occasional thought that I wish I could help them." She immediately regretted saying it out loud.

"I don't think you would be you if you didn't become friends with them. Also, I won't tell Shirley, but I know you and Natalie are up to something." Elvie did look over then, her eyes wide. "Natalie's been muttering to herself, pouring over notebooks for days. You seem distracted, not just about your future but something else. It's alright. You wouldn't be human if you didn't want to change the way things end."

"I didn't think I was allowed to feel human." It came out sharper than she had intended, but Tony just laughed.

"You're allowed to feel human. I wish I had a bit more humanity left."

"Are you taking me off the case?" Elvie asked. She didn't want him to delay it. Better he make the decision now.

"A little late to take you out now. I think at least two of the four North Siders would burn the base down looking for you." When he said that, Elvie blushed. "If it makes you feel any better, you matter to them, too. I see it in every interaction that I watch from your pocket watch."

"How much are you watching?"

"Not much. I used to watch more because I was worried about you. Then I realized I didn't need to be. I never should have worried, you know how to protect yourself, you know your limits...and you have good friends watching out for you." When she didn't say anything else, he sighed. "I'm going back to base. If you need anything you know where to reach me."

Elvie leaned back and looked at the stars. She saw the constellation she had been waiting for. Astrology wasn't necessarily true. She knew that. She knew it was all up to interpretation. Still, as her star sign, the Ram, Aries, appeared overhead she felt herself gain back her confidence. She was a trailblazer, a fighter, a fire starter. And whatever happened next, it was because she made it that way.

Chapter 42

Elvie knocked twice on the door to a Congress Hotel room. She heard someone moving on the other side and waited, patiently. The sound of footsteps approaching the door, trying to tiptoe, had her trying not to roll her eyes and a second later the door in front of her swung open. Victor was standing in front of her, his tie undone, collar open and his jacket off. His dark locks were still perfect looking, not a hair out of place.

"Elvira!" He stood aside and motioned her in.

"Not my name." She grumbled for the second time that day. Victor had been trying to guess if she had a full first name for weeks. Now, he was certain it was Elvira, and she just didn't want to admit it.

"Then tell me what your full name is. Drink?"

"Whiskey, please. How do you know that my name isn't just Elvie?" She turned to look at him, where he stood, stock still, frozen between his living area and the drink case, stunned. "It's been a very long day." Victor's face softened and he nodded.

"Yeah, it has." He poured them each a drink and motioned for her to sit. He sank down next to her, handing her a drink. "I've been in here trying to convince myself to go out and cause some trouble at the speaks but," he took a long drink. "Those kids wore me out." Elvie grinned and took a sip of her own whiskey, it burned but in a good, necessary, way.

"You're really good with them."

"Yeah, I love kids. It helps that I'm a big one myself." Victor drained his glass and leaned back. "So, what's on your mind?"

"What makes you think something's on my mind?"

"Elvie. Elvlita…" he paused and Elvie shook her head. "Damn. Anyway, I've known you a bit now. You never come to my place when you're bored. You always go to Earl's. If he's at Mary's, she'd love to have you over and really meet you. But tonight, you came here. Why?" Elvie leaned her head back against the back of his couch and stared at the ceiling.

"To forget. I think I keep forgetting who I was…who I should be. Maybe I should forget who I am now." She threw back the entire drink and Victor took her glass and his to refill them, when he sat back down they both downed them in one go.

"You're worse than Earl, you know that?" Victor laughed, softly, leaning back into the throw pillows again. "He told me earlier that he was going to go home, down some alcohol and pass out. I don't think he did. Last I heard, he actually was over at Mary and Violet's. But you apparently…"

"I'm surprised you didn't go with him. I heard Mary makes a mean stew." Elvie had been treated to a full review of Mary's stew by Victor a month ago when he had gone there for dinner. She'd never heard him wax poetic about anything but he was practically writing sonnets about that stew.

"Some nights I don't want to watch other people live happy lives with their parents when my mom prefers every other sibling to me." It was a brutally honest answer that Elvie hadn't expected, and she found herself trying to comfort him.

"I'm sorry, D. You deserve a family that loves you and accepts you for you." He waved it away, the way he always did when things got emotional.

"I've got my brother, John. And James. I just…worry about Frank. He's so much like me and I wonder what they will do to avoid another me." Elvie winced inwardly. Frank was going to die in just a few months. In Wisconsin. At an asylum for kids who parents deemed insane because they didn't fit the mold. She wished she could tell Victor that Frank would be okay, but it was such a bald faced lie, even she couldn't spin it well.

"Well, I like you the way you are." She said at last.

"Just not as much as you like Earl." He smiled when Elvie glared at him. "Oh come on. The two of you practically drool over each other. Also, I thought you were never going to stop insulting me when I was picking on him this morning."

"Asshole." She grumbled. "But it's a different kind of like. You are my friend. My very good friend. And Earl is also my very good friend. I just want it to be more. But it can't."

"Why? Because you don't want to make it happen?" Victor shook his head. "It's gonna have to be you. He'll never do it."

"No...because he's not meant for me. He's meant for someone else." She waited for Victor to ask what that meant. Anyone else would have asked what it meant but Victor was quiet. Then, he rose, refilled her glass and his own and sat down. Raising the glass, Elvie went to down this one, too, when Victor spoke.

"What year are you from?" The question was so innocently asked, just like part of a normal conversation but Elvie choked on the alcohol, and fell to coughing and sputtering.

"Sorry?" She gasped, when she was finally able to get air.

"My god, I thought you would have a better poker face." Victor laughed. "That's payback for this morning, by the way." Elvie just stared at him. "Oh, come on. You know so much all the time. I've seen you react to things before they happen. Your car has buttons that I have never seen before, and don't think for a second I didn't notice the speedometer goes up to 250." And then there is that pocket watch." Elvie pulled it out of her jacket and flipped the lid, revealing a normal clock face. Victor leaned over and spun the hour hand all the way around once. The face changed and became the screen that Elvie used. "I've seen you do it a few times. So, again, Miss Townshend, I ask what year are you from?" Elvie met his eyes, and before she could stop it, the entire story came spilling out.

Chapter 43

Elvie stayed in Victor's hotel room that night. She hadn't meant to, but after they stayed up talking until three, Victor had a lot of questions, and after years of keeping the secret, Elvie was too happy to share—the fatigue caused by the alcohol had kicked in. She didn't remember falling asleep on his couch, but when she woke up, there was a blanket over her and a note on the table in his customary scrawl.

Had some leads to follow up on. Called E, he wants you to pick him up from Mary and V's at 8:30. Dr's appointment, I guess. See you at the garage tomorrow. —Victor

Elvie rolled off the couch and reappeared standing on the front step at the base. Opening the door quietly, she slipped inside. She could hear Shirley and Tony talking at a level which indicated they weren't quite fighting but were having a disagreement. Elvie tiptoed upstairs and put on a new suit, brushed her teeth, and snuck back downstairs and froze. Natalie was sitting on a stool in the kitchen. They stared at each other for a second before Elvie held a finger to her own lips, before grabbing a chunk of freshly baked bread off the counter and tried to leave again. Unfortunately, Natalie followed her out the door. Elvie could have disappeared, but it always felt rude to do so to Natalie.

"Are you going to avoid Shirley forever?" she asked Elvie as she walked beside her, heading east toward the Loop.

"I'm not avoiding her. I just want to not deal with her trying to apologize right now." She was tearing the bread into bits, her appetite gone. She tossed the broken parts to some pigeons as she walked.

"Are you okay?" Natalie sounded like she was trying to be patient but Elvie was aggravating her.

"Fine. Freaked out, insecure, neurotic and emotional. So, I'm myself." She gave Natalie an obviously fake smile and Natalie rolled her eyes.

"Elvie, if you need anything, I've got your back."

"Mhmm," Elvie said as she sped up. Once she was out of reach, she could disappear into her space.

"Oh no, lady." Natalie reached out and grabbed her arm. "Elvie. Stop. You can't keep avoiding us."

"I'm not avoiding you. I'm doing my job." She paused. "Okay, I'm also avoiding you. But you guys don't need me around. I'm always a drain on the mood and whatnot."

"Elvie come on, you know that's not—"

"Sorry, gotta go." And she slipped into the In-Between. When she landed in New Mexico, Joe was waiting for her, swinging his legs back off the wall of the sanitorium.

He hopped down and landed in front of Elvie, making a show of the landing. She shook her head at him and he grinned wider. The oldest Weiss child appeared to be a trickster.

"So, do you think today will be the day?" She asked, tilting her head, waiting. The answer every time they had tried was "No." Just a short and simple answer, before she tugged and lost the ability to breathe for several seconds. Today, though, Joe didn't answer immediately. Instead, he frowned, thinking.

"Not today. But very soon." Then he looked at her and held out his hand, as he did everyday. "Still want to try?"

"Always," Elvie grabbed his hand and pulled. She felt one foot make it out onto the side of the living room this time, and just when she was feeling a little too triumphant, her lungs stopped working, and she had to let go. Standing together in the In-Between, though, Joe was grinning from ear to ear.

"We're almost there."

"Only took two months. What is it now, the middle of..." She trailed off and pulled out her pocket watch; the date said May 17, 1924. Two days. There were two days until the raid that was going to throw Chicago into a gang war. There had been no mention of it. And here she thought she was on equal footing with them. Apparently not. She looked up at Joseph, who grimaced. "Something's going to happen on the day of the raid, isn't it?"

"That's the problem." He held out his hands, shrugging. "I don't know for sure. I just...feel like you're going to need some help soon. Very soon. The fact that it's the day that my brother's gang is planning to double cross Torrio and Capone might not have anything to do with it. But..." Elvie had told him about her conversation with Derrick outside of Frank's and suddenly a lot more pieces fell into place. If the attention was on the Gennas, they wouldn't notice anything happening inside Torrio's gang.

"But, given what Derrick said that day, there's been a plan in place for awhile." Joseph nodded again. "But surely...oh, son of a bitch." She was gone before Joseph could register the pure rage that crossed her face.

Chapter 44

Elvie threw the door to base open harder than she ever had. She found herself equal parts glad and annoyed that she no longer could light fires with her emotions. It would have been relaxing to blow the door off right now. The dent it left in the wall would have to suffice. Natalie came rushing down the stairs just Elvie turned and stormed down the basement steps.

"What is going on—"

"Shirley," Elvie was trying, really, she was trying to keep her voice even and calm. It was difficult. The last time she had been this angry was after Rasputin had been so drunk he'd tried to swim in the frozen Neva River. His dive had ended up giving him a bloody nose and a mild concussion. Elvie had had to drag him into the Winter Palace and bribe the maids and cooks to let him warm up in there while she iced his face. The food in the oven had exploded. Elvie would have come up with an explanation just fine, except the cook blamed Rasputin, and Elvie just went along with it, seeing as he was too inebriated and concussed to notice he was being thrown under the proverbial bus. Now, though, this was a different kind of anger, because while she had been getting yelled at for spending too much time with the Northsiders, Bixby and Violet were either oblivious to notice or they were a part of an Interface attack. "Shirley, could you please get Bixby and Violet here....*now*."

"Why? What's the matter?" Shirley pulled up their screens, where their vitals showed that they were perfectly safe and healthy. "They're okay, why do they need—"

"Because the Sieban Brewery raid is the day after tomorrow. Because I've been speaking with a ghost in the In-Between, and he said that he is pretty damn sure that there is going to be something that will happen on that day that will screw things up. And because the Gennas have been a distraction for the past three months and the two people who would know about this particular plan are currently sitting in a restaurant with a white slaver and a syphilitic bastard." Natalie and Shirley stared at her open-mouthed, and then Shirley punched in something on the computer. Thirty seconds went by…sixty seconds…ninety…and then a message from Bixby appeared on the screen.

Will be there this evening. At lunch.

Elvie, doing something that she never, ever did, wheeled Shirley's chair out of the way and typed.

No. You will be here now. Interface attack imminent but I bet you already know that.

They waited and watched the screen. After two minutes the reply appeared.

Leaving now. No sign of the Interface from my post.

By the time Bixby and Violet came down the stairs to the control room, Elvie had paced around the room so many times Shirley had claimed to be getting dizzy. They had finally had to tell Shirley and Tony, who had been summoned back from whatever part of the world he had disappeared to, about Elvie's powers changing. When she found out that Elvie wasn't going to blow the base to pieces, Shirley relaxed considerably.

"So that's why nothing exploded yesterday." Tony said, thoughtfully. "I thought that was weird." Tony had also pointed out that her having this ability made the most sense. "You're the most accident prone. We'll save a ton on bandages."

"They refill themselves and it comes with the base." Natalie had pointed out. Tony had simply replied that it was probably hard on the old house, having to work so hard all the time. Which was when the door to the house opened and Elvie's senses sharpened, her muscles tensed, ready for a fight. Natalie, Tony and Shirley were nervous and edgy. They'd never seen Elvie so angry at one of the others before. She never got angry with the others.

Violet appeared first, her perfectly curled brown hair pinned under a fashionable hat, her full lips painted a deep red, and her brilliant green eyes flashing. She was Elvie's height, and they both had the same shape, a slightly less than classic hourglass, but Violet was softer, not so callused and muscled from years of jobs in rough conditions. Tony had once joked that she was the refined version of Elvie. Standing opposite each other in the control room, it was even more obvious. Elvie's eyes, which she knew were a sharp, icy blue, and her wavy blonde hair a wild mess around her head, dressed in a black, specially tailored suit, took in the other woman in her expensive flapper dress and a cloak, and had to restrain herself from lunging across the room and knocking her refined ass to the ground.

Violet looked towards her and winced. "I shouldn't be surprised, I suppose. Anger always has been your overriding emotion."

"Violet," Tony cut in, both verbally and physically, placing himself between her and Elvie. "Elvie has every reason to be angry. She's heard that Steve and his second in command, Derrick, have been using the Gennas as a decoy while setting up something bigger to happen during the brewery raid."

"Well, shit." Bixby sighed from behind his partner. "That actually makes sense." Everyone looked at him. "I mean, think about it. No one likes the Gennas, right? They're terrible. So, if they cause a little extra trouble where they shouldn't and are seen with Derrick, we won't look elsewhere in the city. They can plan to perfection."

"They've been planning this in your territory." Elvie pointed out. "There's no way they are operating over there with Torrio and Capone knowing about it."

"Wait, are you saying we knew about this?" Bixby started forward. "You can't think that—"

"No, Bixby." Elvie sighed. "I don't think you knew anything about it. But I wonder if Violet's boyfriend does?"

Violet scoffed. "Why would he?"

"He's pretty high up the food chain over there, right? So, if Steve and Derrick do have a foot in the door you would know about it." But Violet just shook her head, laughing.

"Oh, honey. No." She looked condescendingly at Elvie, who had to bite the inside of her cheek to remain calm. "He and I are lovers. He doesn't involve me in the business side of things. We aren't equals. And he has never once said otherwise. Because, surely," Violet's green eyes went ice cold and her lip curled in a tiny sneer. "Elvie, if someone were an equal, they would know about potential upcoming plans." Elvie wished she could close everything off to Violet, that she couldn't find the sensitive spots in someone's brain and pick at and poke them. Like now. "It'd be a nasty way to find out you never belonged somewhere, them hiding plans from you." The two of them stared at each other, and the room seemed to be holding it's breathe. When Elvie looked away first, Natalie looked like she wanted to cry, and Violet let herself have a small triumphant smile before she turned back to Shirley and Tony.

"Is there anything else you need from me? I have to get back to work." She was already halfway up the steps and Natalie, whom Violet always underestimated, spoke up before either of the two in charge could answer.

"Why are you in such a hurry? What's so important that you have to get back to?"

Violet looked her up and down and then flung a smile, a biting, nasty smile at Elvie, who was glaring at her. "I've got a dinner party to attend. A man named Steve is coming over, and I need to be there to get as much information as possible." Tony just managed to grab Elvie before she pounced, and Violet's laughter lingered in her ears for the rest of the day, as Elvie ran herself through battle training and came up with a plan of attack for dealing with Sieban Raid and the Interface in two days' time. Every time she punched another practice dummy, she thought of the smug look on Violet's face as she delivered that parting shot. Violet's lover, whoever he was, was sharing something important with her. And Elvie had been left in the dark by her friends, as she always knew she would be.

Chapter 45

Violet Monahan's place on Oakdale Avenue wasn't too far from the base, and as Elvie, who had been forcibly pushed out the door by Natalie after she said Earl could find his own way to the speakeasy or wherever he wanted to go, was waiting for Earl, she tried to talk herself through the way she was feeling. She had spilled her guts to Victor last night, and he hadn't thought to let her in on the raid. Granted...he knew she knew about the raid, so there really wasn't a reason for him to tell her. But Earl...maybe they hadn't been as close as she had thought. Maybe it was all in her head. Loneliness had finally driven her to delusion. It wasn't Earl's fault, she reasoned, but that didn't stop her from being angry with him. That only made it more annoying that he was running late, which wasn't like him. When he did eventually come out of the building, he was walking slowly, his eyes had dark circles underneath, and they were puffy as if he had been crying. Elvie was guessing he hadn't gotten good news at his doctor's appointment today, and in spite of herself, she felt her anger dissipate almost immediately as he shut the door and sank back into his seat.

"Hi...are you okay?" She asked tentatively as he slid into the seat next to her.

"No." He stared straight ahead. "Can we go to the speak on Fullerton? The one with the best highballs?"

"Of course. Are you sure you're up for it. You don't look so hot."

"Just drive...please." Elvie did as he asked...or ordered, but continued watching him out of the corner of her eye as she drove. It was clear he was antsy. After a block or so, he was flipping restlessly through his prayer book, and as they were pulling onto the street in front of the speakeasy he had requested for the night, she noticed he hadn't flipped in a block or two. He was reading the last page over and over. She had researched what it said a long time ago, and often wondered what he had thought of the last page.

They who have done good shall come forth unto the resurrection of life; but they who have done evil unto the resurrection of judgement.

"You okay?" She asked, again, tentatively. His eyes were fixed on the words, but she couldn't tell if he was reading them or just staring at the page. He had the look of someone who had read something so many times over that they didn't have to focus on the words anymore.

"Yeah, I mean. Nothing I didn't already know. But it's just...let's go get a drink, and I'll tell you."

The place was crowded, but Elvie and Earl found spots at the end of the bar. It was in the corner closest to the offices, so patrons avoided it as a rule.

"Okay, spill," Elvie said after the bartender had dropped off her water and his highball. He didn't even ask their orders.

"So, I'm dying, which I knew, but..." He started, looking down into his glass. He tipped it back, proceeding to drain the whole thing in one shot. He signaled the bartender for another. Elvie knew where this conversation was going, but she realized she wasn't going to have time to comfort him. Earl never drank to excess. One highball made him tipsy. "You and I, we knew I was dying faster than normal people, right? But I found out today, it turns out, I know my expiration date." The bartender set down the highball, and Earl drank it as quickly as the first. He slammed it down on the bar, making the people nearby jump. The. The bartender looked over, and he signaled for a third. Even though she had been bracing herself for this conversation for a week, she still wasn't prepared when he finally spoke the words, "I've got maybe two or three years left." The bartender dropped off the third drink and shot Elvie a pointed look before walking away. "But hey! That's probably all I had left anyway in this line of work." He reached for the glass of alcohol, and Elvie's hand shot out and covered the top of the glass before he could get it to his mouth. She slowly pushed it down.

"Earl, slow down. Drinking yourself into a stupor isn't going to help." She worried she was too harsh but already she could see the alcohol reflected in his eyes. "You might have longer than they said." She slid his drink to her other side, knowing that she was lying. He had a little over two years, but not because of the cancer.

"I could, but I don't. And Elvie…" His voice shook, and, for the first time since she'd met him, he looked frightened."I'm going to hell." He pulled out his prayer book and flipped to the back, even though she knew he had the words memorized, "They who have done good shall come forth unto the resurrection of life, but they who have done evil unto the resurrection of judgement." He looked up at her as he shut the book with shaking hands. "I'm going to hell."

"Earl, let's go somewhere else. Somewhere you can think." He nodded slowly but then reached around her and grabbed the glass throwing it back before she could stop him.

"You aren't the only one who moves fast," he tried a wink and failed, and then whispered loudly, "God, I'm an idiot. Who's dying? Who's dying and going to hell?"

"Let's go, Mr. Weiss."

She managed to get him out of the speak and into her car before the drinks really hit him. It was a ten-minute drive to his place on West Monroe, but in those ten minutes, Elvie learned that the already impulsive Hymie Weiss, when under the influence of spirits, lost his filter between his brain and his mouth. She was thankful he was too inebriated to remember to roll the window down, as he had something to yell at every person they drove past. Between the car and the few feet to his door, he managed to yell at at least ten passing cars, using every expletive he knew in English and Polish, as well as what sounded like a few Sicilian ones. Finally, inside his own house, he wouldn't stop talking. After Elvie deposited him in a chair in his front room and went to find the kitchen, his house was small enough that she could still hear his every word.

"I'm not even married! I'll never have kids. Would have made a lousy father anyway. *I* wouldn't disown them, though, not even if they made poor life decisions as I did. Nope. No, sir-ey," Elvie heard him either kick or run into a wall. He was still talking, though, so she was pretty sure he was relatively okay. She sliced some bread and started toasting it. Then she grabbed the coffee from a carton labeled *kawa* and began brewing that. By now, he had wandered into the kitchen and was still talking like he had just discovered he could. Thankfully, he did sit when Elvie pointed at the table, laying his head on it for a moment. He sat up when she slid the toast across to him, his eyes glassy. She wanted to comfort him, but when he was like this, she knew talking was useless. She had never seen him drunk, but he reminded her of Victor when he was, and she had taken care of him several times.

"Elvie, will you kiss me?" He was ignoring the toast, much to Elvie's dismay. She really needed him to eat, especially if he was at the point of talking about kissing. Although that was normally Victor's first stop, so maybe this was a good sign. "I've always wanted to kiss you. Ever since that first day at lunch. Now that I know I'm going to die in two years... well, I think I should. You know...kiss you. But I think I might be drunk, and I would miss your face." Elvie was thankful she had turned away to pour the coffee because she had to hold back a laugh. He sounded so serious but also very confused, as if he couldn't figure out how he had wound up in that state.

"I'm not going to kiss you." She was thankful he liked his coffee black; maybe it would be easier to get him up to his bed if it took some of the edge off.

"Elvie, why am I the way I am? Why am I always angry? Why do I have completely rotten luck?"

"Because you are strong enough to handle it. Drink." This time she walked around the table and handed him the cup. She stood in front of him, arms crossed as he drank it. Then she slid to toast closer and he finally picked up a piece. He looked at it, confused.

"Why toast?"

"It will soak up the alcohol and help you sober up faster. And hopefully not throw up." She paused. "And it was the fastest thing I could make without looking too hard.

"Why won't you kiss me?" When he turned those big eyes on her again, they were still glassy but more alert, less drunk.

"You would regret it." She said, taking his cup to refill it.

"I would? Or you would?"

"You. I know I wouldn't." He looked down at the toast and took a bite. And when Elvie handed him the new coffee, he drank it just as quickly. He was quiet for a few moments as he ate.

"I wouldn't." He said slowly. "I think I would regret doing it under the influence of alcohol." His speech wasn't slurred anymore, and Elvie smiled at him as she cleared away the dishes. "Elvie. I don't care that I'm going to die. But I wish I wasn't going to hell. And I wish it wasn't going to be cancer."

Elvie kneeled in front of him and took his face in her hands. "Can I tell you a secret?" He nodded. "I don't think you're going to be tortured for all eternity. What I think happens is that we repay for our wrongs, either in another life or in purgatory. And then eventually, we get to go to heaven. Something tells me that you're going to find a way to make up for what you think you've done in this life. Earl, you have more time than you know, don't waste it drinking yourself under a table. You're a lightweight; it doesn't take much." He smiled at her, but then looked down again.

"The war doc's were right. I've got a bad heart."

Those doctors weren't right. You don't have a weak heart. You are strong, smart, and stubborn. I don't think a cancer diagnosis will hold you back." She could see how tired he was, "Let's get you to bed. You're going to feel like crap in the morning."

Chapter 46

After getting Earl into bed and putting a glass of water on the table next to him, Elvie went downstairs and cleaned up his kitchen. Then she walked into the living room and looked around. She should probably type out a quick message on the watch, so they wouldn't come looking for her. She typed out quickly where she was, that she was okay, and that she would be there all night to make sure he was alright in the morning.

The room was sparsely decorated. It was evident that he didn't spend much time at home. He had a phonograph in one corner and a couch and a big, oversized chair in the other. A picture of his family was on top of his fireplace, next to a picture of his chosen family, him, Dean, Victor, and George. They were all smiling and laughing at something behind the camera, and even Earl looked completely at ease. She turned towards the lamp and was about to turn it off, and then curled up on the couch to try to sleep when her eyes caught on the small stack of books.

The Mysterious Affair at Styles

The Secret Adversary

The Murder on the Links

And on top, a fresh copy of *The Man in the Brown Suit*. Elvie picked it up and smiled. A few weeks ago, she had been out with Earl and Victor and seen the new releases in a shop window. She had raced inside and bought one on the spot. Victor hadn't even blinked at it, just continued on with his day. But Earl had asked why she was so excited.

"Agatha Christie is one of my favorite writers." She caught herself and added, "I mean, this is only her fourth book, but I love all the others."

"What's so good about them?" He had asked, taking the book from her and flipping through it. Victor ran into a convience store to pick up something for Cecilia, leaving them alone on the sidewalk.

"They're mysteries but the detectives have...personalities. Especially Tommy and Tuppence in *The Secret Adversary*. And she just has such a way of telling the stories that you really have to keep reading because you want to know what's going to happen next and who did it." She had been gushing and she stopped herself. She always did her best to not word vomit and reign in her passions when talking to anyone, not just people from the past. She looked over at him, embarrassed. "Sorry, I just really love books."

"Don't be sorry. It was...lovely to see you light up like that. You should do it more often."

Victor had come out of the shop then and looked between the two of them, "Alright, lovebirds, let's get a move on." Earl knocked the other man's hat off and walked away. Elvie picked up the hat and stuck it on her own head, and followed after him. "Do you two have to be so annoying?" The three had made it back to the Drucci's place with Elvie still wearing the hat.

The memory brought tears to her eyes. It was such a happy one. Her heart hurt as she thought about how soon, very soon, it would all be over. The events that were coming *had* to happen. Without one, the others wouldn't, and Chicago would never become Chicago. Without those events, the world wouldn't be the same, no matter how much losing it would break her heart.

Chapter 47

The next morning, after spending a mostly sleepless night working on plans for dealing with Steven and Derrick at the Brewery, she had Natalie bring over some clothes. Natalie, while she was a field agent in theory, was in charge of the technology and the well-being of the base, so she spent much of her time there. As such, she was always happy to run errands around town and explore. Elvie let Natalie sit in the living room while she washed and changed as quietly as possible in the bathroom, and when she came out, found her standing at the fireplace mantel, looking at the picture of the North Siders laughing together. When Elvie walked up behind her, she seemed to be fixated on Victor, but all she had said was "He looks...interesting."

Her attention then turned back to Elvie, who was holding out the bag that contained yesterday's clothes. "Violet reported back what happened at dinner last night." Elvie avoided looking at her directly and made a noncommittal sound in her throat. "No word was mentioned about anything other than Johnny Torrio accepting Dean's share of the Sieban Brewery. But..." she trailed off, and Elvie glanced at her.

When Natalie stayed quiet, thoughtful, her gaze drifting back to the picture, absently, Elvie prodded, "but..."

"But I don't think they would have talked about it in front of her. The fact that Steve was there at all seemed...weird. Like a ploy to upset you more than anything. I have no doubt that Steven and Derrick are up to something. But I've watched you all together. There's no way that she's closer to whoever it is she's dating than you and these four."

"Three," Elvie corrected. "George hates my guts."

"He does not, but I think the feeling would be mutual." Elvie snorted and showed Natalie out before sitting on the sofa and amusing herself by reading "The Secret Adversary," until she decided she should start the coffee.

Around eleven, an hour after his usual waking hour, she heard him stumble to the bathroom and then, shortly after, shuffling to the stairs. He slowly made his way down, and Elvie set the coffee and the plate of bacon, eggs, and toast on the table before disappearing back into the living room. He had regarded her suspiciously when he saw her, and now Elvie heard him hesitate before sitting at the table. Earl Weiss was not a happy-go-lucky person at the best of times; his temper was always just on the other side of his mood. Elvie, wanting to live through the rumored omelette to the face story that would happen to Josephine in a year or so, was gathering up her bag, intending to run to the print shop to get a new set of notebooks before trying to come up with a way to get herself an invite to the Brewery the next day. Just as she was finishing up, he called her name.

"Elvie?" His voice was hoarse and groggy still.

"Yeah?" Thankfully, his house was small, so she was able to keep her voice low and still have him hear her without aggravating his head.

"Are you leaving?"

"I have some errands to run before work." She called back, pulling her bag over her head. "Figured you could use some peace and quiet, since I'm sure your head is pounding."

"That it is." She thought she heard him huff a pained laugh before speaking again. "Can I come with you?" She had been almost to the door, her hand outstretched. Slowly, she turned and walked back into the kitchen. He was looking at his plate, but she saw his gaze slide sideways when she appeared in the doorway.

"I figured you wouldn't want someone around when you felt this crappy."

"Well, I'm going to take one of those lovely pills you gave me and then clean up. And...where did you get the clothes?" The night before, she had been in one of my usual pinstripe suits. Today, thanks to Natalie bringing her favorite things over because, as she had said when Elvie smiled at the sight of them, she figured Elvie could use some cheering up, and why not with her favorite clothes? It was a pair of black leggings, a blue shirt with long sleeves that ended around mid thigh and had a black outline and pockets, her black boots, and over the top she was wearing her long, old but comfortable dark blue pirate long coat. Elvie had, over the past three months devolped something of a reputation around town as being oddly dressed. It meant she hadn't blended in well, as her job description said, but it also meant she didn't have to worry so much about looking perfect when she left.

"I had my friend Natalie drop them off. These are my favorites, and she knew I'd been down lately, so she thought they'd cheer me up."

"Oh..." Elvie was about to apologize for letting Natalie into his house, thinking that was the reason he looked so...off. But before she could, he looked up and met her gaze. "You look lovely, that shirt and coat match your eyes. Anyway," he cleared his throat as Elvie blushed, "after I do that stuff, I will be feeling better. Can I come with you? Please?" As the months had gone by, he had gotten more comfortable saying please, but today sounded a bit more desperate than usual. As she had always been unable to resist his saying, 'please,' Elvie didn't even try to fight it this time.

"Of course." Elvie said. Then she went back into the living room, shrugging off her coat and bag. She was just sitting down to read another chapter when he called out again.

"You don't have to hide in there. I won't hurt you."

"I'm good in here. Safely out of the way of food items and cups. When you go upstairs I'll clean up."

"I can do it." He growled. *That*, thought Elvie, *is why I am out here.* To his credit, she *did* hear him take his dishes to the sink, but she also heard him swear loudly when they clattered in the porcelain and the water was only turned on momentarily before she heard him get the glass of water she had set next to the sink and grumble his way back upstairs, complaining under his breath about alcohol and how only complete idiots would do this to themselves everyday.

About thirty minutes later, the time it took for the pills to kick in, Elvie noted, she heard him on the stairs again. She had cleaned up his kitchen and was sitting on his couch again, her legs folded so one was under her, and the other could be used to rest the book on. He came around the couch, another cup of coffee clutched in his hand, and sank down next to her.

"I'm surprised you stayed." He said as he stared straight ahead.

"You said you were coming."

"I meant last night."

"Oh." She didn't know why it would be strange to him. It wasn't like he was in any condition to take care of himself. "Of course, I stayed. I couldn't let you be alone, even if you were a mess." She put the book down. "I don't know how much you remember, but I meant what I said."

"Which bit? I remember some…" He paused and then, he closed his eyes, groaning. "Shit."

"I meant that I know you well enough to know you won't let cancer stop you from anything. Hell, knowing you, you'll use it as an excuse to fight hard, work harder, maybe don't drink harder…" he snorted and then winced, "But you'll be okay." She almost added that maybe he would meet new friends, too, but decided that would be leaning too closely to revealing the future.

"I remember that. And I liked that you don't think I'll immediately be damned forever." He leaned his head back and looked over at her,

"I knew I was going to die early anyway. Between the headaches, my heart, and doing what I do, it was just *awful* to have it confirmed. And then I went over to tell my sister and her husband. They were fighting, so I didn't get a chance. Then I guess I just lost it."

"I've seen you lose it." It had involved her, Victor, George, and Dean, driving out to a deserted beach at night, and Elvie and George tossing bottles of alcohol in the air while the others shot them down, as a way to get Earl's energy out. "Last night was different. That was grief, Earl. It's allowed."

"Hmm." He sighed. His eyes flicked down to her mouth and then away as he sat forward suddenly. "You're reading my Agatha Christie collection, I see."

"Just this one. I love Tommy and Tuppence."

"I haven't started it yet. I just finished *Styles*."

"What did you think of Poirot?"

"He's a prick." Elvie laughed, caught off guard by the sureness of his answer and the deadpan delivery. She was still laughing when she asked why. Amused, he would occasionally laugh at her own hysterics, as he discussed the man's annoying conceitedness and his "*fucking French*." Every time Elvie would try to collect herself, he would impersonate Poirot, and she would collapse into giggles again.

"Sorry," she said at last, breathing hard, tears of laughter running down her cheeks. "I haven't laughed like that in a long time."

"I liked it. Your laugh is like magic." It was getting harder not to grab his tie and pull him in for a kiss, so Elvie changed the subject.

"Shall we go to the print store?" She asked, standing and putting her jacket back on. Earl put his hat on his head and then gestured for her to lead the way. She heard him groan when she opened the front door, and the sunlight hit his eyes.

"Now, I know why I don't drink. And it's got nothin' to do with God."

Chapter 48

They left the print store about an hour later, Elvie's bag now holding a new notebook and set of ink pens, five pencils, and Earl playing with a fountain pen he had picked up and not been able to stop fiddling with, so she had bought it for him. His enthusiasm for it was adorable, and she kept glancing over as they walked, in silence as they were wont to do, watching him roll it through his fingers and twist the cap on and off and repeat.

It turned out that Elvie didn't need to find an excuse to ask about the gang's plans for tomorrow or even to be there. Victor, who was making his way out of an unidentified apartment building, with his tie slightly askew, ran into them a few blocks later. He fell in step with them, so Elvie was sandwiched between them. Earl, jumping at his voice when he greeted them, carefully slid the pen into his pocket and grumbled under his breath in Polish.

"He's hungover and crabby." Elvie stage-whispered to Victor, who laughed loudly.

"Oh, boy. Earl hungover is so fun to screw with."

Earl, glaring at him, switched to Sicilian, which always impressed Elvie, the way he could switch from Polish, to Sicilian, to English and back as if he was simply pressing a button in his brain. "Don't be an asshole, D'Ambrosio. I'll kick your ass from here back to where your ancestors were born."

Victor laughed louder than before and answered, on his own in Polish, which, while he wasn't as fluent as Earl was in his language was still impressive. "Try it, and I'll tell your mother, you prick." Elvie, who could understand them but couldn't always speak the languages correctly, just shook her head. Then, Victor, switching back to English, addressed her. "Have you got plans tomorrow, Elvista?" Elvie's heart rate picked up and only the fact that Earl still had no idea she was from the future, kept her voice steady.

"Not my name. And not really, why?" She waited while Victor dug in his pockets for his keys, they'd just reached his car and none of them felt like walking the rest of the way to the flower shop. Or in Elvie's case, home, as she wasn't supposed to be at the garage until this afternoon. They all climbed in the car, and once the door was shut behind him, with Elvie sat in the back for once and them up front, Earl answered instead of Victor.

"Dean's going to trick Torrio into buying his share in that Sieban brewery. It's set to be raided tomorrow. Double-crossing Torrio will get us out of that peace treaty and get us out of having to play nice with the Gennas.

"We were hoping," Victor finished, "that you could maybe keep an eye on things. You know where no one could see you." Elvie nodded, looking out the window.

"Yeah, sure no problem." Her heart was breaking in her chest and then, as she had since that day at lunch all those months ago, Elvie heard herself talking without meaning to.

"But I really don't think this is the way to do it." Earl turned and looked at her, surprised. Victor glanced at her in the rear view mirror, a look on his face that she couldn't read.

"Why not?" Earl's brow was furrowed and he seemed to have no idea what to do with her not going along with the plan he was outlining.

"Because..." she glanced at Victor in the mirror again but he looked away and fixed his eyes on the road. Well, fine. "Because if you do you're going to make a very powerful enemy. Torrio hates to be tricked, he hates to be caught with his hands dirty and he hates to be embarrassed. If you do all three of those, as this plan will do, you're all signing your own death warrants."

"I don't think we need to be worried about that. Torrio isn't one for violence." Victor pointed out. "Well, he is but he wouldn't do it himself." Earl nodded and then looked at Elvie as if they would make her feel better. Which, which of course, it didn't.

"But Torrio's not the only who hates Dean. Or any of you. What about the Gennas? They would be happy for you all to be out from under the protection of the truce."

"Nah, that Sicilian union leader will keep us—"Earl started but Elvie could feel herself getting angry. He was writing off her concerns, ignoring that she was making valid points.

"He's dying of cancer!" She all but yelled, making both men jump. "And once he's gone then what? It's not going to take long before they take matters into their own hands. And they have friends, nasty, evil friends, in New York who wouldn't hesitate to come help."

"Elvie, it's going to be fine. I understand this isn't your cup of tea, but—" She couldn't take it. It was the slightly condescending tone that did it.

"God damn it all, Henry Wojciechowski," She almost middle named him but decided his birth name was probaby risking her safety enough. "I am from the future and I am telling you that you need to not do this or you will all die in a gang war." She pulled out her watch and showed him how it worked as she talked. "You have to listen to me, I can't let you do this without saying something."

"Elvie, you…you can't be from the…" He glanced at Victor who nodded at Earl and he looked back at Elvie, eyes wide. "Oh…oh…well, that explains…a lot actually. You're a whole damn package of surprises, aren't you?" He paused and Elvie thought, hoped that her words had landed, that he would listen. Except, then she realized, the fact that everything was still around her, that she wasn't dead and broken, meant that he didn't care or want to believe what she had just told him. "Maybe you're wrong. Maybe it won't happen that way."

"Maybe..." Elvie sank back in her seat, which felt too real and too solid around her as tears pricked the back of her eyes. "Maybe it doesn't matter. I just told you everything. I told you I'm from the future. That I know what will happen and I'm still here. You're going to do what you want regardless of what I say and it won't change a damn thing." Her throat was tight as she rubbed her eyes under her glasses. Fine. She'd been a part of histories biggest moments, she could handle this. It wasn't the Romanov Exile, it wasn't the Boston Tea Party, or the French Revolution, It wasn't any of the bloody wars she'd had to witness. It wasn't even a pirate battle. She could handle this. "What time do you need me there tomorrow?" The car rolled into it's parking spot in front of Schofield's and Victor killed the engine, looking at her in the mirror again

"Elvie...it's not—"

"What time, Victor?" Her growl rivaled Earl's, so with a sigh, Victor broke eye contact.

"Four O'Clock, tomorrow morning. Police should be there about five." Elvie nodded and disappeared. She had training to do before the next day.

Chapter 49

Elvie was standing outside the building the next morning at three thirty, fresh from New Mexico and a conversation with Joseph about what he had knew. Admittedly, it wasn't much just that there was an ambushed planned, but not what it was or who it was for, as everyone made there way inside, Elvie, tired, lonely, and angry, walked alongside Dean, who had no idea she was there. She was surprised they had made it this far, considering Dean's eyese were lit up with a secret and she could see that even when he tried he couldn't stop a mischevious smile from spreading across his face.

The Sieben Brewery was a place that Elvie had only seen from the outside. Outside was a big red and white brick building that was nothing special compared to the buildings around it. Inside the huge machinery of the brewery didn't mask some of the echoing. They came to a stop on a walkway overlooking the machines. To his right stood Johnny Torrio. Elvie had only seen him from a distance once or twice. He looked younger than the pictures she remembered. His hair was still wispy, but he looked less haggard and there was an intelligent gleam in his eyes. Clearly, being harassed by a heartbroken gangster bent on revenge ages you quickly.

"Never thought to see you giving up on this business so quickly." Torrio said in his soft voice that was still touched with a Lower East Side accent.

"Well," Dean gave him a self deprecating smile, "what can I say? I'm not made for this business like you are. Figured my shares should go to someone who knows what he's doing and all that." Elvie rolled her eyes skyward and wondered if Earl and Victor knew exactly how thick he was laying it on.

"That is true, kid. And who knows maybe you'll have better luck in a different racket. Have you considered brothels? There's money to be made there." A quick glance told her that Dean's thoughts on prostitutuion were exactly what history said they were. His lip curled involuntary and quickly covered it with a sneeze that would have won him awards on Broadway.

Johnny Torrio was an eel for a lot of reasons but especially because he had kidnapped and broken the will of hundreds of young girls both directly and indirectly and sold them into brothels. Add to that that he was a coward and it was easy to understand why the Northsiders found him insufferable. He was now talking to Dean about something unrelated to the brewery and Elvie tuned them out, taking in, instead the men working with equipment and running around the building on different jobs. No one really stood out as being out of place, and she was wondering if Joseph's intuition had been wrong when she saw him.

It was the same man, Derrick, from the speakeasy on Pierce. He was dressed as if he were a brewery worker but the way he was creeping around the corner near the door was what had gave him away. Once she spotted him, she knew what he was going to do. She appeared right in front of him as he opened his mouth to yell and he managed to get out "John—" before Elvie slapped a hand over his mouth and drug him into the In-Between with her. There was an office area in the back of the building, she knew from studying floorplans the night before and she had materialized them there. It was, thankfully, abandoned and she threw him away from her into the real world as she stepped through.

"Natalie," she kept her voice quiet enough that not even Derrick, who was currently struggling against a dented filing cabinet could hear, but loud and clear enough that the watch could pick up. "Tell Shirley and Tony the Interface just tried to interfere with the Brewery raid." She hoped Natalie got the message because that was all she cared to send. She crossed the room in two easy strides and hauled Derrick to his feet.

"I warned you. And I warned Steve. Still, you both thought it was a good idea to mess with this?" Elvie was angry. Angry that she had to stop him from interfering, angry that they had bothered with this at all, and she was angry that the Interface kept making her life more difficult. She knee'd him hard in the groin and when he doubled over she swung her elbow into his temple. Not hard enough to knock him out but hard enough to make him see stars. She paused to listen to the sounds of the building. She needed to make sure that the raid hadn't started yet. She had to keep him back here until the police found Torrio and Dean.

Unfortunately, the pause gave Derrick a moment to collect himself enough to talk. "I am surprised." He was wheezing, but she had to hand it to him, he got to his feet. "I thought you would want us to stop the raid. Stop the raid, and there's no beer wars. Your friends…your boyfriend…they all live."

She scowled at him, and advanced on him again. "It would have happened later. Sooner or later something got to give. It would have all been the same in the end. Except the future wouldn't exist. Which you know." She had no desire to spend more time with Derrick than necessary. "Pull out your stupid little box and get the fuck out of here."

"They didn't give me a box this time." He growled. "Once I delivered my message I was supposed to just…leave." He lunged for her but Elvie just stepped out of the way. She had just heard the police break in, she could yelling and Dean talking. And a thought occurred to her.

"They really didn't give you a box?" The man simply shook his head, trying to stop the bleeding from his nose. "You were just supposed to walk out of here?"

"Well, not exactly came a voice from behind her and she swung around managed to duck as a metal rod missed her head by inches. Two more enemy agents were standing there. She couldn't remember their names but she knew they were tough and she knew that she couldn't do this alone. She backed towards a wall, watching Derrick smile, cruelly as he pulled brass knuckles onto his fist.

"Karma's a bitch, Elvie Townshend. And the three of us are about to deliver you a good dose." His fist connected with Elvie's ribs and she doubled over. The other two landed a couple of kicks and Elvie managed after a second to right herself and roll out of the way.

"Hey, I'm ready when you are." She said to no one in particular as Derrick advanced on her again. She was seeing stars and she was thankful for her new found healing ability because those ribs were definitely broken.

"Already talking to yourself, huh? I thought you'd be tougher." Derrick pulled his fist back.

"Oh, no. D-bag. You underestimated me, again." She teased with a wink.

He swung, Elvie ducked, sending Derrick carreening over her, reached through the In-Between, wretching hard and Joseph Weiss flew by her, delivering two hard punches to the nameless agents and knocking them out cold. Derrick was laying on the floor with Elvie's boot over his throat.

"I don't think I'm the one karma's looking for, asshole." The other two agents sat up and before Elvie could yell two Joseph to grab them, they had their Snex's out and disappeared.

Elvie was listening to the door. It sounded like things were dying down out on the floor and she grabbed Derrick by his shirt. "Except you aren't getting out of this one." This time she had managed at speed that made her question how much of the In-Between she had even used for this. She dragged the kicking, snarling and bleeding Derrick around the side of the building, with. Joseph followed, staying in the space between, waiting for her finish.

"Hey, baawhs." She slid her voice into the closest she could come to a full blown Chicago twang and the cop closest to her turned around. "Shit." She grumbled. This day just kept getting worse. At least she could drop the accent.

Officer Dan Healy was striding toward her. In three years, Healy would have killed multiple gangsters in the line of duty, most famously would be Victor. She disliked him for that as it was. It wasn't helped that the few times they had met previously she had been bailing someone out of jail and the he had made snide comments under his breath the whole time. Everything in her revolted against him. She almost let Derrick go. She almost left him there rather than give this asshole the satisfaction of making an arrest but she thought of Derrick and Steve wrecking havoc on the timeline in her city and she hardened her resolve.

"Elvie? Dean said he was the only one here." Over his shoulder Elvie could see Dean shaking hands with multiple police officers, his voice carrying as he congratulated the policeman on a job well done. Over the top even for him and being pushed into a car, she could see Torrio piecing it all together and scowling. This was his second Volstead offense. He was going to jail.

"Yeah well, I just happened to be in the area. Saw everything going down. This guy here, he works for Torrio. Thought you might like the honor of arresting him."

"How do I know this isn't some patsy you and Weiss don't like and are trying to get sent upriver?" Healy looked suspiciously at her even as she saw him reach for his cuffs. She couldn't come up with another lie; thankfully, she didn't have to. Derrick chose that moment to take a swing at her. She let it land, knowing it was the best way to get what she wanted. But it still hurt like hell. She was pretty sure that if the bone under her eye wasn't cracked, it was very bruised.

Healy was on Derrick in a heartbeat, "Alright, you piece of shit. I don't know if you are a member of Torrio's outfit or not, but hitting women in front of a police officer is not going to get you out of jail."

Elvie was gingerly touching her face when a thought occurred to her. The Gennas had said they talked to a man named Stephen. It had struck her as odd at the time because Steven never did the dirty work. She would bet good money that Derrick was who they had spoken to about the territory lines.

"Ask the Gennas. They'll tell you that this guy is a real ass."

"Yeah, yeah, Townshend, I've got this. Make yourself scarce before I borrow cuffs and arrest you, too." And so, with one last sneer at Derrick, she vanished when Healy's back was turned. Standing next to Joe in the In-Between, she smiled up at the younger man who was beaming as she moved them towards the door of the base. Even if she hadn't stopped the raid herself, she'd managed something she never thought possible and her mind was full of new ideas and possibilities.

Chapter 50

The door swung open before Elvie even got a chance to knock, or brace Joseph, who was still getting used to stepping into and out of the In-Between and the world of the living. When he had, finally, been able to come with her he had become somehow even more solid. He looked so much like Earl and his brother, Fred, who Elvie had yet to meet, but he seemed to be the connection between their sharp scowls and hard eyes and the soft, round features, and the more expressive eyes of Bruno and Violet, the other two Weiss children. His brown hair wasn't just brown but flecked with blond and red and his cheeks were a healthy pink. He was taller than Elvie by an inch or two and was definitely strong, if the immediate daze suffered by the Interface Goons was anything to go by. Still, she would have liked a second to warn him about the bizarre house and the chaos that it held, which he was about to join.

When she'd gone to New Mexico after leaving Victor and Earl the day before, she had told Joe everything that he hadn't yet figured out about The Pathfinders and their lives. She explained that if she pulled him through, he would have to join them, that he would have to undergo some tests, treatments, vaccinations, and probably a lot of educational lessons. He, with all the fervor of someone who's life was cut too short and who wanted to go on an amazing adventure readily agreed. Elvie had made sure to stress the dangers and the sadness that was going to come with what he was viewing as a magnificent opportunity. She told him all the bad things that had happened to her over the years and the reason that she wore her fingerless gloves all the time. She showed him the scar that curved around her right eye like a crescent mood from having her head slammed into a desk. She also made sure to remind him repeatedly that he would have to follow orders and not revolt against anyone. He had agreed over and over to all of it. He just wanted to help, he had said. He wanted a life that he could be proud of, that he could make a difference in. And after hours of conversation and planning, the two had agreed, that he would follow her to the Brewery and help her when the ambush occurred. It had worked smoother than Elvie had expected and Joseph, later would wonder privately if it wasn't somehow helped by her anger at Earl for not listening to her. They had agreed not to tell anyone that Victor and Earl knew about time travel and let them find out somehow on their own.

Now, standing on her doorstep with a formally deceased person in tow, Elvie was second guessing bringing him back here at all. But Tony just looked between the two of them, gave a sigh that seemed to originate deep down inside of him and stepped out of their way. Shirley met them at the bottom of the stairs.

"Natalie got your message." She gestured behind her where the inventress sat with her legs crossed and her blotters resting on her head in a large office chair, looking proud, yes, but also with her lecture face on, ready to discuss the logistics of adding someone to their team.

When Elvie had told Natalie her plan to pull Joseph through month ago, they had began planning what could go wrong. When it seemed that they couldn't figure out a way that adding Joe to the timeline as one of them could go wrong, if they were galavanting around for however many centuries and hadn't messed everything up, they had started making a list of what vaccinations and health treatments and scan Joseph would need. They'd come up with a comprehensive educational plan to catch him up on everything from 1913, when he died to 2025, when they were from. Next to Natalie, on the desk now, sat a notebook that was full, cover to cover with answers to any possible question that Shirley or Tony could have. And upstairs, hidden from everyone was another notebook of plans for the army that Elvie and Natalie were planning on building if this addition of Joseph worked. But that was a conversation for another day. Righ now, they needed to get through this conversation.

Tony sat down in the chair next to Shirley's giant computer chair. Shirley's chair was a big black, and grey, leather wingback that made her look like a supervillain at times. Tony's chair was basically a stool with a small back that he had dragged over one day when a meeting took so long that his aggitated pacing tired him out. He rubbed his temples and then looked at his co-captain.

"Shirley…can you…can you start? I don't have the capactiy for this today…or ever really."

Bemused, Shirley looked Joseph up and down and then looked at Elvie, who, despite having taken several hard kicks and punches was standing tall and proud, the only one that hadn't healed was the black eye that she had let Derrick deliver. Her bodies punishment, she assumed, for not ducking when she could have. It was definitely worth it. Shirley's eyes traveled to Natalie, in the chair on her other side, another supervillain-esque chair with a supervillain-esque woman sitting in it.

"So," Shirley began slowly, gathering her thoughts. "I'm going to guess… that this has been planned for awhile." All three nodded and Shirley sighed as Tony groaned. She stood and held out a hand to Joe. "I'm Shirley, one of the two captains of The Pathfinders. We aren't really in charge as you can see, but we like to think we are." Joe shook her hand.

"I'm Joseph Weiss. And if you'll have me I would love to join your crew, Captain." He turned to Tony who had stood and held out his hand.

"I'm Tony and even though I already died once and am only a reconstruction of myself made for this mission the four current agents are going to send me back to the grave." As they shook hands, though, Tony's lips twitched. "Maybe you'll be the easy one." Joe's face split into a beautific grin and Natalie took that as her cue. She stood, introduced herself with a handshake and then handed the notebook on the desk to Shirley.

"This is, we believe a comprehensive list of everything Mr. Weiss will need done to determine his health, what he will need to keep him as healthy as us, going forward, and the educational circiculum that we feel will be necessary to keep him from getting overwhelmed as an agent of the Pathfinders."

Elvie, despite the stab to her heart she had felt at the words 'Mr. Weiss,' spoke next. "He is already a very good fighter, but I would be happy to train him in the different fighting styles and the physical fitness exercises to ensure that he is on par with what he could face if he goes up against the Interface in a real battle." Shirley and Tony looked at the notebook as Shirley flipped through it and then at each other, communicating without words they seemed to reach some conclusion, though from the look Tony gave her briefly before he spoke again, she knew she would be getting a lecture later today. But that was for later, for now, with another long suffering, bone weary sigh, Tony gestured for Joe to follow him. "Let's run some tests and see what you've got going on now that you are a physical human again." As they entered the hospital ward Elvie and Natalie looked at Shirley, who just shook her head, exasperated before throwing their arms around each other in a celebratory hug and dance.

Chapter 51

Elvie was sitting at the kitchen counter, an energy drink she had the robotic refrigerator produce in front of her when Tony came upstairs around noon. Joe had come up a little bit ago and he and Natalie were in her workshop together, designing his rooms that needed to be added to the house.

"It'll be a fun change after all the poking and prodding," Natalie had promised as they'd gone up the stairs. When Elvie had left them a short while later they were clearly enjoying themself and Joe's hands, which moved faster when he was excited was gesturing wildly as Natalie nodded over a tablet, adding in her two cents now and again.

She watched as Tony entered the kitchen, poured a cup of coffee from the always fresh coffee pot and stood across from her. They held each other's gaze for a long time, neither willing to give in. The way it always was, Elvie sure she was right, Tony, unwilling to give up control. At last, Tony took a drink, the closest Elvie would get to a victory.

"You realize all the things that could have gone wrong, right?" He asked as she sipped her own drink. Elvie just nodded. "And you are aware that he could still have TB or whatever else he had when he was alive?" Again, Elvie nodded, having learned over time that to actually answer would just upset Tony further.

"He doesn't, by the way." Tony said quietly, and her eyes widened a fraction. "He's perfectly healthy; there isn't even scarring on his lungs from the coughing. It's like he never had it. Your power seems to extend to the time you spent together in the In-Between. Or pulling him out did it. I haven't figured out which, yet." He took another drink.

"I'd tell you to tell me before you do it next time, but I can't say that wouldn't lead to an argument and I can't say an argument would stop you from doing what you want, anyway. Just...chose carefully when you do this, okay?" Elvie nodded again, scarcely trusting herself to say a single word. "And, whatever it is you're planning..." She waited for him to ask, she had her explanation all ready. Hell, she'd made a slideshow if he really needed to see it blown up on a wall. To her further surprise, though, he didn't even hint at wanting a clue to her plan. "Let me know if you need any help with it." He drained his incredibly hot coffee in two gulps and put the cup down with a thud.

"Now, for the part you really won't like and this was the plan before today." Tony crossed him arms across his chest and pulled his shoulders back before continuing. "Starting immediately, your mission in Chicago is a part time, background mission. You will check in here occassionally and there might be things to attend to from time to time but until at least November, you will be doing things elsewhere in the US."

"Where is elsewhere?" Elvie asked resting her head on her hand. She was tired and her head was pounding. Though she had been trying hard not to show it, pulling Joseph through the curtain had taken a lot out of her. Besides, she felt it was time for her to leave for awhile as well. She'd been too attached, she'd been deluded and lonely. She was still lonely but she could fix the other two issues by leaving and if that's what the mission orders were, it was that much easier.

"First stop for all four of you is a vacation."

Elvie's head slipped off her hand and she stared at him, stunned. "Sorry? Since when do we all take one at the same time?"

"You'll all be on call, and of course you'll be helping Joe adjust and train but for the most part you are all to relax. Specifically, we are putting you up in fancy hotels in New York for a month and then you are all free to do what you want for another two months. You should be refreshed by September, which, if I am not mistaken gives you, Elvie two months, to prepare for what you have planned in November."

"I can't just...not do anything for three months."

Tony raised his eyebrows, and Elvie blushed as he finished his lecture. "I have no doubt you will keep busy and find reasons to travel wherever you damn well choose. But you do need a break, so officially...starting tomorrow morning, you are on vacation." He tossed a train ticket down. Her train left Dearborn Street Station the day after tomorrow. "I know you could do it yourself, but Shirley remembered how much you loved trains. You and Natalie will be joined by Bixby and Violet eventually. Do try not to let Violet get to you too much." With a parting wink, he left the kitchen, and Elvie heard him heading off to talk to Natalie upstairs, probably sending Joseph down to Elvie or Shirley before giving her the same speech.

Sure enough, less than three minutes later, Joseph descended the stairs. He was about to continue, clearly headed to Shirley, when he saw Elvie. She waved, and he came in.

"Coffee?" Elvie asked as he sat next to her.

"If it's not too much trouble?" He looked tired and overwhelmed, but Elvie imagined how anyone wouldn't be. Standing, Elvie poured him a mug and paused before handing it to him.

"Black? Or do you want sugar or milk?"

"Black. You can't add anything, or else it takes away the jolt you get." He sounded so sure, as if he had said it a million times before.

"Does it?" Elvie set it in front of him, and he took a long drink.

"Yeah, that's what I always used to tell my brothers. Sure, coffee tastes terrible, but if you add all that other stuff, you lose the bad taste, which is half what wakes you up about it."

"Well, Earl listened, anyway." Elvie sat down next to him again. "How are you holding up?"

"Pretty good. This is all so crazy and a little fast. But...I'm not dead anymore."

"Nope, in fact, it seems you're better than ever." Elvie knocked her can into his mug, and he smiled.

"That trip through was exhausting, though." Joe said as he finished the rest of his mug. Elvie got up and refilled it. Before she could sit back down, Joe picked up the mug and stood. "I know you're probably exhausted. If I'm tired, I can't imagine the energy you used this morning, but do you think you could come downstairs to talk to Shirley with me? She's supposed to give me a list of books to read...Tony made it sound like I was going to be in trouble if I didn't know what they were."

"You won't be," Elvie laughed. "That's just Tony, but yes. Let's go get you ready to learn."

Chapter 52

The doorbell had rang several times over the afternoon and evening, but Elvie hadn't heard it, and no one had told her that it had been for her every time. After she and Joseph got his book from Shirley, Natalie had reappeared to take him to his new rooms, and Elvie had dragged herself up to her own rooms. She hadn't even made it to the shower, just collapsed on her bed and slept from early afternoon to well after the sun was up the next day. When she emerged, freshly showered and dressed in her favorite black and silver pinstripe suit, Bixby and Violet were in the kitchen with Natalie and Joseph. Joseph seemed to be taking everything in stride, still. He must have slept well, because his eyes were sparkling with excitement, and he was showing Natalie something in one of the encyclopedias. Elvie and Violet nodded to each other, but Elvie continued on her way to her boots, jacket, and the door.

She stepped out into the warm, late May sunshine and let it warm her face. She knew where she was going, who she needed to talk to, but she also knew that it was too gorgeous a day to use the In-Between. Besides, she wasn't in a hurry; if anyone was looking for her, they would wait. And so, she walked, heading east and listening once again to the sounds of her favorite city in the world. Cars drove past, and newspaper boys yelled the headlines. She walked until she reached the corner of Monroe and North State Street, where she hopped aboard a passing trolley and rode it until she reached the florist's shop. The door was standing open, and Mr. Schofield and Mr. Crutchfeld greeted her with smiles.

"Are any of the bosses in?" She asked after making small talk, and both men nodded.

"Earl is upstairs; he's been in an awful mood all day. Dean left a while ago. Told him if he couldn't be civil, to stay out of the mechanic's way. Last I heard, Victor had made his way up there, too." William Cruthfeld told her.

"Thank you very much. I'll see you both later!" And before they could reply made her way, as loudly as she possibly could, up the stairs. She stomped her feet and even knocked on the wall a few times, just to be a pain in their sides. The door to the smoking room was open just a crack, and she pushed it the rest of the way open without knocking.

'Who the hell—" Earl was yelling as he turned around, but stopped as soon as he saw her. She stood with her arms crossed in the doorway and grinned.

"That would be me. I am sure that there is absolutely no way you didn't hear me coming."

"I think the nuns over at the school heard you." Earl said, pointedly, and then Victor added, with trademark sincerity,

"I am pretty sure the dead in the old city cemetery heard you." He was sitting on the couch, with his feet on a stool, his hair ruffled, and circles under his eyes. Earl must have been pacing, and judging by the way his hair stuck out from the terrible group he put in it, running his fingers through his own hair repeatedly.

"Only that far?" Elvie sighed theatrically, "I should have been louder." Then she walked over to the couch and perched herself on the arm of it. "I heard you're up here to keep the foul mood of Earl from leaking downstairs."

"That is not what they said," the moody one growled, and Elvie stuck her tongue out.

"It is true, though," Victor muttered under his breath.

"What's got you in such a bad mood?" Elvie didn't usually enjoy aggravating people, but she was still irritated from the other day, and so she added, almost as an afterthought. "Your plan worked perfectly. Not one bridge left unburned."

"We heard." Victor said, yawning. "Dean insisted on celebrating last night. He's still a little tipsy, I think." Earl rolled his eyes and leaned against the desk, arms crossed. Brown eyes fixed on Elvie's.

"There was one queer thing that happened, though."

"Oh?" Elvie asked, her voice neutral and disinterested.

"Yeah, Officer Healer arrested some guy named Derrick." He paused and waited for Elvie to say something, but she just shrugged and looked innocent. "According to Dean, who asked about it at the station, he punched a woman in a long coat with blonde hair."

"Asshole." Elvie deadpanned and brought her fingers up to touch the bruise on her eye which had faded a little while she was asleep.

"Indeed. Thank you…for watching out."

"That's literally my job." Elvie grumbled. "I was serious when I said I was from the future."

"I know." He sighed, looking away. "Victor told me what you told him after you…stormed out of the car, for lack of a better term. Thank you for—"

"Don't. Thank me." Elvie said, abandoning all pretense of not being heartbroken. "I can't change things as much as I want to and whatever happens has to happen so you should definitely *not* thank me. Besides, it's not like I was ever anything other than a hanger-on anyway, right?"

Victor hissed under his breath and Earl looked like she had smacked him. "That's not true at all. I have always told you you were one of us."

"Bullshit." Elvie snapped and stood off the arm of the couch, drawing herself up to her full height. "If I really belonged you wouldn't have waited until you needed help to tell me about the raid. You would have let me in on the plans. But you didn't. You kept me in the dark. I'm nothing more than a fun accessory to the gang. And do you know what hurts? The fact that I wanted so desperately to fit somewhere, for Chicago to be my home, that I let myself believe you."

"Elvie, it wasn't—" Victor began, but Elvie kept going, needing to get out everything she had rehearsed in her head.

"I've been alone for a long time. I don't fit in with the others. I never did. Did you know I'm the only American? Even before my In-Betweenness, I was different. I was just along to fuck things up, everyone said. But, I thought, maybe it'd be different here. I was wrong. I wasn't important enough to you, I never really belonged. George was right, there never could be a place for me here.

"Elvie, I'm—— " Earl stepped forward, and Elvie held up a hand.

"Don't apologize. There's nothing for you to apologize for. This was my fault and I know that. I let myself hope…get attached…whatever." She took in a breath and let it out slowly. Now came the hard part. "I'm leaving town for a bit. I have a stop in New York, and I'll be working odd jobs in different places. I'll be back in Chicago from time to time and I'll stop by and say hi. Later this year, I'll be around for awhile. But for now…this is goodbye. Thank you…for everything you've taught me." And she turned on her heel and left, this time, letting the In-Between carry her away.

Chapter 53

June 7, New York, 1924

For Elvie there were moments of time traveling that stood out as her personal turning points. Most of them were ones that she wouldn't realize until later how pivotal they had been. The night when she met the Marx Brothers was not one of those nights. She knew that night, hell, she knew that moment when she shook Harpo's hand and was introduced the next moment to Chico that this was an event that would change things. Not because she was feeling romantically inclined towards either of them, because there was an air about them that held inspiration for the future. Which was just what she needed.

They were backstage in a Broadway theater. New York City was not one of Elvie's favorite places, by any means. She was staying in a hotel down the street with Natalie and Violet. Bixby had decided to visit Japan for the remaining five months of their forced exile. Violet said she needed some girl time and opted to stay. Whoever her boyfriend was in Chicago was from New York, she said, and he would be inclined to visit her. Elvie had noticed, however, that the longer whoever the man was went without visiting her, the more Violet flirted with anyone around, which was how she ended up at the Marx Brothers show in the first place. Violet had been down on Broadway for most of the day, flirting with a member of the orchestra for the show "I'll Say She Is." When she had gotten invited to the play that night, she asked if her friends could come as well.

"The more the merrier," The man had said. He had clearly had two other Violet's pictured and not Natalie or Elvie. He couldn't exactly say that when the three showed up at the theater that night. Instead, he let all three women watch the show from backstage. Natalie was in a pink potato sack thing with something that resembled sequins and beads that she said the woman down the street had said was the height of fashion. Violet was, of course, over the top stylish in a full length gold beaded dress with white gloves and a hat. Elvie was wearing her customary black but in dress form. It had probably started out as full length evening gown that took away her form, like Violet's and Natalie's dresses but Elvie had cinched the waist in so that the skirt puffed a bit and accentuated her hips and you could tell where her waist was. She had also added a small slit at the bottom, and had her hair down although she was reminded of her bad habit of running her fingers through it.

The show was still an hour away from starting when Elvie and Natalie were watching Violet shamelessly throw herself at an understudy, despite being invited by someone else. All three women jumped when there was a crash from one of the dressing rooms. The door banged open and a girl of five or six ran smack into Elvie. The girl looked up at Elvie and whispered, "Help." And then out of the dressing room came a very angry, Groucho Marx.

"Get back here!" He stomped over to where Elvie, Natalie, and now, a girl, who Elvie recognized as the daughter of Chico Marx, Maxine, were standing. Violet broke away from the understudy and moved closer because in that moment Elvie had made the decision to move the girl behind her, and her entire energy had shifted from standoffish to aggressive defense and Violet was never one to miss a fight. Natalie, too, was watching with interest.

Groucho glared at Elvie. "Get out of the way. This is none of your business." He looked her up and down, "Although you look like you could have business with her father."

"It was an accident, Uncle Groucho," came the voice from behind Elvie. "You startled me. I didn't mean to—"

"You spilled water and juice all over my notebook. Do you have any idea how many brilliant ideas you just destroyed? Now you get back in that room, so we can have this chat in private, you little—"

"She's not going anywhere with you." Elvie snapped and pulled herself up to her full height. Which wasn't tall, but given how short Groucho was certainly made her look more formidable than him. "I sincerely doubt that any of the ideas in your little book were life changing. And anyway, leave it to dry and it will be fine."

"Now you listen here, you fifteen cent—"

"What's the problem, Grouch?" A heavy New York accent broke through, drawing the attention of the group.

"Uncle Harpo," Maxine ran out from behind Elvie and tried to hide in Harpo's trench coat. He was already dressed in his costume, but he was clearly not in character. He was frowning, which was out of place on a face which looked like it wasn't used to serious. "It was just an accident. I was in his room, and I spilled on his notebook. He started yelling, and I ran and this lady was helping me."

"Lady." Scoffed Groucho. "She was butting in. That girl shouldn't be running around backstage anymore anyway. And look she ran into a low class—"

"I have more class in my pinky than you will ever have in your whole life, you walking pile of donkey semen."

"Donkey Semen?" Violet giggled and Natalie was smirking behind her hand. Elvie looked at her and seemed to realize she had spoken out loud.

"That's a new one." The new voice was accented but in the way voices are when they have traveled a little bit of everywhere. The owner of the voice, who might have looked like the other two in the way all siblings do, but who held a confidence and swagger that the other two did not possess, scooped up his daughter in one arm and punched his brother hard in the stomach with the other.

Groucho sputtered and coughed. Chico, pointed at his brother as he doubled over. "First, don't scare my daughter. Second, I heard you were talking funny to my wife again. You know not to do that. Third, you just insulted another woman from what I can tell at least three times and you are lucky she didn't punch you first."

"Go to your room and calm down, baby brother." Harpo added. "You need sleep. I have a feeling you're going to regret this all tomorrow." Groucho glowered at the other two and limped back to his room. Slamming the door behind him.

"Sorry about him," Harpo said, as Chico took Maxine away talking in a soothing voice and making her laugh. "The stories that he got his name from a grouch bag are exaggerated. It's mostly because he's an ass."

"It's fine. I just wanted to help that poor kid. Is she okay?"

"Max'll be good. She's dealt with Groucho being angrier than that. I don't think he was mad at her as much as he was mad at you for standing up to him. Women backstage usually don't, ya see. I'm Harpo, by the way. You must be the three that that orchestra player invited."

"That's us, well me." Violet stuck out her hand. "I'm Violet. These are Natalie and Elvie."

"That's a hell of a name." Harpo shook Elvie's hand, his face was bright and sparkling again. "Short for Elvira?"

"No, just Elvie." She smiled, a genuine smile. His smile was infectious, and in her head she could hear Victor muttering that he'd already tried Elvira.

"So, Donkey Semen?" Chico was back. "It's nice to meet a lady who can come up with something like that faster than Groucho." He extended his hand, and Harpo introduced them all again, except Violet, who had wandered away, annoyed to not be the center of attention.

"Thank you. Although I didn't mean to say that out loud."

"He deserved it. Thanks for helping my girl. Groucho's usually not so bad, but he hasn't slept in a few days. None of us has."

"That's not really an excuse. You two aren't..." Elvie trailed off.

"Piles of Donkey Semen?" Harpo grinned. Elvie blushed, and Natalie did a double-take. Elvie Townsend had just blushed. Where was Violet? Someone else needed to witness this. She glanced around, but Violet was nowhere to be seen.

"Oh balls." Natalie groaned. "She's gone."

"We'd better go find her." It could have been Natalie's imagination, but Elvie looked a bit disappointed.

"No, you stay. You actually seem to be enjoying yourself." Natalie squeezed her friend's arm and wandered off.

"Want a tour?" Both men asked at the same time. As if they had planned it, but the look they gave each other said they hadn't, although it happened all the time. Chico and Harpo each held out an arm, and Elvie took both, letting them lead her around, and enjoyed a good thirty minutes of fun conversation before the two men had to run to start the show.

"But stay, after." Harpo, bending in an exaggerated bow, told her.

"Please do. I may even skip my card game to have dinner tonight," And with a wink and a kiss on the hand, Chico made his way to the stage. If he thought that was going to work on Elvie, he was sorely mistaken. Although it didn't mean she didn't enjoy it.

Chapter 54

October 11, 1924, Chicago

Elvie had been back to Chicago a few times since she left in May. She'd gone to Frank's funeral, of course. She'd helped Victor when he couldn't be consoled afterwards. She'd been around for the arrest of Dean, Earl, and a friend of theirs when they got caught with a hijacked truck full of liquor, but she'd stayed more or less out of the way for that one. She was there when Earl was hospitalized with appendicitis. He'd been in New York when she was in August, leaving on a trip to England that included several Chicago politicians and other bootleggers, but Elvie had been very careful not to cross paths with him. Not that she had to worry too much about it. Keeping Chico out of trouble was something of a mission in and of itself. The number of times she had been in California or Missouri or even the one time she had been allowed overseas since her unspoken grounding when she left Chicago, she'd gotten the warning that something was wrong and sped to wherever the anamoly was usually to find Chico looking sheepish with either another man's wife or a gambling debt that needed to be paid off immediately. She'd stop coming up with excuses to be in the same place as him every time he was in trouble, and he seemed to just accept it as a fortunate twist of fate.

Now, though, Elvie was back in the city that held her heart. She wasn't on a specific mission, but Joseph had come running down the stairs a week ago, saying that someone needed to be in Chicago to make sure nothing went wrong with the upcoming tragedy. He'd met Elvie's eyes when he said it, and she knew that he didn't mean something wouldn't happen, but that she might fail in the next part of their plan, and so she had moved back, taking a room at the Drake. It had taken her a week or two to get everything settled for her move, as Pathfinders rarely actually moved out of the base into another state. Currently, the base was resting on a hillside in what would one day be an extremely famous but was currently a more or less deserted beach, Malibu Lagoon, in California. By the time she was checking into the Drake, Joseph, who had not had a single issue adjusting to life as a Pathfinder, so much so that sometimes they all forgot he was born in 1889 and not 1989, had not slept a night without having the dream of something going wrong. He was shaking and panicking. The first morning she woke in the hotel, she received a phone call from Natalie to tell her that he was planning a party to celebrate not having the dream again. He hadn't had it since.

Elvie had been a bit lonely here. Earl had been in Europe, not that she'd want to see him anyway, she reminded herself. Victor was in New York, as far as she could tell. Or Miami. She was avoiding him as well. Dean was out west, getting ready to order the infamous Tommy Gun that would shape Chicago's history; besides, they hadn't been close. And George was George. She'd spent some time with Delilah and Mickey, but when school had started back up, they were too busy, and she supposed that was a good thing. She found herself wandering the city more and more, and when Earl's ship docked, she knew, on the thirtieth of September, Elvie was wondering if she should check in on him, just to make sure. Which was why she was currently standing in the In-Between, leaning against the corner of Holy Name Cathedral, watching Schofield's.

"You could just go in and see if he's there," came a voice from beside her, and Elvie jumped a mile.

"God damn it, Joe." She snarled and then glanced apologetically at the cathedral next to her, making Joe laugh even harder. "No, I'm not going in there. It's not my place, and besides, he can see me if he looks over here. He can see you, too. So, be careful, I don't want him to know about you, yet." It would just add pressure to her upcoming rescue mission, and she didn't need that.

"No, he can't." Joe looked sadly at the flowershop. "I've tried to get him to see me. Even standing next to you when you were in the In-Between checking on him, he has no idea I'm here."

"You haven't gotten the film lifted yet." She said, referring to the bit of veil that allowed her to eavesdrop on the otherside and Earl to see her. Joe could occasionally eavesdrop, but so far, he wasn't able to do it as well as Elvie. She had over fifty years more experience, though she often reminded him.

"Someday I will. But anyway, I came to tell you that Natalie thinks she figured out what happened with Frank and how we avoid it...next time." Looking back at the shop, Elvie sighed.

"Let's go talk somewhere else," Elvie said, "if he sees me talking to myself, that might raise even more questions." She touched his sleeve, and they reappeared on the roof of an old warehouse that looked out over the lake. Propping herself on the ledge, Elvie waited while Joseph took in the view.

"How did you know about this place?"

"I didn't. Victor told me about it once. I figured since he's not in town, it'd be a safe place to go." She looked back out at the lake where the sun was making the water sparkle. "He was right. It's gorgeous up here." Then she turned back to him, all business. "So, about Frank?"

Back in June, she and Joe had tried to do what they had done with him to Victor's little brother, Frank, who died from a gallbladder problem in a sanatorium. They were there when he died, but no spirit showed up in the In-Between. And Joseph, who could travel between all three planes, had checked the side of the dead and said he wasn't there, either. The working theory was that he hadn't been meant to be part of the Pathfinders and that they had no real way of knowing who he was.

"Natalie said that we are half right." Joseph settled himself on the edge across from her as he talked. "She said he wasn't meant to be part of the gang, but that also, because he died so suddenly, his soul didn't stay around longer than it had to. For him, she's pretty sure, there was no moment between being completely alive and completely dead." Elvie nodded, thoughtfully, as she looked out across the lake. "Do we know..." Joe trailed off, unsure of how to ask the question.

"I don't think he was dead after the first shot." Elvie's voice was soft and far away. "I'll look it up when I get home tonight, but...for all of our sake. I hope not."

"We'll figure something out, Elf." The first time Joe had called her by the pet name, she'd blushed furiously but she was used to it now. She found it endearing that the Weiss siblings all seemed to share the same habits and thoughts despite the years of time since they had seen each other. She'd run into the second oldest, Bernard, and their sister Violet, on the street one day and made an excuse to talk to them. Bernard talked without moving, like Earl and Violet talked with her hands like Joe. They all had the same, dry sense of humor. When she'd gone on her way, she'd found herself thinking how close knit that family was...minus Fred, she reminded herself.

"I know we will." Elvie turned back to look at Joe, her face set, ready to fight. "We have to." They sat quietly for a long time. Joe wasn't as quiet as Earl, which Elvie was fairly certain was due more to having been alone on the other side for so long, but sometimes he would slip into silence. Bixby, who had become fast friends with him, once said it was jarring to be on a mission with him and to wake up, only to find Joseph staring out a window, completely lost in his own world. She was about to suggest they leave the roof when Joseph, sat up and stretched.

"I'm going back to base." His voice was soft and calm, as always. He rarely got worked up about anything. It always made Elvie wonder had actually happened that night in the saloon years ago. One day, she would have to ask him, for now she waved but not before he smiled. "There's someone looking for you down there." And then he was gone.

Elvie frowned and she leaned over the side of the warehouse, where staring up at her, when anyone else would have seen the sky was Earl. He waved to her and, hesitantly, she waved back. She almost let herself go down to see him. Almost let herself hope that things could go back to the way they had been before the raid, but then out of the building across the way emerged his brother in law, Philip and his brother Bruno and he turned. When he glanced back up before he got in the car with them, Elvie was gone.

Chapter 55

November 10, 1924, Chicago, IL
Elvie paced the flowershop's interior, completely unseen by Dean O'Banion as he cut flowers and ran back and forth from the greenhouse making floral arrangements for the funeral of the Sicilian union leader, Mike Merlo, later today. Merlo had finally succumbed the cancer he had been fighting. Unbeknownst to the Northsiders, his death had set into motion Dean's, as well. If they were expecting it, they weren't expecting it before the peace-loving Merlo was at least buried in the ground. The Gennas and the Torrio-Capone gangs, however, believed in striking while the iron was hot. And so, Elvie was here. Waiting. Hoping. Even praying. Because if they had a repeat of what had happened with Frank, she was probably going to lose her mind. She was also going to be in trouble, either way, she figured. She might as well be able to do the thing she was getting in trouble for.

She heard Dean, humming to himself as he arranged some wreaths and then took a phone call. Elvie glanced at the clock on the wall. *Right on schedule,* she thought sadly. After he hung up he disappeared for a second and William Crutchfeld appeared with a broom. Elvie's throat tightened, and she started tapping her fingers restlessly against the railing on the stairs, the glass cabinet, the cash register, whatever she happened to be pacing next to at that second. She didn't *want* Dean to die. Far from it. Elvie never wanted anyone who wasn't truly evil or who didn't deserve it to die. It was how she had ended up with her In-Betweeness anyway. But she would like to get the waiting over with. Her pocketwatch chimed. Natalie had figured out not only how to track her here but also how to send her messages.

Natalie: Joe and I are waiting...any sign of anything yet?

She had no more read the message than she watched a automobile pull up outside and three men, well dressed and polished looking got out. The shortest one, Frankie Yale, was in town from New York specifically for what was about to happen. Her entire being seemed to recoil in disgust as the second man, Angelo Genna, came into the shop, before Salvatore Ammatuna, another of the Genna gang, who Elvie had not had the displeasure of meeting. Behind him, as the door swung shut she saw two more figures in the car, waiting. One, pale and wispy-haired, the other dark and slightly crazed-looking, it was the Murder Twins, John Scalise and Albert Anselmi. Elvie's stomach clenched and she thought she might throw up. These men couldn't rile one bit of sympathy from Elvie, who could usually find something redeeming about a person. There had been times where she couldn't, of course. Some people are just well and truly evil and this felt like one of those times. Keep your head, she reminded herself as the door the workroom opened and Dean stepped out, greeting them and sending Mr. Crutchfield back to the workroom to sweep there instead.

Elvie edged closer as Dean stretched out his hand in greeting. Yale muttered something and Elvie's vision blurred as she focused, solely on Dean. One man held Dean's hand while the other two fired four times. The first shot, to his chest, staggered him. One to his cheek pulled his soul toward Elvie, who, without waiting for the final two shots to find the mark (the other cheek would also be hit, and one shot would hit him in the throat), grabbed his arm and wanked him to the first place she could of where she knew they would be safe, which was the apartment at the top of the Old Water Tower.

Chapter 56

Joe appeared next to her, with Natalie on his other arm. Natalie was getting used to traveling with them and seemed to prefer it to traveling with Tony, which often left her nauseous. Today, she had come to explain what was going on to Dean. It turned out that that was unnecessary.

"It's true then? You're a ghost?" And then, his blue eyes slid to Joe and widened. "Joseph! What the hell are you——? Natalie?" He stared at her and then glanced at where she held on to Joseph, and his eyes narrowed.

"Does Victor know about this?" He gestured between them and Elvie, confused as she was about that last statement and how he knew Natalie, interrupted.

"Dean, you just died. You are dead. And the thing you want to talk to us about is that I'm a ghost and Victor needing to know about Natalie touching Joseph, who also, you should have more important questions about?" Her voice seemed to pull him back to the situation as he took himself in, looking at his body and arms and then back at Elvie.

"Okay." His lyrical voice steady as he seemed to be centering himself. "Let's start from the top? What just happened?" Elvie took the first part, explaining the assassination and why it had happened.

"They certainly didn't waste time," Dean grumbled, sitting slowly at the desk that was still by the window. Elvie sat on the window ledge, where she had sat with Earl on her birthday. Joseph and Natalie waited patiently off to the side. "So, you really are a ghost then?"

"Sort of. I'm between. I can move between the world of the living and the world between life and death."

"Because you tried to do something you shouldn't to the timeline?" Dean looked up at her, and Elvie felt irritation overwhelm her.

"My God, did they tell George, too?" She had been being snarky but when Dean nodded, it was all she could do not to scream. "Anyway. Yes. I have that ability. And we, Natalie and I, are from the future."

"And what about Joey? He's been dead for over ten years." Here, Joseph, or 'Joey,' as he clearly hated to be called told his story. Then, once Dean was nodding, as if this all made perfect sense, Natalie jumped in with a plan for him to come back with them. But only if he wanted.

"Of course I want to," Dean stood, incredulous. "Why wouldn't I want to?" And so Elvie found herself going over all the reasons and rules as she had done with Joseph a few months earlier.

"Also, Dean, if you're just done, if you just want to go see what's next, that's okay, too." She added and when Dean met her eyes, she knew he was thinking of Earl and how he might want to be done existing as well. Elvie was wondering if she would even be able to grab him. His death wouldn't be instant but she could see him immediately chosing where to go before she had a chance. It was why she had been so quick to grab Dean.

"No, I'm not ready to be done. How could I be ready? You've just told me about all these amazing things that I am going to miss. I mean, I still might miss them, but I get a second chance. A do-over. And I can do some good." He looked at each of them and nodded again. "Yes, I want to join you guys." Elvie and Joseph looked at each other, and each nodded. Joe stepped back, pulling Natalie with him and Elvie held out her hand, which Dean looked at alarmed.

"My handshakes aren't nearly as bad the last guy." She joked, hoping to ease his worries and it worked. He raised his eyes to hers and a smile broke out as he gripped her hand. She pulled and at the same time Joseph and Natalie vanished before Elvie and Dean, a very solid, very much alive Dean O'Banion landed on the front step of the house in Malibu. Tony opened the door to the four of them. As they passed him he groaned quietly. "This place is getting crowded. How many more people are we planning on adding?"

Doing her best to look calm, despite the chill and headache, and the pride that Joe hadn't been a fluke, that she had brought someone over with her, not once but twice and they were an actual living human, Elvie stopped at the top of the stairs and shrugged. "Well, at least two off the top of my head."

www.ingramcontent.com/pod-product-compliance
Lightning Source LLC
LaVergne TN
LVHW041701060526
838201LV00043B/514